ONLY FOR LOVE

CRISTIN HARBER

MILL CREEK PRESS

ONLY FOR LOVE

Compilation copyright © 2015 Cristin Harber

ISBN-10: 1942236212
ISBN-13: 978-1-942236-21-4

www.CristinHarber.com

Published in the United States of America.

ACKNOWLEDGMENTS

Thank you, readers, for falling in love with Grayson and Emma! I poured my heart into the Only series and the overwhelming support has been amazing. I am forever grateful for you.

I cannot express how much Team Titan means to me. Every day we have a blast together, and I can't count the amount of times you've made me laugh or made me teary. I *love* how supportive you are, both to me and to each other (even when claiming book boyfriends), and I'm proud to be part of our community. You will never know how much your messages, posts, tweets, shares, and reviews means to me.

Thank you to the wonderful, talented women I get the honor to work with every day. JB Salsbury, Racquel Reck, Claudia Connor, and Sharon Kay. I am forever a friend and always in awe of you.

This series would not have been possible without the support of bloggers, especially Straight Shootin' Book Reviews, Grown Up Fangirl, Kame at TBQ, Danyella at ReadersIsle, Heather at Obsessed With My Shelf, and Stacey at Romance Ever After.

Another huge thank you to the team that makes my dreams come true. Thank you to Julia Sutherland for your heart and your time, to Red Adept for editing and proofing, to Okay Creations and Sarah Hansen for creating a cover that is brilliantly beautiful, and to Inkslinger PR—KP Simmon, Tara Gonzalez, and Amber Noffke—for the creative energy that you ignite.

Finally, thank you to my family who supports me without hesitation.

ONLY FOR HIM

CHAPTER 1

Six Years Ago
Sophomore Year,
Summerland County High School...

GRAYSON

This entire shitty-ass trailer reeks. The stink of cheap liquor and an even cheaper woman hangs in the air as I walk in the door. There's a system I keep for knowing how deep Pops is, and it goes by smell. If he's been smokin' pot, I'm on my own before football practice. No big deal. If the stench of cheap beer fills our place, Pops'll give me hell, but not enough that I can't duck out and escape. I'll be a little banged up, but nothing I can't ignore when Coach Snyder makes me run laps for being late. But if our trailer smells like liquor, I'm screwed.

That's the last thing I need. I forgot my damn football pads this morning and needed to slink in, grab them, and go. But judging by what stinks, that may've been a bad decision.

"Oh!" A woman's slurred surprise drifts down the short hall.

Well... damn.

I turn toward the source of the slurred yip and cheap vanilla aroma. She walks into the room, and I feel her gaze as I assess her level of sobriety. On a scale from buzzed to smashed, she's hovering around a solid tipsy. Smeared red lipstick and years' worth of smoking are written on her too-tan face. That's Pops's type—dive bar skank.

The lady's hair screams "just been fucked," and she hops from one foot to the other, tugging on a stripper-girl shoe. One foot makes it into the see-through plastic, but she drops to the ragged carpet in a mess of drunken giggles.

Great.

"Hey, you," she slurs, her eyes bobbing all over me.

Disgusting. I don't know her name, but I could guess. Bambi. Candi. Mandi. Sandi. I think they make up their names. Statistically, there aren't enough parents in Summerland County naming their kids with names ending in i to allow his screws to all rhyme.

"Didn't know you had a boy, Randall," she coos, more to me than to Pops. "Quite the boy..."

Not only have I been caught at home, but the lady is eyeball fuckin' the shit out of me. Pops's instability makes him jealous, which fuels his anger. Like I'd touch one of his whores.

But now that Pops is done with his woman, he's going to take it out on me for whatever he dreams up—that I'm flirting with his fucks or that I... exist. *Such an asshole.* I exist. I'm his son. His problem. It blows my mind how often he brings his trash back here when he doesn't want them to know I'm alive. In what world does that make sense?

Shirtless and with glassy eyes, Pops sways from

the back room, acting drunk and well-fucked. I hate that look; I always thought that getting laid should chill him out, but it never does. Just makes him angrier. Not that it is hard to do. He can go from passed-out to ready-to-kill in a liquor-stinking breath.

Pops sneers at me, and even though I should expect it, my stomach sinks. He hates me, and as sick as it is, I can't blame him. I ruined our lives.

"Grayson, boy, told you not to come home."

"Randall." The lady, still sitting on her butt, giggles from the floor. "You're too young for a boy that big." She eyes me like she needs another go in Pops's waterbed. Alcohol-fueled lust fires behind her makeup-caked eyelashes.

My skin crawls. Her tongue darts out, licking like she wants to taste me, and a foul shiver runs through me.

Pops swings his glare between me and his piece of ass, and his scowl tightens. "You shoulda stayed doing your football, ROTC, whatever the fuck you do. Not come here."

If I didn't need my shit for football, I wouldn't have come home. I should've skipped practice. I'm never going to make it back in time. With the anger pulsing in our trailer, there's no doubt Pops wants a fight that I won't give him. I can't—I've earned every punch he lands.

Dread rushes into my blood. The thing about a whiskey punch is that it hurts a fuckava lot more than if he's been slamming beers. Even better is when he's stoned. Even if his limp-dick fist balls, there's a good chance he'll pass out before he makes contact.

I swallow the lump in the back of my throat, bracing for what will come. It will suck, especially since he doesn't seem *that* drunk. The more sober he is, the longer he lasts. A shitty fact of life. The guy's up for father of the year.

"I forgot my pads." I try to sidestep him in the narrow living-slash-kitchen area.

He takes two swaying steps. "Boy." Spittle hits the back of my neck, then his fist cracks sloppily on my head.

Son of a bitch. I hadn't braced for that. If a hit's coming, I zone out, not feeling a thing. But him swinging in front of that lady? I shrug it off, ignoring the sting. "Just getting my shit, and I'm out, Pops."

"You ain't goin' nowhere now, boy."

I move toward my room. Practice is in twenty minutes. My teeth grind together. If I can just—

Pops grabs my shoulder, steadying himself, and then leans in. "I said—"

"Think I should be going." The woman gives a smoker's cough.

Even though bench-pressing his weight would be easy, I let Pops whirl me to the counter. It takes everything I have to detach. The counter edge digs into my back, and I know the beating is coming. The confirmation is in his eyes, and one long onceover tells me he's not nearly drunk enough to make this session quick.

I've had fifteen years walking this earth, and I should've known better than trying to sneak in to grab my gear. I'm never going to make practice tonight. Coach Snyder might wonder, but he never asks.

"You knew I had company, you little shit." His voice is cigarette stained. More spittle hits my skin. "Honey," Pops calls to the lady without taking his eyes off me. "I'll call you. Get your ass goin' home now."

"'Kay, honey." She fumbles toward the door, swinging a purse off the couch.

The honey-talk makes me sick. Maybe she doesn't think he'll fight, and I'll just take it. I have a couple inches on him, plus muscle where he has none. I play sports. He smokes anything he can find. I survive on protein bars. Pops trades our food stamps for dime bags and fifths of whatever burns the hardest. Instinct should have my adrenaline going, readying to fight or flight. But it doesn't.

"What's wrong with you?" Pops snaps.

Everything.

But I shake my head slowly and wait, daring him to strike. I'm not afraid of pain. Maybe I even embrace it.

My heart pounds for all the wrong reasons. This is what I deserve but can't wait to escape. As the trailer door slaps shut, he drives home a gut shot.

The hit explodes. I torture myself by staying under his roof, knowing he's the most pathetic, ruined man I've ever met. But I made him that way, and as fucked up as it sounds, it's the only way I think he'll survive. I owe him that much. Long ago, Pops was normal… I was normal… Mom was alive.

Another blow lands, and my breath is gone. I brace for his wheezy left hook. It connects, but I've already started to numb out, thinking the only thoughts that save me from my nightmare.

The sweaty stench of liquor registers as he lands a slap. "Fuck you, boy."

Another slap to my temple, and he grabs my ear, ripping it down. A burn of pain explodes, and I silence my reaction, dropping to my knees. His drunken attack hits more than it misses. The scalp shots hurt, blistering fresh pain into a familiar headache. Blood touches my tongue. Bruises are a part of life. No one looks too hard. This is what I've accepted.

Harder punches rain down, but I'm gone. Numb. I hear the swings more than I feel the impact. I wonder if this is how soldiers detach when they're prisoners of war. I close my eyes and think about the only thing that makes life worth the trials: Emma Kingsley, her sweet smile, and the laugh that make me believe in a future.

Warmth bleeds through me, and I'm aware of her innocence. Sophomore year isn't for finding answers in a girl's face. It's for working my way off first-string JV and figuring out how to pass chemistry.

Another hit strikes my temple. Pops nails that perfect spot, and my balance is off. Pain I will not admit to explodes behind my eyes. Another strike lands. Then a push. I'm down on my back. Violent agony ricochets as Pops's bare foot strikes my ribs. That bastard.

Emma.

I fight to think of her. The only girl I want. The only one I could ever tell about this. But I won't.

I open my eyes. It's the wrong time to say I'm sorry. Our gazes clash, then one sloppy kick flies to my head. A hair of a second before his foot hits, I know I'm going to be out.

CHAPTER 2

Junior Year...

Emma

Irish twins. The thing about sharing classes with my older brother is that we confuse people. Ryan is eleven months older than me. Most assume we are fraternal twins, since we don't look *at all* the same. His hair is dark blond. Mine's more gold. His eyes are hazel; mine are brown. He's a little preppy, a little trendy, which is a good combination on him. But I'm all over the place: maxi dress one day, a jeans-and-shirt combo that's more tomboy than casual the next.

Tonight, it's torn-at-the-knees jeans and a screen-print tee with a pixelated, monochrome design I'd made in photography class. All around me, music thumps. Some of the guys from our class are getting trashed. Some of the girls are, too. But mostly, it's just a typical party.

Courtney and Melanie are in the corner, evil-eyeing me, but I catch them, and they glance away. There's a good chance they're in deep discussion about revoking my BFF card. Fine by me. I just want to leave, and that's why I'm getting their dirty looks. I'm distracted by one Grayson Ford, hottest guy in the room, and my platonic best guy friend. Yay...

He's got a cheerleader following him around, and he isn't ignoring her. Yay, again.

"Hey." Hands clap to my shoulders and spin me around. Courtney's glaring at me. "Would you just go over there already?"

I can't even play dumb. "Nah. What's the point?"

Melanie sidles up. "Yeah, what's the point? Except you two are like star-crossed lovers or something—crazy in love and doing nothing about it."

Crazy love. I've grown up with the perfect example of that. And *that* is not *anything* that I have with Gray. Well, at least it's not mutual because, whether I admit to it or not, I love him and have since I can remember.

Courtney throws her head back, laughing. "First comes love—" Melanie joins in with their rhyme, and in sync, they finish up, "Then comes babies in a baby carriage."

They break into squeals about our future imaginary children. God. But I'm not even going to have this discussion. Pointing to my ear, I mouth, "What? Never..."

My parents *are* crazy in love and, apparently back in the day, humped like rabbits. Totally disgusting, except for kind of cute, which is why there were three of us kids in very short order. Cherry is about a year older than Ryan, and she's the wild child.

Our folks stopped after me, probably because three kids three and under would be enough to send anyone to an asylum. Mom's sanity was likely saved from the loony bin by tying her tubes—which incidentally was the only time our parents would ever, even in passing, touch on the birds and the bees talk. Win-win for all. I like being the baby of the family, our parents are sane, and no one had to sit around for an awkward conversation.

But why I'm thinking about families and babies while staring at Grayson out of the corner of my eye is... pathetic. He's Ryan's best bro and a semi-permanent fixture around our house. Grayson is just Grayson, and even if I've imagined him looking at me the way I do him, it's just not a possibility.

So I'm glad he and Ryan are tight. I'm even happier that I can at least call him my close friend, too. I focus on our long standing friendship. It's been the only way I can justify the homicidal tendencies that provoke my inner ninja warrior chick every single time I see some bippy-boppy, cliquey bitch succeed in capturing his attention.

"Seriously, Emma. You need to chill out or head home." Courtney hip-bumps me.

"Can't." I turn to her, shaking my head. I've masochistically offered to make sure both Ryan and Grayson have a sober ride at the end of the night. And by sober ride, I mean me.

"Right. Well, don't look now, but here comes a certain somebody." Melanie giggles into her red plastic cup. "See ya."

Courtney squeaks. "Eek, see ya!"

They both take off in the absolute most obvious way possible. *Shit, shoot, shit.* Deciding that my thoughts are too transparent, I head for the front door. Some fresh air will fix me up since I'm pretty much the only sober person here.

"Emma?" Grayson calls from behind me.

I pretend like I don't hear and push through the crowd for the door. I'm almost outside when I hear Ryan calling after me, too. He's laughing, and once I'm on the front yard, I turn around to see my brother heading out the door with his arm thrown around a girl I pretty much hate. "Let's go to Whities before we drop them home."

Them? Oh, no. I didn't sign up to chauffeur around Ryan and that girl making out all over the back seat while trying to ignore Grayson, who's looking ten kinds of amazing. And... no way am I heading for a burger run. Just not gonna happen.

The door to the house opens again, and out walks Grayson. My mind freezes then spirals to an immediate love-struck-heartbroken twist when I see Gray with *another her* whom I dislike. Immensely.

She's clinging to his broad chest and giggling as they make their way down the front porch. I hate this, how I feel, how I react. There's always that distant, maybe-one-day kind of hope that this weird vibe is actually not a made-up daydream. But if that's the case, why would he torture me?

"Ems." He shoves away from his clinger. "We leaving?"

At least that shove gives me some very small level of satisfaction, even though she just moves back in again.

"Hey." I jingle my keys then turn to Ryan. "Yes. But we're not going to Whities."

Ryan groans, and I roll my eyes.

Gray sidesteps the girl on his hip. "Why'd you run off a sec ago?"

"I was in sober-girl hell." *No way will I admit to him why.* Everywhere I went tonight, there was a chick trying for his attention.

"So why'd you run for the door just now?" His voice is teasing. He nudges my shoulder with his arm.

I swear, between those arms and that chest, I don't know what to do with myself. I shrug instead, imagining him holding his arm around me, pressing our bodies together. "I was bored. Didn't want to drink, and I have dance in the morning."

My list makes sense, but none of it's true. I can't drink around Grayson for fear that I'll do something stupid. And I like being their sober option because I'm pretty much their *only* option, and that guarantees me more time with him. I'm a Grayson Ford addict. No one will blame me though, and I'm pretty sure there's an *I Dream of Gray* support group at school.

My eyes slide over him. He's perfect. Sweet. Funny. Smart. Tough. A combination of male awesomeness, all in the right blend.

The girl who had been latched to Ryan's chest pulls back from him. "Seriously, Emma, you should try out for the team."

Now the girl under Gray's arm scowls. "Tryouts have been over for forever."

Add her snippy shut down of something I don't even want to do to the list of reasons I hate her.

Ryan's girl smiles at me, and I think that she's actually trying to suck up to me to win him over. "For Emma's talent, I think we'd make an exception." Spoken like a true captain of the cheerleading squad.

Whatever. Art bleeds in my veins. I know I could do well on the cheerleading team, but that's not why I dance. The rhythm, the feelings, with the right music and a focus, I don't dance. I emote. All that poetry in motion stuff comes naturally to me.

"She's not a dancer," Grayson adds. "She's a photographer."

Dancing's fun, but photography is who I am. He knows it. Heat hidden by the evening's dim light hits my cheeks. "That I am. But really, I'm your ride, so in the car. Let's go."

Grayson's girl wraps her arms on him, readying to work some take-me-home magic. But he sidesteps her move, and relief floods me.

"Hey." Gray points down the street. "Becca's in your neighborhood. She'll drop you."

When her mouth hinges open to protest, he leans in to add a more private part to their conversation. Whatever he said works, and after a bit of giggle-fussying, she waves goodbye and almost skips down the sidewalk.

Seriously. I. Hate. Her. Or maybe it's me that I'm hating. Why can't I just tell him? Sighing, I know the answer I've replayed a million times.

He's my friend.

My *best* friend.

It will ruin everything. He's Grayson Ford, the dream boyfriend, the ideal catch. And I'm me: cute but not gorgeous, friendly but not super popular. If Ryan wasn't my brother, I wonder if as many people would even notice I exist. A long time ago, I learned that some *friends* only wanted to hang with me for access to Ryan and Gray. Nice.

Back to chauffeur duty. Ryan's attached at the face to his cheerleader and heading toward the back seat.

Grayson throws his arm around my shoulder and leans in. His lips graze my temple, evidence that he's had his share of keg beer and laughs. "Take me home, Emma."

Ha. If he had *any* clue.

CHAPTER 3

Senior Year...

Emma

A million middle-of-the-night conversations passed through our adjoining air vent as I lay on my bed and my sister Cherry did the same in her room. She used to tell me secrets through the slats while we knocked our heels against the wall and chatted in the dark.

I'm sure our deep, giggles were broadcast to the entire house. They probably gave our folks heart failure because, even when Cherry was a kid, she was a handful. Mom would come up and tell us to go to bed. Dad would come up and tell us to stop scuffing the walls—but then he'd tuck us in. Twenty seconds later, we'd be on our backs again, feet in the air, knocking and scuffing and telling secrets.

When Cherry left for college, everything changed. I lost my sounding board. She might be three years older, but she was my confidant. I saw the world vicariously through her eyes. She never had a negative outlook on life, never thought she wasn't the center of attention, but she always held my hand, doling out amazing, albeit unconventional advice. I really miss her.

Lying on my back with Grayson on my mind, I look at the vent and knock my heels against the wall, trying to imagine what Cherry would say about the debacle at lunch today—

Knock, knock.

I turn my head, and there's my problem. In the span of a second, my languid musings about my festering crush are replaced by the slow mind-meld that is Grayson Ford.

"Hey, Gray." I swear, each day he grows bigger, and his eyes become more vibrant. All he does is work out. Baseball season is about over, yet he's training like he's eyeing the Olympics. I don't get it, but I'm able to appreciate the benefits of his grueling regimen.

"Hey, you. We've gotta talk."

My stomach drops as I swallow the burst of lust that I've become accustomed to when he shows up. I sit up from probably the most unattractive position: legs up, head down, kicked back on my bed. Or maybe it's the most provocative, if I were the provocative type. *I wish I were.*

His eyes track my legs to my face. I really shouldn't lie upside down if there's even the slightest chance he'll show up. A fire heats up my neck and into my cheeks. I don't have a clue about the type of flirting that would be in Gray's league. When it comes to him, I'm an expert on unrequited desire. Perks of being just a friend...

"You ran out of school today like your ass was on fire." He bounds a couple huge steps and flops down next to me. The entire bed shifts, and the addictive scent of his soap invades my space.

I turn to my side and take in his profile. Shower-wet hair, cheeks that are starting to chisel as he grows into a physique that doesn't look remind me of any other guy's in our school. He's more of a man every day, and I feel more like an awkward nerd girl.

"Tell me you're not pissed about earlier." He turns to his side to face me, and I bite my lip. He takes up most of my twin bed. Mom and Dad would freak if it were anyone but Grayson. Their "no boys in my room" rule was carved into stone during my freshman year when Ryan's friends started hanging around—sniffing around, as Dad says. But I say that's a big, fat laugh. Their room-rule doesn't apply to Gray, though.

He reaches over our heads and grabs my iPod, shoving an ear bud in his ear and one in mine. A few scrolls later, music blasts. It's kinda emo, a little deep, nothing that I expect he'd choose. The vocals croon about heartache, about how the future is a blur. The beat drops low, and the bass rolls through my body. Even though Gray's so close, or maybe because of it, I feel my blood thumping.

"Now that..." Slowly, he nabs the lone ear bud from me. Our eyes lock. "I'd pay to see you dance to."

"Grayson," I whisper as a fever hits my neck, bleeding through me. When he looks like this—acts like it too—I don't know what's for real and what's in my head.

"Been talking to your wall?"

I stifle a cringe. He knows me so well it hurts. "Something like that."

"About me?" He smiles, but it's not a joke. Everything feels different. His voice sounds different. His touches have been longer, his stares deeper, and right now, he's not pulling back from his question. "Nothing to say, Ems?"

Without an answer to give him, I roll back to stare at the ceiling.

He groans. "You're mad at me, right?"

Shoot. We're going to have to talk about today. But I'm clueless. It's like having what I want served on a platter, but it's not real.

He nudges my shoulder. "Say something."

If I stay quiet another second, he's going to think I'm nuts. Protecting my heart is my top priority, but I can't let go of the hope. "Kelly Reynolds will probably hate me for the rest of my life."

It's the best thing I've got, talking about something besides him and me but staying on topic. Not bad. But Grayson's deep laugh surrounds me.

I turn to face him again, and his brilliant smile makes his perfect face radiate. "Kelly Reynolds is a slut."

True, but that isn't my issue with her. "She thinks I asked you to Sadie Hawkins."

"You were going to." Confident and handsome. The total package.

"Oh, my God." I can't breathe. What the hell's going on between us? *Downplay, downplay, downplay.* I can't handle him right now. Smiling like he's dropping jokes, I nudge him back. "No way. You were bottom of my list, seriously, deep on the backup pile if I couldn't nab a date."

A brooding scowl darkens his face. "Like you couldn't swing any date you wanted."

"Not quite..."

He elbows me but lingers longer than he should. The heavy beat of my pulse thumps in my neck. I feel it in my wrists, and my mouth waters. What is it with us?

"Shit, Ems. I don't know what to do here."

I jerk back. Wait. What? My stomach's in my

throat, my skin has shiver bumps, I can't inch away, and he's not moving.

"Gray?" But I forget everything else I want to say because I want to hear him say those words again. Then I'll believe that whatever this is I feel is not just in my head.

He pushes a few strands of hair off my cheek, and it's surreal. My breaths are shallow. My mind races. Confliction and confusion battle for forefront in my mind. He's the only boy I'll ever trust enough to blush in front of, if that makes sense, which it doesn't. I blame stupid love.

"Tell me a story, Emma." He inches closer. "Tell me something that takes us far away from here."

That's his thing. He hates *here*, which I don't entirely get. But he loves that I'm a dreamer, that I can transport us far away when we close our eyes. It's something we've done since we were kids, and even when I can't breathe lying next to him, the familiarity is as intoxicating as it is soothing.

Okay. I can do this. "Eyes closed, Gray."

"Closed."

I breathe in deeply and think of something that moves us away from now. I can't think of anything because I've never loved a moment as much as this one.

"Are your eyes still closed, Emma?"

They are. I nod. "Yup."

There's a shift of his weight as he moves on the bed, coming closer. "Keep them closed."

My lungs ache. My heart's exploding, and my senses are hyper-alive. My lips part, wanting to tell him a story, wanting to kiss him more than I want to breathe. My eyelashes flutter.

"*Closed*, Ems." His low voice rakes over me.

I'm dying. In heaven. Right now.

His side touches my side. The heat from his body covers mine. His soft breaths torture my cheek... my chin... then hover over my lips.

Unable to control myself, I feel my hips shift. My chin tilts up. Anticipation squeezes deep into my soul. He's watching me. My eyes are still shut, but I can feel his gaze as his finger touches my hair, sliding down the strands to the slope of my collarbone.

I'm ready—swooning, melting, *panting*—for a kiss.

"God, you are beautiful, Ems," he whispers.

My eyes open, and my mind spins. The vibrant green of his are inches away.

"What are we doing?"

"I'm memorizing what takes me away. What saves me."

"You've—" My whispering voice cracks, but I don't care how I sound. I'm toeing the cusp of all I ever wanted.

"We're done ignoring us." His hand cups my face, fingers stroking my cheeks down to my chin. When my lips part, his eyes drop to my mouth, focusing on my lips.

I've been kissed. Dates. Dares. However they've happened, I've had a few solid moments of PG-rated hookups. *Nothing* I have *ever* experienced has *anything* on this moment, and Gray's lips haven't even touched mine.

His heavy weight lies atop of me, but one arm props him up, so I'm not crushed. I can't think. Just feel. A kiss has never been more meant to be. Then his lips touch mine. I breathe him in.

He groans into my mouth, and I let his tongue sweep mine. Hungry for more of him, I wrap my arms around his shoulders, scarcely believing this is happening. Knowing how big and broad Gray is, that's one thing. Wrapping myself around him, feeling him hold me, kiss me—it's insane.

His hands thread into my hair, and it's like we've unleashed a fire. His hips flex to mine. His erection pushes into my stomach. Without thought, I'm biting his lip, scratching my fingers into his back—

A noise startles us. We're frozen, panting, connected and staring into each other's eyes.

"Garage," I mumble against his lips.

He hugs me close; then we separate, rolling to opposite ends. All I can do is stare at Grayson and smile like a loon.

He chuckles and tilts his head, a crooked half smile on his face. "What—"

The bedroom door opens. Dad and Ryan were out running some kind of man-errands that I wasn't invited to and didn't want to go on. Thank God.

"Hi, sweetie pie." My dad pops his head in. "Oh, hey, Grayson." Then Dad laughs like what just happened has no chance of ever happening between Gray and me. "No boys in your room with the door closed."

"Hey, Mr. Kingsley."

"Right. Gotcha. Sorry." The way those three words fumble out of my stuttering mouth should've been a neon blinking sign that screamed obvious. But apparently, Dad's stuck in oblivious mode.

"I meant to tell you, son, great job last Friday." Then Dad smiles at me. "Guess this guy will always be an exception in this house."

He turns to leave, *shuts the door*, and there Grayson and I are, still silent and staring. I slap my hands over my mouth, certain insane, nervous giggles are going to explode at any second. Gray's the epitome of cool collectedness. Must be nice.

Pound, pound. Ryan thumps on my door as he walks past. "Gray in there?"

Grayson's eyes trail toward the door, then he stands. "So…"

"So…" Please don't ruin anything. Please don't say anything like *whoopsie* or *oh, shit, why did that happen?*

He leans against my wall, and his green eyes are on fire. A smile that melts me catches on his lips. "Get ready to get your Sadie Hawkins on."

My mind is already doodling *Mrs. Grayson Ford* in imaginary notebooks. He has no clue where my head is. But given that I didn't see what just happened coming *at all*, maybe I have no clue where his head is either.

He lifts his chin to say goodbye. Then he's gone. Down the hall, Grayson and Ryan bro out. I listen to their muffled voices while I press my fingers against my mouth. My lips feel swollen. My entire body feels… explosive.

Finally, I drop back to my bed and kick my feet up. Cherry needs to weigh in on this situation. I grab my phone and see a text message from Grayson.

Grayson: NO MORE STORIES. THAT'S ALL I'VE EVER NEEDED.

CHAPTER 4

Emma

I'm so glad this week is over. After kissing Gray and walking around like a grinning lovesick puppy for about twenty-four hours, I immediately realized I was going to screw this up. For the rest of that day, I hid in my room, blowing up Cherry's phone with emergency SOS texts. When she called me, her advice was perfect. Then she dropped the same message, but a thousand times more concise, into a text.

Cherry: WHATEVER YOU DO, DON'T LET HIM GO. HE'S PERFECT.

Yeah, no kidding. But how wasn't I going to screw up? I have no idea what to do about kissing Gray, other than finding a kickass dress for Sadie Hawkins. Then I scroll back to her next text.

Cherry: WHAT ARE YOU GONNA TELL RYAN?!

The thing is Ryan would handle it well. We're all friends, and Gray's not a dick. Still, telling Ryan, that's unnerving. But there's nothing to tell Ryan if I can't pull my act together and stop avoiding Gray.

I've been a complete baby about it. In my defense, it was the world's most perfect kiss. I still get the feels thinking about it. As far as I can tell, there's a significant chance that it can't get any better than it was in my bed.

Well, in my imagination, it can. But real life?

Sadie Hawkins is tomorrow night, and I have no choice but to see him since I'm his date and all. Shit. The slow pound of my heart begins its predictable cadence, thinking of the dress that took three days of shopping to find. The blue fabric and curving fit have one purpose: explain to Grayson what I want when I can't manage to talk.

Scrolling back to Cherry's text—shit—I catch the time, and I'm late. I grab my camera bag and bolt downstairs. If there's any way I'm going to hit the sunset that curves over Three Sisters Mountain, I needed to be in my car five minutes ago.

If I skip around the Parkway and hit the 613 Bypass, I can get there. I need this shot. Everything is tied into it. The perfect picture lands the final, perfect grade and pretty much secures my acceptance into Trydan College's uber-elite art program. I'm already lined up to attend next fall, but if I don't secure a seat in that program, what's the point?

I jump the last two stairs, spin around the corner, and slam into an unexpected wall of muscle.

"Ems."

Grayson... Shit. "Hey, um, sorry."

I right myself, slinging the camera bag back on my shoulder, but I can't tear away from him. How did

I not know he was here? As much as I've avoided him, now I don't want to go anywhere. Every second counts as the setting sun's light shifts over the thick forest cap. But his hands, his gaze. God, I'm not going anywhere to take that photo.

His hands move to my biceps, steadying me when I haven't realized I'm swaying. "You good?"

I nod. Yup, totally good. What's the question? What isn't the question? Because that thing where I can't think, breathe, function, move... I spiral into total Grayson reaction.

He lets me go and crosses muscular arms over an expansive chest. "You've been avoiding me."

"No. Not really." I cringe. "Maybe."

"Can't do that, Ems." He steps forward. His hand is on my side, backing me against the wall.

Oh, God. What if he kisses me again? I don't think I can keep upright. "I know. It's okay. I just..." Have no idea what to say or do.

"Want to tell me why?"

Ha. No way. "I was shopping after school this week."

"Haven't seen you at lunch, haven't seen you text, haven't seen you at all."

"Well, um..."

"We're still good for tomorrow?" His brows are up, but his smile is down. A concern mars his handsome face, and nodding is the only thing I can do to confirm Sadie Hawkins.

"See, this is the thing." He leans closer. "Me kissing you, you disappearing, that's my nightmare."

His nightmare?

He leans down. His face comes closer. "We've been tight since we were six. Don't let anything screw that up." The strongest guy I know shows a slice of vulnerability. "You don't know what you mean to me, Emma."

I... what? "Gray—"

His stomach touches mine. His hands move up and palm my cheeks. This guy could have *anyone* at school. But he's here in my house, saying this, doing this.

"I don't get it." My eyes sting. I can't explain why. Between the not breathing and the not thinking, tearing up couldn't come at a worst time. But my head's all over the place. My love, it's too strong, and if he ever knew... Whatever's burning between us, it's enough to make my daydreams seem like a possibility.

"What don't you get?" His thumbs caress my cheeks.

"This."

He pulls back and snags my hand. My camera bag drops off my shoulder, landing at the base of the stairs as he drags me back up. The closer we come to my room, the more my stinging eyes and breathing problems rage.

Then we're in my room. He shuts the door, and everything inside me tingles. My folks aren't home. My brother's in the basement. Just me and Gray behind my closed bedroom door.

"Sit down, Emma."

If he hadn't given me a little push, there's a chance I would've obeyed and dropped to the floor right there. Carefully, I sit on my bed, watching him pace, lost in silence. The twist on his face is confusing.

"Gray?"

He stops and turns to me. "You're the only one who can do that."

"Do what?" I whisper, uncertain of... everything.

"Stop my head. Freeze my mind. Bring me to another place. Or keep me where I need to be."

"Where's that?"

"I thought far away." He rubs his temples. "School's over in, what, three weeks?"

"Yeah."

"Then you're off to Trydan."

"In a few months." Biting my lip, I don't know where he's going with this. He hasn't said anything about college. I know he's had a couple of scouts talk to him at school, but discussions about the future— just like his home life—are off-limits. I know where, or if, he's going to college like I know what his bedroom looks like: I don't.

And he won't talk about it. I've tried more than once. His father is an asshole. That's all he's ever shared, but I picked up on that the few times I've seen his dad over the years. More than once, I've seen Grayson with bruises that he blames on football, though I've never seen Ryan like that. Gray's home life is bad. I figured that out long ago when I started telling him stories. The future is what he avoids.

He crosses his thick arms, making his muscles flex. "This week fuckin' sucked."

I blink. "Why?"

"God," he growls. "Are you that blind?"

My eyes go wide. My heart slams in my chest. "No—"

He drops to his knees in front of my bed. His hands tear into my hair. His mouth finds mine, pulling me to him. This isn't a kiss. It's a pleading. No one's ever touched me like he does. It's hard and hot, and I didn't know kisses like this existed outside the movies.

"I'm sorry." I kiss him, bite him. God, I need him. "I'm scared of you."

He breaks from me, breathing hard. "*What?*"

"What if what you want isn't what I want?" I bite

my lip. "What if I'm so far past..."

His arms wrap around me, and Gray pulls me with him as he crawls onto my bed. "Don't doubt this."

I nod, and his mouth finds my neck. Everything inside my body ignites. Deep in me, I'm dying for him, all lust-drunk and love-crazy. His hips flex, pushing his weight between my legs. My hands claw into his shirt, ripping to get under it and palm his skin, and when I do, he moans as my fingernails dig into his hot flesh.

But then he stops. I'm panting, my mouth open against his. His eyes freeze on mine, his breaths the mirror of mine. I feel his hard-on between my legs, thick and hard.

"You can't hide from me. You have no idea..." He blinks. "Promise me."

I nod.

"Good."

"Are you sure... about us?" Because I can't believe it. Wrapping my head around him and me, it's almost impossible. Very Cinderella—just a fairy tale come to life.

He grabs my hand and presses it to the bulge in his pants. I want to jerk away. I know my mouth's hanging open. That's so... so, oh my God. It's an asshole move, but it's not. It's... I don't know what it is. But it's forward, beyond anything I know how to comprehend.

"Emma." He lets my hand go. "You're adorable. And cute. Sweet. Better to me than anyone's ever been."

What does any of that have to do with us? "So is everybody else."

"Pretty doesn't begin to describe you, Ems. You're..."

"Awkward with a camera stuck to my face."

"The one I dream about."

My heart freezes. "Grayson..." *I love you.*

"You have no idea when it comes to what I think about you."

The sun has set. My room's light is turning a deep purple, and there's an urge to hug and hold him that has nothing to do with the kiss that just happened.

He leans over to kiss me. This time it's slow. He tastes like mint, and I'm mesmerized by the lazy roll of his mouth. Grayson holds my hip. His fingers flex, and his thumb scores back and forth over the slip of bare skin under my shirt. We could stay here for hours. Maybe we will.

His teeth tug my bottom lip. "I gotta run."

My chest is tight, and I crave his hands, his mouth everywhere. But everyone will be home soon, and my total inexperience is going to put me into a position where I want more than I know what to do about. "Okay."

One more kiss, and he leaves me on my back. "Bye, Ems."

"Bye." I kick my feet to the wall and wish Cherry was on the other side. Instead, I text her, expecting her to reply with something like, *go find that boy and jump him.* Maybe someday soon, I will.

CHAPTER 5

Emma

Today, we killed the juniors in the powder-puff game. Football's no joke, and even though it was all fun and games, I'm sore. I swallow a couple of Tylenol before Grayson picks me up because nothing's slowing me down for tonight's Sadie Hawkins, not sore muscles or nervous stomach twinges or the excited anticipation of walking in on his arm, knowing there's more than a good chance his lips will be on mine sometime tonight.

The doorbell rings, and my stomach jumps.

"Gray's here." Mom made such a fuss when Ryan's date picked him up that maybe she's not having the same holy shit moment I am. Grayson used the doorbell? In what world does that happen? He just walks in. He may even have a key because I know he's been here when we haven't.

One last twirl before my mirror, and the blue dress seems smaller and tighter than anything I'm used to wearing. I can't explain how much I love it.

My heart pounds, wondering what his reaction will be.

I fumble for my purse. Again, one more time, just in case, I spin in front of the mirror. Maybe this dress is too much? It's just a stupid Sadie Hawkins—

"Emma?" Mom's heels come closer.

Right. I can do this. He likes me. I love him. No pressure. Shit, shoot, shit… Okay.

I head to the stairs, each step closer to my big reveal, and I can't fight the giddy smile on my face. He's bringing out a part of me that I've always had but kept hidden.

As I stand at the top of the stairs, Mom stops mid-conversation with an unseen Grayson and gapes. "William," she calls to my dad. "Honey, come see Emma."

Dad's in the background, futzing with whatever he's doing. Neither Mom nor Dad would have expected this. It's just a dance with Gray. But it's so much more, and this dress announces it. At least in my mind it does.

As I descend the stairs, my eyes track to Grayson, and the desire on his face makes my chest feel tight. A nervous grin I can't hide crosses my face, and he steps forward. He's wearing a suit that makes him look like a movie star ready for the red carpet. His broad shoulders in the dark jacket are large but lean. The stark white shirt unbuttoned at the collar epitomizes sexy. Everything about him screams out of my league. He's just so… Grayson.

His lips part as he walks to me. "Wow."

One word. But the effect he has on me is nothing short of epic. Under his scrutiny, I'm red-carpet worthy alongside him. Words like pretty or beautiful, even sexy, don't begin to cover how he makes me feel. A dangerously chaste kiss lands on my cheek, and he breathes deep. "Hell of a dress."

Holy. Shit. And three days of non-stop shopping is now totally worth it. One of his hands grazes across my bare shoulder, and the need to throw myself against his hard body is unbearable.

Dad meanders into the room and glances me up and down. "Gorgeous, sweetie pie." Then he turns to Grayson and claps him on the back. "Keep an eye on her for me."

Dad chuckles and pulls Mom under his arm. They have no idea. I think they think that Grayson's my pity date and that I asked him because there's no one else I could-would-should ask. Dad's subtle warning isn't for Gray. It's for Gray to keep others away. Mom and Dad always said I didn't know how the world saw me. Maybe they were right. But it doesn't matter. Gray's the only one I care about.

When we leave my house, his large hand spans the small of my back. He has me close, and my stomach is on rotation, flip after flop. This feels like one of those chick flicks where I just know everything will come together in the end.

"I like you in a suit, Gray."

He tucks me into the passenger seat, crouches down, and catches my hand as I reach for my seatbelt. His hand is strong and confident. "I like you any way you come."

Then he pulls back to shut the door. I don't even know this guy anymore, but I can't get enough. Ten minutes later, we're at school and heading inside, his hand holding mine. Strings of lights sparkle overhead, glittering like stars and transforming the gym into something worth remembering.

When Gray told Kelly I'm his date, it never occurred to me that I'm actually going to *be* his date.

Four years of high school, countless dances, and he's always been my dream guy. Probably everybody else's too.

I catch a glance of Ryan talking with his date, some floozy that surely gave him a BJ before they got here. That's what happens. People hook up. They hang out.

My stomach flutters. Dating doesn't really exist. People can be fuck buddies. Then after a couple of weeks, they're heartbroken or they're not, but they move on. At least that's how it seems to me. No one really *dates*. It's old and awkward. But Gray and me? It's been two weeks of nervous moments, hot kisses, and awesomeness. So whatever it's called, I love it.

Shifting in heels that I should never have worn, I scan right to left. It's a sea of dresses and suits. Couples who have been watching the dance floor are now looking at me. At *us*. The stares are like a chokehold.

"Gray..." I lean against him.

The whole gym sees me on his arm, hand in hand, when I realize that even *Gray* is looking at me. Blood rushes in my neck, screams in my ears. My lungs go tight, and that has nothing to do with the dress I poured myself into. He leans over and presses his lips to my temple. "Let them talk."

Ryan sees us, studies our handhold, and I can see him processing the Gray-me couple. After a few long seconds, my brother gives Grayson a chin lift and me a smile. It's the Ryan Kingsley stamp of approval.

Gray's lips drag across my forehead, and I sway into him. The whispers start as we walk farther in. Their eyes follow the football star-art nerd combo. They're used to seeing us like *us* over the years, not like this, arms connected, bodies touching. This is different. His fingers are intertwined with mine. He's so close and smells like clean, soapy heaven.

"People are looking at us."

His hand squeezes. "Good."

"Kelly Reynolds is drooling over you."

He laughs. "And every dude here's doing the same for you."

What? I bite my lip but lean into him. "Liar."

Gray whips me around, arms around my waist, backing me to the dance floor where everyone who isn't staring is dancing. The music is fast, the beat strong. But we're almost slow dancing, and the motion leaves me desperate and anxious, wanting more of him than I've had.

I corral all of my nerves and bravery into one giant question. "So is this some kind of boyfriend-girlfriend thing?"

He slows even though we are already moving at a swaying crawl. My throat tightens. This can't be good. Panic scares away the bravery, and my foolishness is debilitating.

With narrow eyes, he inches closer. "Is that what you want?"

Is he kidding me? I blink, afraid to give my answer. "I..."

I'm unsure how it's even possible, but his arms hold me closer. His breath touches my ear. "You could do so much better than me."

Laughing uncomfortably, I don't understand any of this. He wants me, or he doesn't. The hand holding and hugging isn't a move for a fuck buddy. It's all so genuine it hurts.

"Why say that, Gray?"

"Hm?"

"You're playing *you* down to *me?* I mean, it's *you.* Everyone in this gym would die to be me this second."

He chuckles. "I don't play me down."

"You do." It's like we see-saw who's confident and who's in disbelief. "You have everything."

"What I have is…" A lost, pained expression passes across his face. "We need to talk."

"Hey, you two—" Mr. Snyder, my junior year history teacher and one of Gray's coaches, taps my shoulder. "Give it some breathing room."

A hot blush crawls onto my cheeks. "Oh, yeah. Sorry"

Gray doesn't let go. "Just dancing, Coach."

Mr. Snyder's brows furrow, and he scowls at Gray. "*Of course*, Grayson. Some space please, Miss Kingsley."

What the heck is that attitude coming from his coach?

"She's fine. Right, Emma?"

"Yeah, of course."

"Not going to tell you again." Mr. Snyder's watching me, acting as if he's protecting me.

"But—"

"That's okay. We're out of here. C'mon." Grayson snags my hand, and I feel a hundred eyeballs follow us toward the gym door.

We've only been here a few minutes, but with his wanting to talk and my wanting to do anything but talk, I follow without question.

Mr. Snyder's steps are hot on our trail. "Once you leave, you can't re-enter."

"No prob." Grayson doesn't turn around.

"Wait," Mr. Snyder snaps.

I peer over my shoulder, slowing my date down.

My teacher's gaze drifts to our entwined hands. "Miss Kinglsey, do *you* want to stay here?"

My eyes peel back in surprise. "What? No."

Gray steps closer. "Coach—"

Mr. Snyder ignores him. "If you need a ride,

Emma, I'm sure *your brother* or one of your friends can—"

"Nice. Thanks, Coach." Grayson scoffs, and the sarcasm rolls. "Let's go, Ems."

I nod, letting him pull me out the door. Another quick look over my shoulder, and Mr. Snyder's worry shakes me. Gray keeps me with him. We reach his car, and he sets me in it, shuts the door, and storms to the driver's seat. When he gets in, he slams the door and scowls out the windshield.

"What's... going on?" I'm lost. Everything warm and fuzzy is gone, which I hate.

He turns his head. "Really?"

"Uh, yeah."

"Shit, Ems." He throws his head back, and his laughter fills the car with an uneasiness that is lost on me.

"Gray, seriously. What was that?"

"That's everyone's concern for you with me, verbalized."

My forehead pinches. "I don't get it."

"You're like... innocent. And I'm not."

"No, I'm not."

He laughs. "You are, baby, and I'm the guy who can nail any chick in this school." He shakes his head. "Coach Snyder knows it."

Yup. I'm a virgin. *Everyone* probably assumes that. "Oh..."

"Yeah."

"He thinks... what, you're going to..." I cover my smile with my hands. "Defile me?" I want to be embarrassed that my teacher ran after me to protect—what? —my honor. But can't. Not now. Not with Grayson. A giggle I can't stop bursts out.

"Defile?" His grin hitches to the side, and I see softness in his green eyes. "Something like that."

Again, I muster my bravery and hold it deep. Before I can think my thoughts through, my mouth's moving, and my heart's screaming. "What if a girl like me wants to be defiled?"

If I lose my virginity, it has to be to him. Right? Someone I love? Someone I want? Someone who's always been there and who I trust to never disappear?

The softness in his eyes disappears. "Don't say that."

"Oh." My face falls. Everything falls. He wants me, but not like that? Not that much?

His fingers catch my chin, turning me so that I face him. "Ems, nothing about you should ever be defiled."

I blink. "Okay."

Whatever word he wants to use, I'm ready. I don't know when or where, but I want Grayson Ford to be my first.

Really, I want him to be my only.

"It's just that the future is confusing. And sex is whatever, but sex with you... that's not. It's..." He shakes his head.

I shrug to hide my disappointment, completely heartbroken. What is this between us? And who knew *not* having sex was hurtful too?

Gray clears his throat. "Ems... It's the 'you and me' thing again. I'm..."

"You've never had a problem getting a date," I offer, jealous. "I certainly don't think you have a problem sleeping with—"

"Come on, Emma. Don't be like that. It's just that you are..."

I hate every second he doesn't finish that sentence.

"I'm a virgin." Tears burn my eyes. "That's it. It's because I'm a virgin."

CHAPTER 6

GRAYSON

Virgin. My head drops, and I rub my temples, mumbling something along the lines of I can't say no to her anymore. Truth is, even I don't know what I'm saying. I'm trying not to beg, trying not to run, needing to touch her, taste her. But I let her words run through my head. Even if I can't offer Emma anything that she deserves, I can't say no. The girl's had my heart since before I knew it went missing.

"Gray?" she whispers.

I'm unable to give her a response. My mind reels. She wants us. I want us. I picture her naked, pressed against me, and I'm going to fall apart.

And to be her first… That's enough to make me wish I'd never touched another girl, that we were each other's firsts. It's selfish, but even if I'm gone, even if she's in college, living some incredible life one day, she'll have to remember me.

I turn the engine over and drive.

"Where we going?"

Some place I can have her alone, look into her

eyes, and run my hands all over her. Blood thumps in my chest. "My place."

"Your place?"

I should expect the shock in her voice. How many years have I known her, and how often has she been over? Never. I think maybe she's always known that it's not a good place, that it's my hell. But Pops has been on a bender for a few days already, and he hasn't been home. Times like this, he won't show up for a week, maybe two, and those spells of abandonment are the happiest memories I have.

Until now.

"Yeah." Turning toward her, I catch her eyes. "You good with that?"

However she wants to take that, I mean it. Is she good with me and her? Is she good with a shitty trailer?

"I'm good as long as I'm with you." Her fingers tangle with mine as I drive away from school.

God, I love her so much that my heart aches.

We drive down Route 6 and hit the entrance for my place. It's on a weedy plot, and the metal rust-bucket box isn't any better inside. But it's home, and tonight, it's ours.

Killing the engine, I give her a nod and jump out to grab her door. Emma's an angel, everything perfect and right and innocent in the world with buttery blonde hair and brown eyes so light they twinkle in the moonlight. She blinks with a nervous hesitation that brings me to my knees.

I take her hand in mine and squeeze, tugging her and that sinful dress beside me. "The place isn't much to look at. But we'll be alone."

"Really?"

The sweetness in her voice cuts straight through me. I've fucked, I've screwed, but this... this isn't anything like I've gone near before. My heart picks up its pace. My throat tightens, and something powerful bleeds through me.

After we push through the door and I hit a light and bring her down the short hall, I can tell her "really." But until she's in my room, in my bed, it won't feel real.

Emma drops her hand from mine and locks her arm around my waist. We push through my door, and she leans against me so I can hold her close. Short, quick bursts of breaths fall from her lips, and I'm suddenly so hard I hurt. Her hands run up my chest, and the longer she touches me, the more sure she seems.

"This is what you want, baby?" And I pray that she says yes, that she didn't see the crap trailer and remember that I'm a nobody who hides shitty circumstances well.

"Yes." She nods. "More than anything."

That's all I need. Our lips lock. I find the zipper on the back of her dress and drag it down. It hangs loose, and for as many times as I've imagined her naked, I'm barely able to control my hands slipping behind the fabric to touch bare skin.

Her hands freeze on the buttons on my shirt. Where she was soft and hot, she's gone rigid in my arms.

Hugging her tight, I crush her hands between us. "Ems? You good?"

"I..." She bites her lip nervously. "Don't know what I'm doing."

So sweet. God, so sweet. "Yeah, you do. Whatever you want, you do."

She catches my eyes, and I see it then: the curiosity and hunger, the desperate want both of us failed to ignore.

"Yeah? Just... take what I want?"

"Absolutely."

I can promise her the world, promise to take care of her, make her feel amazing, but that's not what she needs. Just a push of confidence is all she wants, something she thinks I have in spades. My lips touch her forehead, her cheeks. My fingers trace the contours of her back, skimming the slope of her spine. Shivers erupt under my touch, and she shimmies and lets the dress fall to the ground. Emma Kingsley is standing in my bedroom in lingerie and high heels. "Christ."

There's nothing to do but drop to my knees and love her. My mouth finds her belly, and as I swirl my tongue over her stomach, I unbutton my shirt and shrug it off.

"I like this." Her fingers trail my bare shoulders, sliding up and into my hair. Then she reaches behind to unclasp her bra. "So much."

Breasts bared to me, she has no idea, no fuckin' clue how much I like this too, how I could come right now. "You okay?"

She nods and sighs loud enough that I feel it in my groin.

"Good." My chest is tight. I hook her arms, hold her to me, and pull us down, bare chest to bare chest.

"More than okay." Her hands rub my back, my biceps. Her hips flex for mine. Her kisses run deeper, stronger. The girl tests her teeth on me, scraping softly enough I want to pay attention but hard enough I'll just enjoy the damn feel of it.

"Fuck, I like that, Ems."

The smile on her face, the way she comes alive, means tonight's meant to be.

She looks away. "So do you have condoms or whatever, 'cause I'm not..."

"Yeah." But I have all night with her. No way could I rush this. "We'll get there."

"Promise?" Her eyes are back on me, confidence on fire, arousal making her demanding.

I nod. "But we've got a checklist first."

"We do?" She laughs.

Nodding again, I run my fingertips from her chin to the top of her chest. "I'm going to kiss you here." Then lower over the swell of her breast, teasing the nipple. "Here again." Then palm the mound between her legs. "Then here."

She sucks in a breath. "Gray."

"Unless you don't want me to."

Her eyes go wide. "I do." Her face turns serious. "Thank you."

"What for?"

"The best night of my life."

Shit. I'm done. I can't stay off of her. With every kiss and touch, she laughs, whispers, and moans. It's a deadly combination, and the sounds are mine to keep. This night, it's the best I'll ever have too.

Her fingernails bite into my flesh as my fingers slide beneath her panties. She moves against me, and I'm going to lose myself if she keeps that up. But God, I want her too. I want to see her come. I want to watch it and own it, to know I did that, gave that to her.

"Grayson." Her breaths are ragged, and even as I work my fingers between her legs, I'm flexing my hips to her side. "Gray... God..."

Her body clenches, her thighs press together, she juts her hips up, and I feel her climax down to my soul. It's the only thing I can focus on. Hell, the world can stop spinning and I wouldn't notice—

A dark, nasty cackle comes from the hall. I jump. Emma jumps.

"Finally nailing that tart. That's my boy," Pops snarls from the dim hallway.

A chill freezes over us, and he staggers into my room.

"Oh, God," Emma's embarrassed cry shreds me, and for a snap of a second, I don't know what to do. Protect her and kill him. I'm angrier than I can fathom. But what the fuck did I think would happen? Nothing good comes in this trailer. Nothing. Ever.

"First time with this one?" Pops falters after a bad step, and a cigarette tucked behind his ear falls to the floor.

"What the fuck?" I growl. Never do I say a word. Never do I handle my shit with him. I'm stronger, bigger, more of a man than he'll ever be, but because I ruined his life, I've taken his crap, his attacks, the vulgar nature of his existence.

Until now.

He hurt the one person who saves me. I toss my covers over her but stare at him. "Get out!"

He steps closer, cigarette and whiskey stench rolling off of him. He claps off-cadence, chuckling to himself like I'm the night's entertainment. "Don't let me stop you."

Jesus. The pressure in my head nears dangerous levels, but I swallow away my reaction. That doesn't mean I haven't come up with a list of what should happen. Maim. Kill. Bury. "Out."

"You're all the time eye-fuckin' my women." Pops sways in the middle of the room, and I'm on my feet. "Think you're big man." He coughs and slurs. "Think you can take from me, and I can't take from you."

I snag her dress from the floor and toss it on the bed. "Get dressed, Ems. Take my car. Go. I'll—"

Pops' drunken right hook catches me on the back of the head. I didn't see it coming and don't feel it now. All I can process is the look of complete disgust on her face.

I turn to the greasy-haired bastard. "Don't do this now."

Like the sleaze he is, Pops laughs. "Years, you don't got shit to say. Get a girl in your bed, you're a big dick with a motor mouth."

"Emma, come on. Take my car—" He shoves me. Humiliation curls deep in my gut. I know I deserve his anger but not like this. Not in front of Emma. I spin to him. "Enough!"

He cough-laughs and throws a fist. I dodge it like all the others I could've dodged my whole life but didn't. His drunken eyes go wide. His mouth parts enough to show he didn't expect to miss. I never move. But tonight I do because Emma's frozen in place.

Her eyes say everything's changed, that maybe she's disappointed or disgusted. Maybe she now knows I live here with him on this side of town for a reason. Whatever's in her mind, I'm no longer what she knows. Embarrassed fear grips me.

"Emma." I reach for her, and she jolts back to reality.

"Shit." She grabs her dress, clutching it to her chest, and tears slide down her cheeks. "Shit, shoot, shit."

Fiery anger builds in my chest. It's red, hot, and rabid. I can't see, can't breathe, and I growl toward Pops. "Get out. Get the fuck out."

He rushes me, hands outstretched. Enough. Fuck him. I'm done. As his fists start their drunken descent, I unleash years of fury. A roar blasts from deep within me. My blows strike with scary accuracy. Head shot. Gut shot. Right hook, left hook. Each lands with impact. Vengeance takes over my limbs. I'm not thinking or feeling. Only doing.

I grab him and slam us against the wall, my hands around his neck. One. Two. Three. And he's done. Out. I let go, and he drops, crumpling on the ground, and I don't give a shit. A cold sweat's taken over my body, and my lungs pound. Adrenaline fueled me, but now I'm starved for oxygen, for sanity.

I glance over at my bed. Emma's tears flow freely. Her bottom lip quivers as she stares at Pops, and then eyes track back to mine.

Fuck me. My hands go clammy. My throat closes up. Adrenaline abates, letting my throbbing head and racing blood slow. Never in my eighteen years have I felt her scrutiny. Never. But now, there it is. Pity. Fright. Confusion.

Unsteadily, she stands, dressing without looking at me. She presses her lips together. "Are you okay?"

I nod, humiliation back, making me angry all over again. This is my life. That is my dad. This is where I live, where I'm trapped. As much as I hide from it at school, *this is me*. And I can't escape.

I look down at Pops, still out. Tonight was supposed to be perfect, the best night ever.

"I have to go." She slides off the bed.

My head drops. "I know…"

"This is what happens. Isn't it, Gray? The football bruises that Ryan never has. The—"

"Don't." I shake my head. I can't let her go there because *I* can't go there. "Forget it." But she deserves as much of the truth as I can stomach. "I've never hit him back before." I rub my temples, still studying the carpet. "Never."

She gasps the softest, saddest breath. "Really?"

Ha. There's a fucked-up logic I could never explain.

"You're twice his size. Why?" She bites her bottom lip. "It doesn't matter. You don't have to—"

"Stop." She's pitying me. God, fuck me, she's trying to map out some life solution for me. "You have to get out." I choke on the shame. "Please. He wasn't supposed to be here."

"I'm so sorry." Her shoulders slump, and her chin's down.

Slowly, I shift and shake my head, a complete disgrace. "Take my car home. Give Ryan the key. We'll just forget tonight..." Forget us because I'll never be able to face her again. All over, I've gone from angry to embarrassed.

Pops stirs on the floor. I'm not going to be here when he wakes up, and neither is she. "Go, Ems."

Tears brim in her eyes. We're breaking apart before we ever started. Part of me wants to beg her to forget this side of me. Another part wants to rejoice that someone knows how deeply I hurt, but I shake my head. "It's not supposed to be like this. It's..."

I can't sugarcoat an explanation. I grab my keys, force them into her hand, then drag Emma to the front door of the trailer I've never been able to escape.

"Please don't—"

"Just go."

She nods and obeys, leaving in silence. The front door slaps shut, and I punch the wall. I'm angry. Heartbroken. Devastated. And completely alone.

CHAPTER 7

GRAYSON

Only a few lights shine down, and sweat beads down my back. I couldn't stay home but had nowhere to go except here, the batting cages where the owner lets me have access anytime day or night. The lights are always on and the gate is always open. It's just me, the ball, and the bat pushing toward midnight.

It's been hours since Emma left my place and I grabbed the keys to Pops's truck. If I stop pushing myself, I'll have to deal with the fallout from tonight. Pops is gonna kill me. He would even if I hadn't borrowed his truck while he was sawing Zs on the floor. Emma's never going to see me the same way. And me. If I look in a damn mirror, I'll be sick. I wanted to leave the second school's over. Running away from my past is an alright way to go once everyone else heads to college. But now I need a plan.

Clicks pop from down range, and the mechanical arm launches another baseball toward me. I'm past even a decent form. I'm exhausted. My muscles scream. One ball after the next, I can't stop swinging, sick over the future, knowing that I had the world fooled until tonight.

Finally nailing that tart. Pops's words reverberate in my head. Another ball flies. Swinging, I embrace the burn in my back, the ache in my arms. A satisfying crack echoes as it flies, another home run that doesn't go anywhere.

The clicks and pops signal another one inbound.

I need to talk to Ryan. He always trusted me with Emma, would never have a problem with me being with her. There's no way he'd think I could hurt her. Because I couldn't. *I can't.* But I did. Fuck me, I did.

The Kingsleys are the only family I've had, even if they aren't really mine. I shake my head, grinding my hands on the grip. A ball flies. Crack. Another one heading for the fence. I should text Ryan. If Emma showed up at home in tears with my car, he's gonna have a problem with me. Their parents will too. My stomach drops. None of that matters, though, not when she's been the only thing that's allowed me to survive, and now she's gone.

All because of Pops. And Mom. Shit, what would my mom do? What would she think? Why couldn't this have been better for her? For us? My mind churns.

Just another one. I can see her face. Vividly. Even when I was a kid, her perfect make-up confused me. She was so pretty. So lost. I want to throw up. God, I can't shake her eyes on me in my memories. I'm going fuckin' nuts. Everyone's in my head: Pops, Ryan, and now Mom. *Just another one, honey. Another minute, Grayson. It'll be okay. It'll always be okay with another one.*

Fuck! It's not okay. It was never okay. Why did she burden me with this? Rage blinds me, and I throw the bat, screaming into the night. The clink and clash of it hitting the fence does nothing to reduce the pounding in my head. I tear my hands into my hair, and it's too short, too tight to grab. I'm seconds away from collapsing, from a complete nervous breakdown.

"Take a breath, son."

Whirling around, I'm sweat-drenched and face-to-face with our ROTC adviser, Marcus Waylon. "What're you doing here?"

"Chaperoning that dance, saw the shit with Snyder. Then I drive by, and you're out here, alone?" He clucks his tongue. "Had to pull in."

Waylon isn't much older than me. He maybe graduated a few years ago. He didn't do college. Did do the military. He's here not because he wants to be anywhere near this side of the United States, but because he's on Uncle Sam's payroll, and they put him here in Virginia as an Army recruiter.

He walks closer. I blink, searching for words, gasping for breaths. Shit knows what he must think about me right now. I flex my aching fingers. "What'd you want, sir?"

He takes another step closer and glares. "Better question, Ford, is what're you doing?"

Trying to outrun my nightmares, hide from my pain. I take a deep breath. My pulse is thumping in my temples, my neck. Trying to slow my heart rate, I make him wait a minute. "Working out. Hitting the cages."

"Baseball season's over." Waylon's arms cross. "Try again."

Avoiding the two people I can't control, Pops and Emma. "Blowing off steam."

He nods. "I talked to Coach. He said—"

C'mon on already. What is it with tonight? "That

prick? Seriously. That goddamn prick thinks—"

"You don't know what he thinks." Waylon grabs and tosses my ignored bottle of water.

I catch it and guzzle half, thinking of how both Snyder and Waylon must think of me. I know what the world sees. I let them see it: good looks, good grades, good at sports. Package trifecta. I get it. But, man, they're wrong. Everyone's wrong. "Coach thinks Emma isn't—"

"I know what's going on with you at home."

Well, fuck me. My hand crushes the plastic bottle. "Yeah. Right." I scuff my shoe into the dirt. "Of course, you do."

Waylon ignores my attitude. "It's easy enough to figure out once you get past all your cocky bravado."

"Easy. Right." First Snyder, now Waylon, both guys I would've thought would be on my side. I'm just as smart as Pops thinks I am. All the voices, doubts, memories, they start to choke me again. Everyone's in my head. Pops. Emma. Ryan. Mom. Snyder. Waylon. It's too much. My sore fingers knead my neck, locking in my hair. I can't catch my breath. The pressure's too much on my lungs. In my head. My throat's closing up.

"Take a breath." Waylon steps closer. "Calm down."

Shit, I can't calm down, can't make it stop. "I need to get out of here."

"Where you going to go?"

Where am I going tonight? Not home. Not the Kingsleys', not after everything with Emma. My chest hurts again. A virgin. She's *my* virgin. She's my world, my heart.

I can't believe how things fell apart. I ruined it— ruined us—and I'm not even sure I can survive the next ten minutes, let alone the rest of school. Emma's the only thing that saves me. Shit, I can't breathe. That look on her face? My dream, my savior, I've lost her tonight, and my heart's going to explode.

A hand claps on my back. I startle, my head shoots up and I'm dizzy with panic.

Waylon's face is serious. "Let's go."

That's all he says before he turns and heads towards the parking lot. I have no reason to go with him, none to stay at the batting cages, and nowhere else to go. A lonely exhaustion hugs me, and unable to see anything but pain, humiliation, and desperation, I follow.

CHAPTER 8

Three weeks later...

Emma

Cherry: YOU SURE YOU'RE GOOD?

That's the fifth text message from Cherry today. I'd spilled my guts when she came in for graduation. We spent a whole weekend bitching about boys, enough to scare Ryan away from all questions about where Grayson has been, but even my brother's caught on, giving the occasional *it's-okay* grin.

After Cherry went back to college, she started a daily text message campaign. Her goal was to ready me for today: D-day. Or rather B-week. Beach week.

In our town, every senior takes the week after graduation, teams up with their friends, and rents a house for a week of celebration. A few of us rented a beach house. My small group obviously includes Grayson, so for the fifth time today, I lie and text Cherry back.

Emma: DOING AWESOME. SERIOUSLY, NO WORRIES.

It takes her two seconds to call me out on it.

Cherry: LIAR. CALL ME IF YOU NEED ME. XX

Yeah, I need her in a major way, but what am I going to do? Have my big sister come home and bunk with me? Besides, I don't want her around Grayson. She's got a heart like mine, and she's a fixer, a planner, and after what I confided in her, she wants to show up at Grayson's place and do something about his dad.

The problem, we decided, is that he's eighteen. He could leave. But leave what? Go where? If he won't talk to me, then I'm left to my own thoughts, which haven't been great. I groan. I'm so confused.

"Hey, hon?" Mom knocks softly and walks in. She's had an eye on me for the last few weeks, and I'm pretty sure that Cherry ratted me out after graduation. Not that she told Mom I offered up myself in bed, but I'm sure Mom knows there was a falling out between me and Gray.

It's been weeks since the Sadie Hawkins disaster. Gray can do his thing, and I'll do mine. He hasn't been to lunch. He hasn't returned a phone call or text, nothing online. Nothing. I almost caught him when I came out of the school darkroom, but he ditched down a hall right when the bell rang, and I was stuck staring after him and holding a handful of photography supplies.

Gray's still hanging with everyone *but* me *and* still going to the beach house. I'm not sure what to do, especially on the ride out there with Ryan and Gray. How should I act? What do I say? Maybe ignore it all? Whatever I do, it won't matter. My heart's still bleeding. I lost him, and it hasn't made me love him any less.

Judging by the pictures from the rental site, there's a chance it will be just like school. We'll never bump into each other, given how big that house is. I could always follow him around like some PI ninja, but that's pathetic, just like how I feel.

Ugh, I stifle a groan and turn to Mom. "Hey."

"Have you talked to Ryan this morning?"

"No." I shake my head. "What's up?"

"He was up all night, sick."

My eyebrows rise. "What?"

She leans against the door jam. "I think he has food poisoning, but either way, he's going to miss the first day or two of beach week."

Shit, shoot, shit. Nervous excitement at the thought of a car ride alone with Grayson rolls through me. It's at my brother's expense, which kinda makes me an awful person. "Yeah, okay."

Maybe Ryan's hungover from his spiral of post-grad partying. Mom leaves, and I grab my phone. After a few minutes of texting Ryan to no avail, I roll out of bed and knock on his door.

No answer, so I nudge open the door. He doesn't seem hungover, just sleepy. But he sounds like shit, croaky and gross.

"Don't come in here, Emma." He pulls the pillow over his head.

"No prob." Germs aren't my thing. I would bathe in hand sanitizer if I could. Getting sick is a nightmare.

Okay. Alright. Shit. Okay. What do I do? We're supposed to leave, like... right now.

"Have fun." He coughs. "Catch up with you guys soon as I can."

If Ryan, Grayson, and I are supposed to ride

together, does that mean now it's just Gray and me? I bite my lip. It seems benign enough except my pulse thumps. But would Gray ride with just me?

Of course he would. Right? He might be avoiding me, but he's not an asshole.

Gray's gotta be mature enough to sit in a car and, at the very least, ignore me for a couple of hours. What if I can't handle the close quarters alone with him? Maybe I should call up Courtney or Melanie and ride with them, just to save everyone an awful few hours. Time is ticking and—

"Emma," Mom calls from downstairs.

My stomach leaps into my throat. It's go time. Grayson must be here already. I head that way, stopping on the final step, nerves firing. *Please don't let him leave when he finds out Ryan won't join us.* I'm not sure I could handle such direct avoidance.

"Emma, get down here, hon. Gray's—" She rounds the corner and steps toward me, her face confused. "Hey, Gray's here."

I peek over Mom's shoulder, and he's inching toward the door. My world spins just seeing him. He's beautiful, handsome, so tall and strong. I think the last few months have changed him from a boy to more of a man. He's just so… Gray.

Knowing his lips had been on mine and why he won't talk to me makes my soul ache. Down to the very base of my body, I hurt. I miss him. Forget that I love him and that I want to hold him. I need him with a desperation I can't explain, and I want him to know that what happened with his dad, it's unacceptable, but it's not worth losing us over.

"Emma?" Mom gives me a onceover. It's like she can sense something's off but can't put two and two together. Maybe I was wrong about Cherry giving her any gossipy details.

Here goes nothing. "Hey, Gray."

He turns, and piercing green eyes draw me to him. "Ems."

The only word I've heard from him in weeks and it has to be Ems. I'm lightheaded.

"Alright, you two." Mom gives me a hug. "Have fun. Give me kisses, Emma."

I kiss her cheek, but my brow drops as I find the courage to tell him he's stuck with me. "Oh, um. Ryan's riding out later."

Grayson's jaw flexes. "Right. That's what your mom said." He shoves his hands in his pockets, his giant shoulders hulking. But his eyes still hold mine. "Okay, let's go."

His obvious discomfort around me is painful. I can't do this. Maybe this was a bad idea, riding with him. "Ya know... I'll hitch a ride. Or drive myself."

Mom laughs. "You're not driving yourself to the beach, Emma. My God. Grayson, her bag is in the mudroom. You two need anything? You're good on cash? Dad shoved another couple twenties in your bag after he said bye this morning."

Numbly, I can't think of an argument that doesn't make me sound pathetic. I stare at the hardwood floor. Grayson passes me, and I hear him grab my bag. When he walks by, my bag thrown over his shoulder, his soapy scent makes my mouth water and my eyes tear. I want that so bad. I want him. So much. So pathetic.

At my door, he turns. "You need anything else?"

Um... Yeah. You. Back to normal with me. But really, I do need my purse and toiletry bag. "Give me a minute."

I run upstairs, grab my crap, and text Cherry.

Emma: THINGS ARE MORE COMPLICATED. BUT I'LL SURVIVE. CALL YOU LATER.

She doesn't ping me back, and there's no option but to get into Gray's car. Actually, there are a million options. The truth is, I'm hurting so much, missing him even more, and I refuse to miss a chance to sit next to him, even if it's in uncomfortable silence, for the next few hours.

"Bye, Mom."

From somewhere, she shouts back, and then I'm out the door to meet him at his car. Each nervous step feels heavier than the next, and by the time my hand touches the door handle, I'm concerned I'll puke from nerves. So much for saving the friendship.

"Hey," he mumbles.

"Hey." I climb in and trap myself next to him. Delicious insanity. I want to hug him, hold him, kiss him, scream at him, plead for words, beg for a conversation. But I just buckle my seatbelt.

He backs out. It's a three-hour drive to the beach. When we show up, we won't be alone. Courtney and Melanie left this morning. Trevor and James arrived last night. Our drive out is my only chance at... what? Everything.

My bravery is pooling again, despite our awkward silence. I bite my lips to keep quiet, but I know it won't work.

We merge onto the highway. His overwhelming presence fills his car, and when I take in his broad shoulders and strong jaw, it's more than my broken mind can handle. The thing about being heartbroken is that I'm so ruined that I don't care if it happens again. I'm blinded by love. Blinded by heartbreak.

Just... blind when it comes to him. I can't see anything past how I feel.

"You okay over there?" His voice interrupts my thoughts.

"What?"

"You're..." His hand flexes on the steering wheel. "Growling or something."

"I didn't growl."

He changes lanes, looking more at me than his blind spot. "So what was that?"

"I'm just...not okay. I want to scream. Or cry. Probably both. Because of you."

He rubs a hand over his face and into his hair.

If it wouldn't kill us on the highway, I would shake him. First, because my hands would be on him again, and it would be temporary heaven. But second, isn't it possible to rattle someone so hard that whatever is wrong with them—with us—slips away? "You told me I can't hide from you. You made me promise I wouldn't avoid you, Gray. *Promise.*"

"Yeah, I know," he mumbles.

"What is it, a double standard?"

The radio station comes back from commercial, and his thumbs beat on the steering wheel. "You wouldn't understand, and I can't explain it."

He turns the music up. Riding with him was an awful idea, and now I can't breathe. My skin crawls. The seatbelt chokes me, and the air conditioning is blowing full blast, but it won't take the edge off the heat eating me alive.

"Everything was awesome. It was... perfect. And when—"

"Drop it, Ems. I can't talk to you about it."

My fingernails bite into my palms as I ball my fists in my lap. "Try me. Talk to me. Just say anything."

"I can't."

"Damn it, Gray. *Try!*"

Surprised, he turns his head. His eyes stay with me like we're not flying down the road. "Ems—"

"Stop with the Ems. Stops with *everything*," I scream. "Stop what's wrong. Stop it, stop it."

"Jesus, Emma, calm down. I'm not doing anything."

"Except you are." My body curls in on itself, and my head shakes. The sadness and loss is overwhelming. I just ache. My stuttering breaths fall ragged between my lips. A tear slips free.

"It's for the best—"

"I don't believe you." The guy who made me feel like I was so much more than some art nerd who happened to be his friend—that guy held me, kissed me. He made me want to give all of me to him.

"You'd never understand." His hand reaches over to find mine, and it sends a strike of lightning straight to my heart. "It's always been about you."

My eyes sink shut, and my mind spins. He's driving with his left hand. His right hand firmly holds my tight fist. His fingers flex and squeeze like he's trying to tell me something. I don't get it. But I do feel it.

I don't know why he runs from me, but I swear we're not over. He can fight, but if there's one gift he's given me over the past few weeks, or maybe even the years we've been building to this point, it's this car ride.

I take my other hand and clasp it over his, sandwiching our hands. Gray lets out a slow breath, and I hope that he sees we're not lost. Not yet. He's running, and I'll stop him. Save him. Grayson's the strongest guy I know, but right now, it feels like I'm holding him afloat.

"Emma, I did something that I can't get out of."

I swallow and wonder if this has to do with his dad or something else. "Okay."

"And I keep pretending if I don't know it's coming, maybe it won't happen."

Kind of like how I'm not thinking about Trydan. When the fall semester starts, I won't see him every day. It isn't that far away. Being a couple of states over isn't that big of a deal unless he asks me to stay, and then it would be... a yes?

Would I give up school and the photography program for Grayson?

Yeah. No question.

Everyone would call me foolish. They'd say I'm too young, that love doesn't come this quickly. But no one would know how long it's been or how deeply I love.

"You can tell me anything. I'll do anything. For you." For us...

He clears his throat. "That's what I'm afraid of." His hand squeezes mine. "Let's pretend next week isn't coming. Deal?"

I just swore I'd do anything for him. Of course he knows my answer. "Deal."

But already, I'm trying to map out my plan on how to make 'us' a 'we.'

CHAPTER 9

Emma

The beach house is rowdy. The guys are here. Ryan finally made it, and Trevor and James are a complete headache. Courtney and Melanie are gossiping, maybe—probably—about me. Ryan's had his eye on Gray, who's not kept his hands off of me, which earned me a quick conversation about Gray being both our friend, that he's the good guy we've always known, and that if something's going to happen while we're all here, Ryan wouldn't surprised.

Okay... Apparently, my brother missed the last few weeks of me moping around but seems totally honed in on the smile I can't hide now. But Ryan's right, and Gray and I are moving to a good place as beach week ticks on.

On day one, the heaviness of the car ride left us both fatigued. When everyone went out that night, we stayed in. Movies on the couch. We started on opposite ends, but by the time the credits rolled, I'd fallen asleep with my head in Gray's lap, his hand lazily toying with my hair. What had happened between us weeks ago hovered somewhere between healing and ignored.

On day two, we were at the beach all day. Volleyball and games of chicken in the ocean. No one else went up on Gray's shoulders. They didn't try, so he didn't have to say no. We were connected at the hip except when I was squealing and screaming in the water, sitting high on his neck. His hands held my calves. His thumbs trailed my skin. And even with a million people around and freezing cold Atlantic Ocean water spraying us, my skin burned from his touch.

My Gray was coming back. The future wasn't in his head, and his eyes were only on me. I loved it. Loved him. God, so much.

On day three, I laid on the beach with the girls. They had twenty questions about us, none of which I would answer, mostly because I didn't know. But I didn't miss his glances when I lounged out of his reach with the girls. They were long and lazy. Ryan, Trevor, and James gave him some hell, to which he replied with a laughing middle finger. The guys backed off, the girls swooned, and I melted any time Grayson came near.

And that brings us to now, to my eyes tracking his beautiful body. For the better part of several days, he's only worn board shorts. Every sexy muscle is on display. I'd known for the last few months that Gray had been slamming extra workouts before and after school. I'm reaping the benefits. Ryan, Trevor, and James look fine. They take care of themselves. But Grayson Ford looks like a beach god. A couple of days' worth of sun has kissed him, and he's beyond words. But no lines have been crossed, no amazing consequences of our unacknowledged flirting. Even though we've been side-by-side nonstop, that's all it's been.

I'm done.

And I think he's done.

Each day, his eyes stay on me longer. His hands touch more boldly. Our laughs are too loud, our gazes too deep. If he doesn't kiss me soon, there's a very good chance I will implode. Just ka-blamy.

"We're gonna grill out. Heading to the store for steaks, beer, and whatever else," Ryan shouts from the front door. "Anyone coming, let's go."

Courtney and Melanie push past hi; the guys do too. It's just Gray and me waiting.

"You going?" I ask.

He steps closer, not answering. His hair is damp, having just showered, and sticking with his beach week uniform, he's back in shorts that hang dangerously low on his hips. I swallow, trying to ignore the V where his stomach muscles lead to his hipbones. But I can't. My eyes slide over him, and there is a distinct bulge in his dark shorts that can't be missed. The thumping of my pulse begins in my neck.

"Gray—"

The front door closes behind Ryan, and Grayson's on me. My body sings. His mouth takes mine. The kiss is rough, his possessive hands are greedy, and he's breathing like *I'm* breathing.

My bikini allows our bare stomachs to touch, and it sends me into carnal overdrive. All my senses are alive and infused with him. Sexy sounds make me purr. His lips devour mine and have me crawling and clinging to him. I let go of my hesitations and live in the moment, grasping his thick biceps.

Gray's hands run roughly over me. He palms and squeezes my breasts before he slides up and tears his fingers into my hair. Using the wall for leverage, I hook my legs around his hips, and he grabs my thighs, holding me in place.

"We're okay?" he growls against my neck.

"Yes…" I'm nodding into his kiss, arching into his mouth.

"Fuck me, I missed you."

I'm nodding more, hanging onto him for everything I've got. "You have no idea." Tears well in my eyes, and what started hot and hungry slows.

He senses me, knows me so well. Gray cups my cheeks, pushing me inches away. His eyes bore into me, removing every vulnerable layer I have. "You're all that's right in my head. You get that?"

No. Not a chance. "I'm whatever you need."

He nods. His lips dance over mine. He tastes so familiar, smells like my greatest weakness. How does he have the whole world fooled?

"Emma, no joke. If I didn't have you, I'd—" He shakes his head. "I need you, always have, in a way you'll never know."

"But I want to."

His eyes close tight. "No. You don't."

Hugging my body to his, I want to meld together. "Whatever's in your head, I wish you could trust me with it."

Placing a soft kiss to my temple, he sighs. "You want to know about Pops?"

I nod.

"Baby, it's dark and dangerous, and I don't think you could ever forgive me, ever be with the kind of person I am."

My heart squeezes. "Grayson, I will take you however you come. Don't you get that?"

"I deserve everything he's thrown at me. But that night? In front of you? I couldn't see straight, couldn't think." He closes his eyes, breathes deeply, then his green eyes open. "Haven't seen Pops since that night."

"He's just... gone?"

Grayson nods. "He has his reasons for hating me... but the look on your face. He hurt you, Emma, and I attacked just like he does. Fuck me, I'm not him and don't want you to think of me like that."

"I don't."

"I saw it in your eyes. You didn't want me, and I didn't blame you. But damn it, that hurt."

I kiss him, lightly at first, then stronger. "I want you in every way. Trust me. Believe me." My lips press to his again, and I kiss him hard, deep, needing to show him that there's nothing he can say that will make me walk away.

"Believe you." He clasps my face, holding my mouth to his. The kiss is intense. Consuming. I can't breathe, and I don't care. I just need him.

A noise outside tears us apart.

Ryan's car has pulled up to the beach house, and everyone is piling out. I'm panting. He's flushed. My lips feel swollen. My nipples are painfully hard and visibly outlined in my bikini top.

"Shit." Grayson's grip flexes. "You good for a minute?"

What does that even mean? I nod, slowing my breaths on purpose. "Yeah."

Grayson and his erection move to a kitchen chair, and I fumble, making sure my bathing suit is where it should be. It's not, and I fix it right as Courtney and Melanie walk in the door, their mouths moving a mile a minute, jabbering about whatever, with arms full of grocery bags. The guys are behind them with a case of beer—which means Ryan's priceless ID worked yet again—and a bag of charcoal for the grill.

One stare from Melanie, and I know I'm busted. Twenty seconds ago, I couldn't breathe. Of course it would be obvious that *something* was happening. She bursts out in giggles, raising a knowing eyebrow. It sets off a chain reaction with Courtney.

"Christ, man. The kitchen?" Ryan mumbles but has nothing more to say.

Grayson ignores them, stands to grab my hand, and tugs. "Let's go."

He wastes no time in showing us to the room he's sharing with Ryan, and he slides the lock on the door. I bite my lip, unsteady under Gray's intense stare.

"What are we doing?" I whisper.

"Ignoring the future."

My heart falls and jumps. Again with his fear of tomorrow, but does that mean he'll give me what I want?

"I'm not going to sleep with you, Emma. Not here. Like this. Not... now."

"Okay." Good. This isn't how I want it anyway, in some room he shares with my brother after we were basically caught making out. Nothing romantic about that. And I want it all: the future, the man, the feelings, and the emotion.

"But I am going to memorize every inch of your body."

Holy crap, I can't even begin to process what that will entail. The way he said it was predatory, and even as I stare, turned on and disillusioned, the timber of his voice crawls through me, sliding down my spine.

"Lie down, Ems."

And carefully, nervously, I do. When he sits beside me, the bed dips. He's by my ankles, and I'm lying stick straight. Again, my breaths fall faster just because of him, and it's so obvious on my back in my bathing suit. Not much to hide behind. But he looms over me with his giant, tan shoulders beautifully within reach. The definition of his chest is scarily sharp.

We watch each other until I realize that I'm no longer stiff and straight but relaxed, loose, and aroused. His hand picks up my right foot. It tickles, and I twitch, which makes him smile.

"Easy, baby."

Baby. My heart stops. That's it. I'm done. If *Ems* did something magical to me before, *baby* knocked me stratospheric. I ease for him. Relax for him. I'll do anything for him, but now all I do is exist as his strong hands glide up my calf and over my knee to massage my thigh. He spends a delicious eternity repeating the unhurried move before switching to my other leg. The process is repeated in its slow entirety. I'm putty in his hands, and as much as I want to touch him, that's apparently not what our moment now is about.

"Turn over," he whispers, and I do.

Gray toys with my hair, brushing it off my shoulders. His fingers trace my spine, running and rubbing my skin, making me squirm. Then he loosens the knot at my neck and the clasp at my back, letting my bikini top fall off even though I'm on my stomach.

"You're perfect. You know that, right?" He draws closer to me.

His body lies parallel but shifts and folds over me. His kiss stuns me when it touches the nape of my neck and slides down my back, following the same path his fingers took. As my skin erupts into shivers, I twist to him, needing so much more, but he holds me in place, kissing my back, all the way to the base of my spine, right to the top of the bikini bottoms.

I lick my lips. "I'm perfect when I'm with you."

He turns me over, my chest bare to him. I don't move to cover or shy away. I've never felt more beautiful than right now. His eyes drink me in, and whatever his fear of the future is, I believe it can be dealt with.

"Sleep with me tonight." His fingertips skim over my skin. "Like *sleep*."

The genuine carefulness in his words stills my heart. I nod. The sun hasn't set, we haven't had dinner, but if he wants to go to bed now, kissing and sleeping until tomorrow, I've never been more ready for bed.

And that's what we do. We kiss and touch and whisper, and long after the sunlight turns to dark, we sleep. His breathing evens out before I tumble into dreams. "I love you, Grayson Ford."

Even though I'm certain he's asleep, his arms flex around me, and this is what happiness means to me.

CHAPTER 10

Emma

Saturday night's here, and I'm sitting on Grayson's leg watching Courtney and Ryan lose at beer pong. Maybe it's unnoticeable to anyone else, but Ryan is losing on purpose. He and Courtney have had this thing all week, and it's shifted the looks from Gray and me to them. Thankfully, though, sitting on Gray's leg, letting him run his fingers up and down my arm, I don't care if anyone has an opinion.

The only thing Ryan's said is that it sucks to have a roommate who locks him out of the room, which made me blush. And made Courtney blush. So thinking back on it, Ryan wasn't too pissed at all about Gray commandeering their shared bedroom for nights *with me*. He wanted it for himself.

But right now, heaviness hangs on Grayson's face. It's not obvious, and when pressed for more, all he gives is a placating smile. I can read him well after the days spent together behind closed doors. The sounds I've made for him would be mortifying if not for how amazing they feel. The way his hands play... Grayson's the only person in the world that I'll let see this side of me. The more intimately he touches me, the bolder I am, and when it's my turn, I become more... alive. More me.

Heat hits my cheeks. I know I'm blushing and trying unsuccessfully to hide my smile. Tucking my face into his bare shoulder, I let my lips press to his skin. It warms my memories. I have thoughts of last night with his mouth over me, in between my thighs, and then my first time tasting him... My belly somersaults.

I love it. Love him. Love everything about us.

"What are you smiling at?" His voice tickles my ear.

"Nothing." I might be able to love what we've done, but telling him about my mini-fantasy of wrapping my lips around him and sucking again... Well, I'm going to need a few weeks before I'm comfortable saying that.

He chuckles, and I know he knows. "How about nothing I haven't replayed a hundred times today, too?"

Holy shit, cue belly flip. "Oh my God, Gray."

His hands tighten around my waist, and I squirm. It's becoming one of the things I do most because, when he touches me, I know what comes next.

"Let's get out of here." He lifts me up, and I squeak in giddy surprise. "We're headed to the beach."

Gray heads for the door, holding me against his soapy-scented chest, and grabs a beach blanket from a pile by the door. I'm weightless, supported in his muscular arms. When we hit the sand, I snuggle close. "What are we going to do?"

"What do you want to do, baby?"

"You." I kiss his shoulder.

He clutches me closer, and the scruff from his cheek scratches against my skin. "Just you and me and the ocean right now."

My chest feels tight. The waves crash in the background. The last few days, I've been honest with everything I've said to him. But there have been some thoughts and concerns that have gone unvoiced, mostly about his crazy future fears. "It's romantic."

Distant lights from the beach house give soft shade to his face. "Didn't bring you out here for romance. Just had to get away, be with you."

Gray sets me down and spreads the blanket. In a whoosh, I'm back in his arms, on my back, and he's holding himself over me. But then he rolls us over so I'm on his chest. Forever ticks by, his thick arms clinging to me like he's scared that tomorrow, when we drive home, everything will be forgotten.

He clears his throat. "I have to tell you something."

This again. He starts; then he stops. Whatever *it* is, it's driving him crazy. Me, not so much. Nothing he can say will change how I feel. Young love, maybe. But it's deep. It's burned into my soul.

I prop up on his chest and stare into a face shadowed by the night. "Okay."

"Fuck me." He groans. "I'm not as strong as you think I am."

I nod. "Probably stronger."

"Not like that, Ems. Like… I'm broken inside, and you, you're perfect."

"You're my perfection." He looks away, and I bring his face back to mine. "Just tell me already. Whatever it is, it's killing you and ruining my romance on the beach." Giving him a half-grin and a quiet laugh, I'm dying to help him free himself of this imaginary burden.

"What if we only had tonight?"

I laugh into the salty air. "Well, you know what I'd want." Dropping my mouth to his, I kiss him and let his tongue sweep into my mouth. "The world's ending, and I want you. It's the apocalypse? My last thought is to be next to you, making love to you."

I can't believe I just said that. My blood rushes.

He hugs me close, murmuring against my lips. "You have no idea."

No, I don't. Not if he won't tell me. Instead of pleading with him again, I press my lips to his.

He pulls back. "Emma, I messed up, but I have to wonder if everything happens for a reason. You're going to college. You've got the world lined up—"

That's what his future issue is? "Grayson. Stop."

"It's—"

"Listen." Plastered on his chest, I lean up and cup his cheeks. Breathing in deeply and knowing the truth, I close my eyes and pray whatever hurts him can just heal, that whatever secret he thinks will cause irreparable harm disappears.

"Listening, baby." Even in the dark, his eyes are the most beautiful shade of green I've ever seen.

"I love you, Grayson." My heart seizes. Even though it's the truth, it's out there, and I can't hide or take it back. "You're my best friend, and I'm in love with you."

His eyes search mine in the dark. Silence hangs. Then his hands cup my cheeks, too. We hold each other like that.

"Promise?"

I nod.

"God, baby." He blows out, and I'm not sure whether it's relief or terror. "I love you, too."

Oh, yes. His words are quiet and sweet, but my heart and soul soar. Already lying on top of him, I hug him and bring my gaze back to his. His lips touch mine, and he kisses me. Strong hands rub my back, my bottom. He threads his fingers into my hair. His length hardens between us, and I'm wound so tight, my skin sizzles from the inside out.

"I want this, Gray. I'm giving everything I have to you. Please."

His lips don't leave mine. His hands hold me tighter. "Emma..."

I kiss him. "As long as you never say goodbye to me, we will always be okay in the end. I want you to be my first..." ...and my last, though *that* I don't have the guts to say.

His soft eyelashes sink shut, our bodies meld, and he kisses me back. "I love you."

"Never tell me goodbye."

He stiffens, staring deep into me. Then he blinks, nods, and kisses, his tongue teasing mine. "Ems—"

"Never mind. No more talking. Please?"

With a look so long and deep that it steals my breath, he finally nods and turns me onto my back. It takes seconds for him to remove my bikini, and smiling, I shed him of his shorts. His mouth is on my neck, behind my ear. Warm air blows over us as our hands intertwine. He's so careful with me, kissing me deeply, hugging me close.

"I love you, baby. I do." One hand slips free of our grasp and teases between my legs. He sucks a long breath against my skin, and so do I. Gray teases me until I'm almost grinding against him, and then he presses fingers inside me. It's heaven. It's still so new, so insane, but I've never been more ready for more.

I'm moaning as he works me. "I'm so... Please. Please..."

His mouth meets mine. His hand guides himself close. The head of him touches me, and my heart's pounding. I'm drunk for wanting this, needing him. And as he pushes against me, our eyes lock. "Yes."

"Okay?" he breathes against me.

God, he's holding back, and I'm surging forward. "Please." It's the only thing I can manage. I'm begging. Pleading. The fullness is shocking, the stretching painful. Uncertainty paints his face, but I'm nodding and urging.

"Oh. God." Inch by inch. He moves into me, and my jaw hinges open, my back arching off the blanket. I gulp and gasp.

"Okay?" he says again. Restraint shows in his jaw.

"Don't stop. God." I hurt as much as I love this. The pain abates, and my hips flex toward his. He reads me. He always does. And slowly he slides deeper, only to withdraw and torture me again.

"Fuck me," he groans. "Love this."

I'm without words, but my teeth find his bottom lip, my body's reacting to his, and what happens is more than I can hope for.

I love him. "I love you."

Then Grayson Ford takes over. Slowly, deeply, he rides into me. My legs wrap around him, and he goes faster. My teeth bite into his shoulder, my mind wound tight as my body. When I begin to spiral toward my climax, he knows it. It's an explosion, and we're lost in each other. He comes with me, and it's the best moment of my life, feeling him inside me, feeling me shatter because he made me.

Our breathing levels while slow kisses steal the night away. His hands cover my back, and carefully, he pulls away from me. I'm in his arms, knowing this is how forever feels. Contentment settles in my chest.

Finally, wordlessly, we dress, and I'm back against him. He carries me to bed. It's the middle of the night, maybe close to morning. My eyelids hang in sated, almost-slumber while he arranges the pillows and tucks me in.

"I'll never forget tonight." He kisses my temple, and the comfortable haven of his arms, my pillow, and blanket call to me. "Love you forever."

Slowly, happily, I slip to sleep.

CHAPTER 11

Present Day...

GRAYSON

"Go, go, go! Get your asses moving." Orders bark in my earpiece from a man who can't see the shit-storm around Maddox and me.

Mortar fire screams from every direction. Smoke clouds the night air, and my lungs burn. Sulfur burns in my nostrils, and I'm choking on adrenaline. Fight. Survive. Those are my goals. I push against the crumbling wall, breathing hard, wishing like hell there is a break in the insurgent attack we never saw coming.

"Go!"

Shit, man. If we have some place to go, our asses would be moving as ordered. Fuck me. But we are blind, trapped in a dilapidated hut on the outskirts of a town that didn't want us here to begin with.

A bullet hits the wall above me. Another one strikes closer, lower, just a few feet off. I'm not getting shot and left to die in this sandbox. I look over at Maddox, the only other man standing. The ground shakes as a mortar lands outside. Our unit has been decimated. We've got nothing, no ammo, no backup, no support except the asshole in our ears telling us to go.

"Go where?" Maddox shouts. His voice breaks. He's scared. God, man, I'm scared. We're done. No way we see tomorrow. It just can't happen.

"Air support's in there in two minutes. Make it 'til then, boys. You goddamn make it until that bird shows up."

An explosion rocks the hut's roof. It's caving in around us. Dust bites into my eyes. Chunks of plaster rain down. I grab Maddox, pulling him with me, and we run with no idea where to go. We blast through what's left of the door, and cool air smacks me.

I drop, dragging Maddox. All our brothers-in-war died around us, coughing up blood, screaming out in pain. Maddox is in shock. I'd be in the same state of mind, except I long ago lost mine.

"C'mon." I've got him by his shoulder, pushing him to keep my grueling pace. Don't know where we're going, but we gotta get there. Gotta live. I have a plan, have had it for three years. The only thing I need to do is stay alive, fulfill my army contract, and find my way home—to a place almost scarier than war, where memories and mistakes are just as real as bullets and IEDs.

Blasts explode and light the sky. It's yards away and not firing at us. Air support. Fuck me, thank God. Relief floods my mind. I can do this, totally survive this night. Maddox will, too.

"Ford, you there?"

I nod, panting from exertion. "Affirmative, sir."

"Extraction helo coming in hot. Head east, two hundred yards. Remain for pick up."

"Roger that." I signal Maddox; he signals back. There's a wall ahead. We'll be in the open for fifty yards, but we will get to that wall. We'll have partial concealment on the way to our pickup. That's our cover. That's where we can hunker down and breathe. "Ready?"

Maddox gives a thumbs up. He's back, at least enough to run.

"Let's go."

We run. My pulse races as we close in on the wall, and—thump—I turn around. The world slows.

"Gray!" Maddox reaches for me. Even in the dark night, I see his face twist. He's been hit. Mid-run, he's falling down. Blood coats his face, and just that fast, his expression is gone.

"Maddox!" I dive next to his body. "Don't do this, man. We're almost out. C'mon. C'mon!"

His eyes are wide, his mouth open. But he's gone. Dead. I scream into the night. "No! Damn it!"

"Jesus, fuck," comes in my ear. "Ford. Go."

My eyes pinch. Emma. She's the only thing that will get me out of here. I drop and roll, then zigzag toward the pickup location.

A new voice breaks into my earpiece. "Alpha, bravo, one-one, extraction team here. Arriving in one minute, boys."

My throat stings. "Just me. Last man standing."

There's a pause, and for a second, I wonder if they're assessing the risk of picking me up. One man. They've already lost the team. Why risk the helo, the men, all to save one guy? Doom wrecks my hope.

Garbled noise pops in my headset. White noise and static. The earpiece crackles again.

"Roger that, Ford?"

"No. Repeat."

"We're coming in hot, dropping a line. You grab it and tie on. You've got one shot out of hell. You got that, son?"

They're still coming. "Got it."

"Ten seconds."

I fumble for the extraction spot, see the clearing, and run all out.

"Three, two…"

"Here!" The quiet thumps of the stealth chopper arrive.

A line with a hook drops mere yards away. I run after it, pushing my body to reach the only way out of this hellhole. My muscles scream. My head spins. I can't breathe, but I grab the rope. Most of my equipment is gone. I have nothing to secure myself to it. No harness. No carabiners. Shit. Okay. I thread the line through my nylon belt, clip it to itself, then wrap both fists around it. One tug and my body jars in pain as the belt rips into my back, and my feet leave the ground. I hang on, gritting my teeth as the chopper pulls out but stays low.

The wind is harsh. The faster we move, the harder I grip, trying to absorb some of the impact of the line and the feeling of my belt tearing into my back. The chopper pulls right. Then left. We're evading attack. They're protecting me from sniper fire while I'm hanging like some American bull's eye.

I don't know the plan. I can't hear my earpiece any more. Will they pull me up? Will we land and load me in? Whatever they're doing, there's a firefight behind us, and we need to clear the attack zone.

Deep, brilliant, violent pain rips in my side. My nerves scream. I scream. Pain I wasn't expecting overpowers me. Shocks me. I can't hang on. Can't hold myself up. I'm losing my grip. My belt's the only thing that catches me.

Fire burns in my side. I'm shot with no idea how much I'm bleeding. My body dangles and spins out of control on the line. I'm dizzy and dim. Blood is on my tongue, and my life is on my mind. I've done two things wrong in my life: killed my mother and left the girl I loved.

Brutal regret ricochets through my body. The memories I use to fight my hell won't come. Emma's face is dark, blank. I can't remember her kiss, her taste—God, I'm dying. I can't even hear her voice. I've got nothing, no memory of the only girl who made me run, the only one who could save me.

CHAPTER 12

Emma

"Two minutes, Ginger."

Shit, shoot, shit. The reflection in the mirror isn't doing me any favors tonight. But there isn't time to fix what can't be changed. My hair is sprayed into place, and my boobs are squeezed to look like they are way bigger than they are.

"Ginger!"

God, I hate Wednesday nights. The only thing that can save tonight is... glitter, which I hate. Grabbing the can, I shake it up, close my eyes, and spray down.

My music thumps from above. No way was that two minutes. I have no time to wait for my shimmer to dry. Cursing, I shuffle in shoes that want to kill me and head up the narrow stairs. The higher I climb, the heavier the smoke stinks. My eyes burn, threatening the barely dry fake eyelashes I just glued in place.

"Ginger Raine!" The announcer's baritone still

booms through the crappy sound system, making what has to be one of the stupidest stripper names in history echo around me.

"Ta da. I'm here." I wave to Bruno and take in the place.

Packed, even on a weeknight. But it always is. They come to see me. I'm the stupid marquis name. If there ever was a career high point that was completely humiliating, I had that nailed.

This is what I do well. I sell the idea of sex. Of want. Of having an untouchable fantasy.

Because I am one.

Ginger Raine is my only salvation. My biggest secret. She's the once-a-week moneymaker that lets me live my life somewhat comfortably. I've got a future waiting for me, and it has nothing to do with the G-string I'm about to show.

"Work it." Bruno nods as I step onto stage.

The lights are hot. The floor is mine. A hundred eyes are on me, and my smile molds onto my face. It's not even that I'm gorgeous; it's that my smile says so much to the men watching the stage. I learned early on a blink of an eye or a sway of my hips does wicked good things for my wallet.

If it weren't for that, I'd be home and wouldn't hate Wednesdays.

A crescendo of pop beats and bass hits crawl from the speakers. This is work. That's all it is as I mentally drift to another place where I'm dancing for one person, the only boy I ever loved, the only one who ever had me.

What if we just have tonight? The tremble of a memory runs down my spine. Years ago, his hands curled over my naked shoulders, sliding down my bare back, and tonight I drop my head and roll my body remembering how I cried for more. Slowly, my hips sway, remembering the only thing that makes me good at my job.

My eyes close. It's just Grayson and me, all night long. This is my torture every Wednesday. It is also my moneymaker. Bruno says he's never seen a girl bring so much tension to the stage. Guess that's a compliment.

I'm numb to this room. When I drop to my knees, my body lies. It begs each man to touch me, to run their paycheck over my curves. I do it all without seeing a soul.

I'm crawling, gyrating, moaning, and the cash falls. Dollars rain down, and lost in a dream of a man I can never have again, I roll in my take. Fingers scratch my skin as they shove ones into my G-string. My knees slide under the carpet of money as I arch my back. Their bills stick to my skin. Only when the music ends does my autopilot trance shut down enough to sway my near-naked ass away.

The night has only just begun. It'd make me sick if I hadn't developed have-no-choice thick skin.

"Give Ginger Raine a few minutes, and she'll be on the floor. If you have a dream, she'll make it come true." The announcer promises the same thing every week to the crowd at the Emerald Gentleman's Club.

I'm their biggest cock tease. No matter what Bruno tries to bait me with and what the announcer promises, I dance, and that's it. Any release that men want can be found on their own.

Bruno is stage left, holding a clove cigarette in his thick fingers. He nods to the beat of the music. "Good girl."

He rocks a Rastafarian look, but it's coupled somehow with a body builder's physique. His bouncers are all similar versions of him. How there's a contingent of Rasta bodybuilders available in the semi-metropolitan area outside Summerland, Virginia, I have no idea. But he's found them.

"I try." But I can't keep trying if I don't head downstairs and change.

"Emma." He's blocking my path to the stairs. Tonight, his thick dreads are tied into some ginormous manly bunch at the back of his head, making him seem every bit the dread-head owner. He's sexy. He knows it. His powerful body is in a tailored suit that hangs perfectly on his bulky muscles. Between that and owning this place, his ego is as big as his personality.

Almost every girl to walk onto his stage has been with him, not because he makes it a requirement but because they can't stay away. Until they never come back. It's not a job for the stable, even if Emerald's Gentlemen Club is about as high class as exists around here. It's not a profession that screams lengthy job history. My two years with Bruno are outliers, and because of that, we've developed a rapport. In his own way, he cares.

"Where's your head tonight? You went deeper than normal."

My sad smile tells him everything he needs to know. Bruno never flirts with me. My guess would be because he knows most of my story. For as hard as he acts, I think he actually wants to help. Why else would he have hired me back in the day when my body was a little soft?

"Just doing the gig."

"You're too young." He shakes his head. "To live like you're that old."

It's almost like he wants to fix my past by supporting my future. I don't know if that even makes sense. It's just what it is. I'm his marquis girl, so he wants to take care of his meal ticket.

But he's also convinced that being twenty means that eventually, I need to let loose and party *with* someone, preferably one of the patrons. That way he'd make a little, I'd get a little, and everyone would be happy. In his mind, a good old-fashioned, screaming orgasm—from a *person*, not a vibrator— would be life altering.

Well, no thank you. Did that once, and it *was* life altering. That's about as much paradigm shift as I could handle.

"I need a couple minutes, Bruno. Seriously, I'm fine, and I promise I'll make us good money."

His hand lands on my shoulder, and his fingers give me a squeeze. "You raked in more money in the last hour than ever before."

"Yay, me. That's a good thing. Right?"

He smirks sarcastically. "Emma, you cleaned out wallets. So I know you're in your head."

"You give me this same speech every week."

Nodding, he looks over my shoulder. "Just want to keep you working for as long as possible."

"Got it."

"And..." He paints on a smile that can only mean vulgarity ahead. "If you feel the need to blow someone, make him pay first."

"I'll remember that." My eyes roll. The shit that comes out of his mouth is so foul that it's not. Sex is business. To Bruno, it's no different buying someone an ice cream, a Rolex, or an orgasm. Each provides pleasure.

He moves aside, and I teeter-totter down the stairs, heading to my vanity. A quick once-over of my makeup and that damn glitter spray, and I'm good. I check my phone. It's blinking with a text message from Cherry. She knows I'm at work, and my stomach drops.

Cherry: CALL ME.

Shit. I swipe the screen and call back. My mind's running fast as the music's dropping upstairs. The phone's ringing, and I'm trying to stay grounded. *Nothing's wrong.* I tie on my corset and slip on some thigh-highs. No answer, voice mail.

Biting my lip, I think, it's probably nothing, but my heart's beating faster. "Hey, it's me. Just checking on everything. Call me back."

The room feels like it's closing in, but if something was really wrong, Cherry would've called and texted something like SOS or ASAP. Something. Anything. I grab a black see-through robe and sash it so my boobs are on display.

My phone rings, and I jump for it. "Cherry? Everything okay—"

"Emma, oh my God."

My pulse skyrockets. "What?"

"We went for ice cream. I saw Julie, who was with Trevor and—"

"Cherry, *what?*"

"Grayson Ford's unit was attacked. They said no one survived." Cherry's voice cracks. "I'm so sorry."

I falter, stumbling back to my chair. "God..."

Bile churns in my stomach. I want to be sick. I want to run away from tonight, throw my phone away, and pretend what she said is wrong, that he's just far away, never to be heard from. Death is final. My hopes... I always had hopes. "Oh, God..."

Footsteps creak at the top of the stairs. "Emma. Get up here. Folks are restless."

I swallow over the lump in my throat. "Okay… I have to go."

Ending the call, I'm numb. But I have to go to work. I need to… just do something. Otherwise, the overwhelming loss might kill me in my chair. "Coming."

Slowly, I push back up the stairs and zero in on my prospects for the night. It's easy to map who'll be up for private time. I can close my eyes and hide my tears. I've lost my Grayson, but at least I have our daughter.

ONLY FOR HER

CHAPTER 13

Emma

There's a very good chance that, standing here in the knee-high grass surrounding Randall Ford's rusted trailer, I'm going to be sick. It looks the same as it did the night I ran from Grayson's bed, the same as when I showed up after beach week three years ago, worried sick and looking for him. Both of those times, Randall made my life hell. I keep waiting for that demented, drunk bastard to die, but he just keeps living.

Ragtag curtains are pulled over the windows. Burnt-orange rust stains streak down from the roof line. I steel myself. According to Summerland County gossip, Grayson died. But that doesn't mean much. The county grapevine also said he left town because he knocked me up. I almost wish that was true—how awful had that morning been, waking up without him. Gray was gone—but not because he knew I was pregnant.

The front door snaps open. Randall steps out, only

to stop and lean against the door frame. He looks ancient compared to the last time I saw him, when I nerved up and asked where Grayson was. His cackling response and door slam is still burned into my memory.

"You again?" Randall coughs.

I nod. This jerk holds the answer. He's sadistic. It's written all over his haggard face. His glassy eyes narrow, his mouth purses into some kind of smile, and he looks as if he stinks of a bar.

I straighten my back and square my shoulders. I have one question—might as well get to it. "Is Grayson dead?"

Inwardly, I cringe. Saying the words makes them seem all the more real. Tears spring into my eyes. I need to know, need to mourn. I'm drowning without the truth. All I know is what people have whispered and that there's been no word of a funeral.

Randall pulls a smoke from behind his ear and lights it. He takes a few long drags and steps down the rickety porch. "You come all the way o'er here jussfer that? Shit." He spits then draws on the cigarette again. "Gotta be better ways than to bother me wit that sonobitch's problems."

I might want to puke with nerves, but I've toughened up in the last few years since he's seen me. "That sonobitch is your *son*, Randall. I know exactly how you treated him."

"My son. Ha." He tilts his head. "Little Emma Kingsley grew a set, did she?"

"What do you know about Grayson?"

"What do you know?" He snarls as he coughs. "Come here to see if that bastard of his can get whatever's left of his benefits?"

My stomach drops, and I stagger back, recoiling at the mention of my daughter and the all-but-certain confirmation of Gray's passing. "Something's wrong with you."

"Blame the boy. I do." He flicks his cigarette at me and turns for the door but looks back. "Stop coming by. There's nothing here for you."

The wind blows, and even though it's a warm June day, I'm shivering. So much hatred. So much disgust. Part of me can't blame Grayson for leaving. The trailer door snaps shut, and I'm left standing in weeds, wondering how I'll move past the death of a man I haven't seen in years but think about every day.

GRAYSON

Trapped in the dark. I'm exhausted and struggling, reaching for escape. I keep surfacing, almost waking. I know it. Can feel it. My body hurts. My mind's tortured.

Screams echo. Shots blast. I feel the heat, the burn, the terror. The ground shakes. Walls and rocks crumble down. Dirt in my eyes, grit in my mouth. Sulfur burns in my nose. I can't see anyone, and they can't see me.

But I feel it. Feel them. Everyone I've let down. My unit. Their blood hangs in the air. Death coats my senses. Their faces flash, one after the other. I can't close my eyes, can't break away.

There's a break in the noise. A woman... in the middle of my hell, I hear a voice. Hope flourishes only to freeze and tear away. She's not my savior. Not my Emma.

Just... my mother?

Just another one, Gray-baby. Find me another one.

One more time, sweetie. Such a good boy. Bring it to me.

I'm going to be sick. War is better than the living room of my childhood. Desperate fear chokes me. I'm torn. Confused. I want her to stop, to go away, to get help. To stop guilting me. I want to help Mom as much as I wanted to save my unit.

I blink in the dark, fight to get away. Her sweet voice calls me, and I can't say no.

Bring me one more, Gray-baby.

Stupid, stupid, stupid. Tears clog my throat. I always did what she said, and I killed her. Dead. Eyes wide open. Lipsticked mouth hung slack. Dead.

"Mom!" I scream but know my mouth isn't moving. I'm trapped in the dark, fighting a body that won't wake up. "Mom!"

Then, with sudden clarity, I see her face. "Gray-baby."

"No!" A cold shudder runs through me, and I can't break free.

Extraction team voices mix with my Pops's. Their words are a blur, indistinguishable, but I know their meaning. Everything is my fault.

My head hurts. Pain radiates. If I can't wake up, I want to die.

Pops's voice spins in my head, his words a tumble of nonsense mixed with his drunk cackle.

"Help her!" Her lifeless face stares at me. It morphs to the desert night where I was the last man standing. "Help them..."

Nothing changes. I fall away from the edge of waking into the hell that I deserve. The only thing that could ever save me was Emma's voice, and I've lost that forever.

CHAPTER 14

Emma

Business Statistics is going to kill me. The formulas in my textbook make even less sense now that they're scrawled across a whiteboard at the front of the classroom. The professor hasn't bothered to show up to class all semester, and I'm ninety-nine percent sure that his assistant is as well versed in this crap as me. My brain will explode soon if I can't figure this out.

"If you have questions, follow up with Professor Baker during office hours. Thanks." The assistant tosses down the dry erase marker and heads out the door before a single question can be answered.

Ugh. I'm going to fail this class, which means I'll lose my internship. I might only do assistant shit, but pouring coffee and taking notes will pay off one day, semesters from now, with a *creative* job at the only decent marketing firm within a twenty-five mile radius. I need this internship because I need *that* job. One day.

And I'm never going to make it to office hours. Ever.

Shit, shoot, shit. I bite my lip and slam my book shut.

"Makes as much sense to you as me."

I look over my shoulder. Two guys. One's cute, my age. Seems popular enough. He always sits near me and more than occasionally catches my eye and smiles. The other is super-hot and an asshole. I don't have time to chat with either of them, but unlucky for me, the guy trying for conversation is the hot asshole.

"Something like that," I say. No need to be rude, but I've seen him in action in the halls. I shove my stuff in my bag and check my phone. I have seventeen minutes to make it across campus, get Cally, and load us into the car. Then, if there's no traffic, we can do a quick dinner and bath before she goes to bed and my mom comes over so I can go to work.

When I walk out the classroom door, the hottie's feet follow.

"Hey, wait up."

I don't. Can't. I'm on a schedule.

He's by my side, his arm wrapping around my back. "Gorgeous, wait—"

"Hands off." If there's one thing that stripping at Emerald's has taught me, it's not to take shit from hot guys who put their hands on me. I might look and act like a wallflower at school, but that's a façade.

"Sorry." He easily keeps pace with my power walk.

I glance at him and his confident smile. "You normally get away with pet names and touching people you don't know?"

His smile broadens. "Usually."

My eyes roll. "Right. I'm late. So… I can't help with stats."

"Actually, this class is a piece of cake for me. I was just trying to get your attention."

Ha. "I really have to go."

"What's your name? Emma, right?"

"Oh my god. Seriously, you... don't want this conversation. I'll make it easy for you. Walk away. You'll be thankful."

His eyes twinkle, and a challenge sparkles in his eyes. "Let me be the judge of that. Bunch of us are getting some beers tonight down at Seven's. It'd be cool to hang out."

I try to walk faster, making me slightly out of breath, but it doesn't seem to faze him. "Not twenty-one yet."

"They don't care."

This I already know about Seven's but not from experience. "I can't."

"Gorgeous, you can."

The second gorgeous pisses me off, then his hand touches my back and curls around my shoulder to slow me down. I stop abruptly and turn toward his mega-watt smile. He thinks he knows the next move. A mixture of cocky and sexy radiates off him and makes me think he doesn't have to try too hard. Hell, he looks so self-assured that I bet he wouldn't be surprised if I dropped to my knees in public to get a taste of him. Jerk.

My molars gnash, and I take a breath. Adding the same bit of sex to my voice that I use at Emerald's, I ask, "What's your name?"

"Sam—"

"Look, Sam. I was polite, but then you pushed. I said don't touch, and you did. So now you get the full explanation that I tried to warn you about." His mouth opens to say something, but I shake my head. "I work three jobs. *Three*. And only two pay. I'm busting my behind across campus to get to day care. To pick up *my daughter*. Whose daddy just *died*. I'm mourning him even though I haven't seen him in *years*. I'm the walking, talking, breathing definition of baggage."

Sam's jaw continues to hang. "Uh..."

"Thanks for the invite. But when a chick tells you to back off, it might be that she's not playing coy. It's that she wants you to *back the hell off.* Get me?"

"Shit. Sorry," he mumbles.

Yeah, I bet.

"If you want..." But he trails off, and I'm walking away anyhow.

I don't want anything from anyone. I can and do support myself and my baby, though it's almost killing me. Taking help is hard. I have my pride, but I'm also mired in my own version of punishment. Carelessness isn't an excuse to take from others. I flat-out refuse cash from my family, though I do accept their time and help. They watch Cally a few times a week, but only so I can earn a living. Not so I can go have drinks with hot guys who want to sneak me into bars.

My phone buzzes, caller ID reading Delightful Diner.

I hit the green circle to take the call. "Hello?"

"Hey, honey." Jan, the lady who owns the place, only calls about shift changes. "Don't need you in tonight. Things are too slow."

Shoot... "You sure? I can work whatever hours you need."

"I know, Emma. Sorry, honey. Don't need any hours tonight."

I chew the inside of my cheek. "No problem. Call me if that changes. I'll be there."

"Know you will, honey."

My stomach sinks. I really needed that shift. My phone buzzes again, and I check the screen, hoping it's Jan again. Nope. Just my brother.

"Hey, Ryan."

"You're moving."

"Ha. No. I'm planning on moving soon." But not when diner shifts keep getting canceled. "I just have to—"

"Look, Emma, I had another call out to your complex today. Dad and I were talking—"

I love Ryan, but that brand-new, shiny rookie badge is going to drive me insane. "My apartment is safe. You know that."

"It's your neighbors who are sketch. A couple years ago, it was fine. Now? Shit changes."

"Not telling me anything I don't already know," I mumble and push open the door for day care, waving at the girl at the desk. "I have to go. Cally and I are running behind."

"Dad put first and last month's down for you. You can afford everything in between. Sign the paperwork. You can move in immediately."

"What!" I spin away from the receptionist, ready to tear into him then call my dad to do the same. But I can't. God, I'm grateful. I hate needing them, but I'm drowning. I pull in a breath and drop my head.

"Emma, you need a break. Take it, okay?"

"Ryan, I don't..."

"You're month-to-month now, right? Almost the same rent, so you have no reason not to."

It would be so nice to leave that apartment, and I've been saving so one day I could. "I want to do it myself."

"Emma, look... I owe you."

He's been even more protective since we all heard about Grayson. It's weird. When Ryan found out I was pregnant, I thought he would be sick, then I was scared he would kill Gray and his chances at the police academy. But eventually Ryan calmed down, in a very protective kind of way. Grayson was a name not to be mentioned around Ryan, but now that it's back in circulation, thanks to county gossip, the protective claws are back.

"No, sweetie. It's me who owes everyone," I say.

He huffs, sounding frustrated in my ear. "Please sign the lease. We'll take care of the move."

"I can't."

"Dammit, Emma. Just say yes."

Whoa. "Easy there."

"You're my baby sister. This is… just something I have to help you do."

I hate the baby sister argument. "We're almost the same age."

"I'm responsible for you."

This again. God love him. "No. You're not. But I'll talk to Dad, okay? See what I can do. Deal?"

"One day we'll all be on the same page." He sighs. "Kiss Cally for me."

"Mommy!"

I turn toward Cally's voice. "Gotta go. Love ya. Bye."

My little girl's running toward me, arms outstretched. I scoop her into a hug, sign her out, and hit the door.

"You have a good time with your friends?" I ask.

"No! My hair got pwulled and I cwolored on da wall." Cally took a breath. "Timeout for me."

Rolling my lips to hide my smile, I can't stand how stinking cute she is. Even if it's her explaining why she was in time out. "Probably shouldn't have drawn on the wall."

"Mommy." She buries her head into my shoulder as we head toward the parking lot. "I wanna go to sleep. Story?"

Oh… I sigh. "Sure thing, snugglebug."

A story makes her bad day go away. My heart squeezes. Like daddy, like daughter.

CHAPTER 15

GRAYSON

Aches and pains. It's the only thing I can register. That, and my tongue feels like sandpaper. Slowly, I blink my eyes open. Everything is white. Searing light streams through a window. I look down and around. I'm in bed. In a hospital? Equipment is on both sides of me, monitors hooked to my arms and chest. Taking a deep breath, I turn and—oh, damn. Pain slices through my side. I moan, fight to catch my breath, and drop back.

My mind struggles to find the missing pieces, and a headache throbs. Dark flashes of action and memories of the insurgent attack—the voices, the screams. Everyone's dead. Everyone... except me? Empty clips and useless weapons. By the time the extraction team arrived, I was the last man standing.

Constant pain consumes me. Gunshot wound? The memory of exploding pain surfaces. What else... broken ribs? Cracked bones? Have to be, because I can't breathe. But still, I'm alive. Out of everyone, why me?

Emma.

I shake my head. A cold sweat drenches me. I had begged God to let me make it right. To stay alive and see my girl. A desperate shudder runs through me. It's too late. It has to be. It's been three fuckin' years since I last saw her. They've been hell. I bitched out on a shot at love, at happiness. She's not my girl. Not anymore.

All alone, I come apart.

Emma would've waited for me after basic, would've waited through these goddamn deployments. I'm a self-fulfilling fuckin' prophecy. I'm everything Pops expected: a piece of shit, not good enough to do anything but ruin lives, ruin myself. I've been out fightin' and doing my damnedest to forget that I love her. That I was too pussy, too jacked in the head to mumble the word "good-bye" and hope that she'd wait.

Nausea hits me. Regret shreds me. Emma's moved on. Why wait for a man who never came back to bed? A girl like her probably has a boyfriend. Or a husband? Bile burns my throat. My hands tear into my hair, and my pain spikes again. How had I never thought about her moving on?

"You're up!" A nurse walks in, heading for a bottle on the wall, and snaps me from a nervous breakdown. She squirts sanitizer on her hands, rubs them together, then snaps on gloves. "Time to take a look at your side, honey."

I groan, hands still in my hair.

"You okay? Remembering again?" She sits on a rolling chair and scoots over.

"What?"

"Memory still foggy? That's the painkillers. Give it a few minutes. The cobwebs will disappear."

I don't know what to say. I don't remember this woman. Flashbacks hit me... cracked ribs. Discharge papers. Maybe? I can't remember what's real, what's a dream.

With a few well-practiced moves, the nurse lifts the covers, moves my gown, re-bandages me, and smiles. "Looks great. Probably still feels awful. I'll let the doctors know you're up, okay? And your girl."

My girl? "She's here?"

The nurse smiles again and snaps off her gloves. "Arrived a bit ago. She's a wild one, that's for sure."

Wild one? Oh... no. Shit. "Um—"

"Grayson!" Behind the nurse, in walks crazy Mazie. That's a face I could never forget. "You're awake."

"Maze—"

"I've been waiting forever for you to wake up."

The nurse heads for the door. "Well, I'll let you two be."

"Wait, no." But my words are muffled by Mazie's smothering hug. "Ow, shit, Maze. That hurts."

She finally pops up. "Hey, you."

This can't be happening. My head's pounding. When I left Emma and ended up at basic training at Fort Benning, then stationed in the same place, I spent enough time with Mazie that we became close friends. She was one of the boys and always knew what was in my head. I told her, probably too many times, that I was in love with Emma.

Sitting up, I ignore the sense of loss that I woke up to her, not Emma. "You have to stop telling people we're getting married."

"That lines always works." She shrugs. "Gets me in the door. I was worried about you."

I nod.

"Word travels fast. I'm really sorry, Gray. Just—" She rolls her lips together. The bubbly, near-manic girl I know is speechless. Don't blame her though. "I thought you were dead. Everyone did. The reports that filtered back were wrong. No one knew anything."

I should've been. Better men than me died. Guys with wives, with children. I take a deep, painful breath, needing a subject change. "I'm back in Georgia?"

She shakes her head. "No. Walter Reed."

"Maryland?"

She nods. "Yeah, sweetie."

Not far from Virginia—not far from Summerland County. Not that Emma's there anymore. She had college and… life. "Why'd you come up?"

"When I heard you survived, I figured no one would come check on you."

That's what happens when you walk away from everyone. My head's spinning. I want her to leave so I can be alone in my misery. "Don't worry about me."

"Someone has to check on you. Besides, I needed a change of scenery. You know how I am."

For as much I want one girl, she wants any guy, so long as he has a tag around his neck and loves just her. Our backgrounds have eerily similar histories, and while I've run from Emma, Mazie's run to any soldier with half an interest, always getting hurt. She's a tag chaser at heart. Really, she's not one hundred percent right in the head, and that's why she's my crazy Mazie.

The guys would get a kick out of her being up here.

The guys… are all dead.

Flashes and explosions rock in my head. I smell fear, taste death. It's revolting. Their screams. The blood. As though I'm living a nightmare, it hits hard and fast. Bile rushes up my throat. My stomach churns; I can't breathe. "I'm gonna be sick."

"Oh! Eek. Um." She grabs a trash can and shoves it under my face just in time.

Shit. God. My wound kills.

I try to block out the sounds from the room around me. My memory explodes with pain. Mazie's talking fast, and rough hands switch the trash can for a bag. My pain radiates as I heave. My gut roils. Everything sucks in a way I can't handle.

Finally, it subsides, whatever it was. My heart beat slows. Cold sweats stop rushing over my body. I take a breath as my stomach calms, and I drop back. I won't open my eyes, won't talk to anyone. The nurse and a doctor are talking. I hear their murmurs, their questions as they mumble words like *trigger*, *stress*, and *attack*. I don't care. All I want is Emma. I need her, and I fight for her memory. A story. A smile. Anything. But it's all blank.

"This will help you," the nurse says by my IV.

A slight hit of warmth bleeds into me through the drip in my arm. My muscles relax, but not my mind.

Until… finally, it's quiet around me. Sleep pulls me toward its dark, heavy hold. Struggling, I open my eyes to see Mazie sit in a chair near me.

"I'm…" I work my numb jaw, running my tongue over my teeth. My body has odd sensations, all pin prickles and fuzzy feels. "Tired."

"Should be. They gave you a knock-out shot." Her eyes are red, her cheeks tear-stained. "I'm sorry." She tucks her knees up and wraps her arms around them. "I shouldn't have been so… cavalier. I'm sorry. I shouldn't have mentioned the guys. Or stupid gossip."

I shake my head, dizzy with exhaustion but not in nearly as much pain. Crazy Mazie is more messed up than me. "It's just a thing."

"Panic attack or something."

"Maybe." My fists feel heavy. So does my soul. I rub my knuckles into my eyes. My skin feels fuzzy and funny. I want to say something, figure out how to make the hurt lessen. "I was the last guy. No one else made it home."

"I know," she whispers.

"I can't see Emma's face anymore. You know, that's always been my fix. It's not working." I drop my hands and tears burn. "It's been too long."

When I focus on Mazie, she's watching me and hugs her legs tighter to her chest. "Maybe it's time you fix it?"

My tongue is thick, dry. I chew on my bottom lip, but it's numb like the rest of me. Everything except my mind. "Maybe."

But first, I have to fix me. Not just my side but what's in my head. Then I can find Emma and fix... everything.

Chapter 16

Two weeks later...

Emma

"Cally, Cally, Cally, honey." I've been home for three hours of power sleep. "Please, baby, get up."

If I don't make it to class on time, Professor Dickhead will call me out as he's done the past two times. The jerk swears by a three-strikes rule, and today is not the day I'm losing my place in Business Management 201.

But if I don't get my precious baby out of bed, dressed, and into the car, we'll never make it to the community college's child care.

"Mama, don't wanna."

Oh, baby. Me neither. I'm exhausted. Funneling coffee. I overslept by three minutes, which shouldn't be that big of a deal, but I have life planned to a T. I drop to my knees and cuddle her head. "I know that, snugglebug. But up, up, and"—I scoop her out of bed—"out."

Droopy-eyed with bedhead, she rubs her face and looks around. "Sleepy."

I nod. "Yuppers, me too."

She looks around, acknowledging her new bedroom. The excitement on her face makes this fast move worth it.

"C'mon. Super-fast breakfast, then we gotta roll."

Cally buries her head into my neck. "Want a muffin."

"Good thing that's what we have."

I hustle her down to the kitchen, and she devours a banana muffin, finishing faster than I would've bet. Thank goodness. That shaves minutes off the schedule. We can totally do this. It's my mantra. Cally and I are a team. We can survive anything, do anything, manage it on our own with just a few helping hands.

Like Cherry, who babysits at my place on Wednesday nights while I'm at Emerald's, and my parents, who watch Cally for any shift I can pick up at the Delightful Diner, where I sling pancakes. Who knew it was possible to hate the smell of butter and batter.

I groan for so many reasons. But this morning, there's no time to lament barely getting by. Because if I do that, we fail, and right now, we're so close to making it with more than just a couple of dollars a paycheck.

Cally's in her clothes, trying to brush her teeth, and batting away my help. She's like me—a little stubborn but going to do it on her own if it kills her—and I love that about her.

"Clean!" Teeth bared and lips smiling, she nods for approval to hop off the stool.

"Super clean, cuddlebug." I hook her around the waist, grab my bag, granola bar, and coffee, and we're out the door.

I check my phone after she's in her car seat and

I'm stuck at a red light. "We're totally going to make it on time."

Cally beams from the backseat. "'Cause we're magical!"

"You know it."

The kid steals my heart every day. And maybe she's right. Magic might let me make it into class before Professor Dickhead does his daily dickheaded duties.

Seventeen minutes later, I screech into class after dropping off Cally a few buildings over.

"Very close, Miss Kingsley." Professor Dickhead shuts the door behind me and launches into a verbatim recounting of exactly what the textbook read.

My lungs pound because I ran across campus, but I made it. I tumble into my seat. All I have to do is keep this up another semester or two, combined with a couple of online classes, and my godforsaken no-pay internship will turn into a real dollars-in-the-bank-account job that pays more than school credits and gift card bonuses.

I'm in this for the future, for Cally. So I can raise my baby girl and eventually have a college degree and job security. But until then, I'm completely exhausted, doing the best I know how.

CHAPTER 17

Emma

TGIF.

Thursdays are always the worst, because I've been on the clock at Emerald's, then classes, then the Delightful Diner, and then my internship. I'm sitting in a client meeting and taking notes for Jeremy Rossdale, my boss, the managing partner of Creative Dynamic Worldwide. With the exception of a couple of hours' sleep, I've been on the job for twenty-four hours in a row. Somewhere in there, I played a solid game of hide-n-seek and dried Cally's tears when we couldn't find anything that was packed.

Moving with a two-year-old? Not easy.

But it's Friday—no classes and my only job that doesn't require physical labor, even if it's also the only job that doesn't pay. The internship's lack of a steady paycheck might blow, but I have a promise from Jeremy: if I get my college degree while doing mundane intern work, I will be hired as an entry-level marketing executive and have a foot in the door for if and when the art department hires. Meaning I'll be paid to do something with a camera, even if it's just brainstorm shoots.

Still, the potential for a paycheck and benefits? Yeah, that I'll bust my butt to get. It'll be a dream-come-true job, mostly because my clothes will stay on and my paycheck will be direct deposited. No writhing and crawling on the floor for bills, no carrying trays of coffee and half-eaten pancakes for coins.

The internship is my long-tail approach to success. Eat that, Professor Dickhead.

I try to stifle a yawn and fiddle with the yarn-and-bead bracelet Cally made me last night. It's pink and purple. When she showed it to me, she did a dance and sang a nonsensical song that still makes my eyes burn with tears. Such a cute kid.

My mom came over after Cally went to sleep so I could pick up a shift at the diner. I wore the bracelet, and all three of the truckers who came in for coffee and hash browns remarked about it.

Staying busy has served a secondary purpose recently. The last few weeks have been a roller coaster. Summerland County gossip has buzzed for days about Grayson dying overseas, and my trip to see Pops went about as well as a disaster.

But on the upside, my twenty-first birthday is almost here, and I've finally been able to scrape together enough money, with a little assistance from my folks, to move Cally and me from our one-bedroom teeny-tiny, should-be-called-a-studio apartment to a real, albeit still teeny-tiny, house. I picked up the keys earlier this week.

God, I need some coffee if I'm going to make through moving. My phone flashes with a text from Sarah, my best friend and fellow marketing intern.

Sarah: MEANT TO TELL YOU, I DROVE BY! SUPER CUTE HOUSE. WAY TO GO YOU. YOU DON'T EVEN TOUCH YOUR NEIGHBORS, IT'S REALLY SOMETHING. PROUD OF YOU.

I roll my lips to keep from smiling. The new house rocks. I'm bursting to get everything out of the apartment and into the house so it will finally feel real. Dad and Ryan moved the beds, a lot of boxes, and our necessities this week. Cherry will take Cally tonight for an auntie slumber party so I can unpack boxes.

My phone rings, and I silence it. The caller ID shows an unfamiliar number. Jeremy looks over, his nose pinched.

I mouth, "Sorry."

Again, I fiddle with the bracelet and take all the notes he'll need. My handwriting is perfect, but I'll have them typed and in his inbox before he leaves for the weekend.

My phone rings again, same number. Two calls in a row make me think of emergency situations. Cally fell. Got sick. Got lost. My stomach twists.

"I think that about wraps this up." Jeremy stands. "Emma, need clarification on anything before we break?"

"No, sir. Got it all." I tap my notepad, which is covered in details. He asks to be polite, but never in my time with him have I missed something he needs.

"Better get that." Jeremy nods at my phone.

"Right. Thanks." I slip out of the conference room and head toward the privacy of the hallway to answer. "Hello?"

"Hey, Ems." The nervous scratch of a faraway voice reaches into my soul, wrapping its brutal tentacles around me.

No one calls me Ems. No one but Grayson Ford. The boy I dream of, the man I dance for, the reason I'm still living, and the source of all my desperation. My throat tightens to the point that I think I'm going to choke, and an intense pounding in my chest finds its way to my ears. There is no way I just heard what I did.

"Grayson?"

It's him. The him who ruined my life. Who *made* my life. Who confused my mind to the point that I can't figure out if I've been destroyed or set free. The him who… is… dead.

I tremble and press against the wall, feeling a wave of weakness. I'm unsure if I'll crumble to the floor, praise God, or just melt.

"You're—alive?" My voice breaks. Tears spill. I want to throw my phone and run. But I can't.

"Yeah… maybe not the guy you knew, but it's me."

There's a gravity to his voice that rolls through me. Three years have passed since he broke my heart. Three weeks since Randall confirmed Grayson had died.

Gray was supposed to be my best friend. He was supposed to be the one I loved forever. But he never saw the tears stream down my face. Never knew the hurt and humiliation and anguish. He just disappeared into the night, and I had to hear from the county gossip machine that he was in boot camp at Fort Benning. I didn't even know if it was true. I even thought about just showing up there one day.

I cried myself to sleep for what seemed like an eternity, waiting for him to call, to explain. To do something that would show I hadn't been in love with a soulless liar. But I was.

And still, I am.

Pathetic.

"You there?" His voice is deeper. Darker, as if he's damaged. There's something to it, almost as if I can touch the coarseness running through him.

"I'm here." I can't hang up. An overwhelming hope bleeds through me, wishing that somehow, errors of the past will magically mend.

"Been a while."

I'm wordless.

He mumbles something, and it sounds as though his hand runs over his mouth. I can picture him threading his fingers into his hair.

"You're mad. I get it. I deserve it, that's the goddamn truth."

Mad? Is he kidding me? I survived my freshman year at community college while pregnant, a newborn's constant waking while pushing myself to work *three* jobs, then I mourned him. *Mourned!*

"I'm not mad. I'm—" I take a deep breath, trying to fend off a screwed-up mixture of vicious anger and nervous breakdown. "I'm at work."

"We gotta talk."

What? My shirt is strangling me. My stockings are too tight. Coming unglued seems too easy, and I hurt, so deeply and so raw, that I'm shaking. Crumbling.

"Emma?"

Two options: talk or hang up. But I do neither. I'm in shock. Like clinical what-the-fuck-do-I-do-now shock. I swallow the knot in my throat and force my mind-mouth connection to forge something. Anything. "I'm here."

I want to sound mature. Maybe even unaffected.

At the very least, I want to sound as if the tornado that is my life didn't start the night he walked away. The love of my life—whom I hate—has come back from the dead? All I want to do is kill him! Or maybe hug him. I don't know.

"Hell, Ems," he growls. "I'm sorry."

My lips pull between my teeth as I fail to ignore the shivers skimming across my shoulders. He sounds like a man. Like sex and heat. His words coat me, holding me, and I hate my visceral response to just his voice.

But it's been years... "You don't get to call me Ems. Never. Not again. No one calls me that." Even though it's one of the sweetest sounds I've ever heard. If a word could hug and forgive, *Ems* could do that.

Grayson's breath drifts into the phone and whisks over me, stirring me to the point that I can't stand. I head to the intern office space, and my chair catches me as I fall, wondering the whys and the nows of this call. No matter what I think, I can't muster enough of a regret to hang up.

"Emma..."

As it turns out, my drawn-out first name has the same sinful effect as "Ems." I hate it—and really don't. "What?"

"I need a minute." As fast as my heart rate picks up—I'm nervous and protective of my world—he tacks on a growly, "please."

The word has just enough sweet Grayson Ford attached to it. Memories tumble through my mind, all ignited by his rough, graveled timbre. I pinch the bridge of my nose, knowing I should be angry. I *should be* a woman scorned. But I'm not. I've always had the hope that this call might happen. And God, when I thought he'd died, I fell apart.

"The guy you knew... he's gone. But some things don't change, Emma, and you saving me is one of them."

My heart can't decide whether to pound or clench. It's hurting. I'm reliving the million pieces of my shattered heart that I've hidden. Despite his haunting memories and living paycheck to paycheck, my life is good right now. Maybe it'll be better if he stays the unrequited dream-come-true that I dance for every Wednesday. At least that way, I'll never know what it's like to be devastated twice in a lifetime.

"Okay. I'll lay it out for you," Grayson says. "I have... regrets."

That pulls me out of my head. "Regrets?" *Regrets!* "Are you kidding me?" My blood pressure rises, and I can't even fathom a response. I just... he has *no* idea. Holy shit, I can't breathe. "Shut up, Gray. Don't say anything else."

Anger pounds in my head. I've had a life to live, complete with major what-the-fuck-should-I-do-now moments. Soul searching and delayed regret has never been on the agenda. Only two mouths to feed and responsibilities. "Take your regret and—"

"You never deserved me leaving. I never wanted to go. It's—you deserve an apology."

"Yeah, I do." My lungs want to explode, and I swear to Jesus, the room starts to spin. This is what I've waited to hear for so long.

"I'm sorry, Ems. Leaving you killed me. Ruined me. I'm fucked for having done it, and I'm asking for your forgiveness."

Dropping my head back, I stare at the ceiling and take inventory of my feelings after his big confession. Nothing's changed. They're just words. What did I think would happen?

Am I any happier? No.

Angrier? Nope.

Euphoric? In love? Relieved? No, no, and no one more damn time.

Well, that isn't true. I'll always love him. But still, we aren't the same high school kids. What a realization. I'm different now. I bite my lip, thankful I don't have the monumental task of trying to explain to Cally that she actually had a dad but he died. "I have to get back to work."

He clears his throat. "Work?"

I nod as if he can see me. "My boss is gonna have a fit if I don't get back."

What more am I supposed to say? *All's forgiven?* My inner subconscious is a demented, two-faced traitor. *I love you. Leave me alone.*

"Then I'll call you later."

"What? Why?" He doesn't get to show up when he feels like it. "I wanted to hear that from you for forever. And now I have." I choke. "I thought you were dead!"

Silence lingers. "Shit. I shouldn't have called like this."

"No! Yes, you should have. But you should've done it years ago. You should have done it when I was heartbroken and alone. When I gave you everything and you walked away. *Everything.* Do you get that!"

"Ems—"

"No! Not with the Ems."

"Sweet Jesus, fuck me. You have no idea. I just needed to hear your voice again."

"God, you're a selfish prick. You can't be serious. I needed your voice *years* ago." Holy crap, I'm sweating I'm so angry. "Your voice. Your help. You! I needed you to be here. You have no damn idea how much."

I slam the phone down and bury my eyes into my elbow. I refuse to cry at work over the boy who left me so long ago. So I won't. Mind over matter. But I turn my head and stare at my phone. It stares back at me, its screen showing that Grayson's still with me. As I always thought he'd be. Dammit! I'm so messed up in the head. I pick it up. "Gray?"

Why couldn't I have said his full name? Hearing Grayson's harsh breath only serves to torture me. The sound is too long, too longing. Too perfect and everything that I remember.

"Ems."

I don't fight my nickname. Not this time. My eyelids sink shut, and I feel his voice as though I could feel his arms around me. But then my heart freezes. What does he know? What does he want? My maternal instinct flares. "I have to—"

"Emma." Sarah raps on the office door.

I squeak, turning my head her way. "Hey."

She raises her eyebrows. "You're needed in the copy room. Get a move on. Let's go, go. G. O."

"On the phone." I gesture toward it.

She shakes her head, smiling. "That better be the president asking you to broker peace in the Middle East. Anything short of that, and you're going to hear it from me."

What is that about?

"It's okay, Emma," Grayson interrupts my thoughts. "I'll figure out a different way to work this out."

"Um—" But the call ends before I can respond. Do I want him to call me later? Hell yes. But not really. My hands are trembling. Confusion will give me a migraine because… I'm also ten kinds of turned on right now. Shit, shoot, shit.

"What is going on with this rosy-cheek thing you have happening now?" Sarah has one eyebrow raised. "Everything okay?"

"I—" I'm stuck in my seat, my phone glued to my hand. Panic joyrides through my system, crashing and clipping every part of me that hurts along the way. "My face is rosy?"

"Sweetheart, if you have some piece of man-candy calling you, promising you dirty things that make your cheeks pink like that, *and* you haven't told me, we're going to have to reevaluate the topics of our coffee break gossip sessions."

My eyes drop back to my cell. Gray's gone. He was just in my ear, and now he's gone. I illuminate the screen. His number is there. I don't know what to do with it. Save it? Delete it? What do I do with the last five minutes?

"Hey, space cadet." Sarah leans farther into the office. "Copy room. It's important. Post haste, move your caboose." She tilts her head, studying me. "No joke. You okay?"

"I... don't know."

Her gaze drops pointedly to my phone. "Who was that?"

"Grayson Ford."

Sarah's mouth falls open. "Wait, *Grayson-Grayson*? I thought—he's... *alive*?"

I can't explain how I feel. "Grayson-Grayson. The love of my life is alive and just called to say, three years later, he was sorry. He sounded like a dick. With a voice... and he was a bossy jerk."

"Bossy?"

"Demanding, maybe."

"About?"

"Forgiveness."

"Oh..." Sarah drops into an empty chair on the other side of my desk. "Well, holy jizzballs."

I nod. "How did he even get my number?"

She scowls. "No idea. So... what did you say?"

I ignore her question and cringe. "He called me Ems." Even now, that makes my stomach flutter.

"Emma," she draws out, "what did you say?"

"Nothing that I should have." I shrug, unable to defend my actions. There should have been name-calling or at least a verbal jab or two. And we had a major amount of things to catch up on... "He said he's calling me again. Later."

"So does he know about our girl?" Sarah has never met Grayson, but she's wiped enough tears and heard my story a thousand times, enough to know the father of my baby doesn't know he's a daddy. "Emma? Shit, sweetheart, snap out of it."

I chew my lip. "I *want* him to call me later. How fucked up am I?" Totally, one hundred percent fucked up. But love makes me stupid; love hates smart decisions. It's all about the feels. Hurts are a distant memory that I can't admit exist. "Wait. Oh my God. Do you think he knows about Cally?"

Sarah's eyes dart to my framed pictures on my desk. "Well—"

"Well?" I bounce from surprisingly, angrily aroused to ready to puke. "He deserves to know. But I'm terrified."

"Why?"

"God, why not? He could want..." My head shakes. "Rights. Custody. Or worse, want nothing. I haven't seen him in years. I know nothing about him except he's *alive.*"

She groans. "Well... wow. Alright, I don't know what to say."

I stand and push my hands against the desk, letting my head hang. I can do this. Go back to work. Survive a few hours. Forget about Grayson. Go home to my new house, unpack some boxes, and relax. Cally's spending the night with my sister. Maybe I'll answer the phone if Grayson calls. *If* he calls. Which he won't. Right?

My phone buzzes. The screen shows a text message.

Unknown number: I'LL FIX WHAT I FUCKED UP. PREPARE YOURSELF, EMS, I'M COMING FOR YOU AND I WANT FORGIVENESS.

CHAPTER 18

Emma

"Surprise!" A dozen faces stare at me, smiling and beaming. There's a cake in the center of the break room table.

I'm in a Grayson-Ford-is-alive stupor, and now I have to play happy at a surprise party.

"Happy birthday," comes from several co-workers.

One of the managers elbows another. "Wow, think we got her?"

"She's so stinkin' sweet. That might be the best surprise face ever."

Holy crap. My office threw me a surprise party? I might be a lowly intern and even a stripper, but I'm not ungrateful. I pull it together fast. "Thank you!"

Sarah squeezes me, a public act of friendship, a private act of support. Then she nudges me toward the cake. The candles are burning low, the wax melting onto the white sheet cake. Scrolled in magenta icing is "Happy 21st Birthday!" Next to the cake are paper plates and plastic forks.

"Birthday girl cuts the cake. And get a move on."
A marketing exec known for his sweet tooth
chuckles.

"Come on." Sarah tugs me to the table and cuts the
first slices before Eileen, our office receptionist, butts
in.

Jeremy pushes his glasses higher on his nose.
"Emma, this is from the office." He reaches under the
table and pulls out a basket. "I'm not sure we've ever
had an intern work so hard."

They've probably never had an intern so hard up
and ready to make a better life.

"Open it!"

I step forward and eye the cellophane wrap. "It's
beautiful."

"Well, you can thank Sarah and Eileen for that."

Some of the guys eat cake and urge me to open the
basket. Whatever is underneath all the plastic, it's
got everyone excited. This feels like more than the
standard present our office pulls together. Tearing it
open, I see bright pink shredded paper then smaller
presents, individually wrapped.

I tear open the first one. It's a cookbook, and the
title makes me giggle. *1001 Ways to Make Ramen
Noodles.* Holding it up, I can't help but laugh. That's
all I eat because they're super cheap. Less moolah
spent on me, more spent on Cally.

Eileen stops cutting cake. "If you're going to eat
that crap every day, might as well change it up a
little."

"Thanks." I open the next few gifts. A pink fuzzy
pen holder for my desk. A framed picture from our
company retreat, which I was only able to spend a
few hours at, and an envelope. I pull it out, and
everyone steps closer. It's a letter, but with everyone
staring at me, I'm nervous. "What's this?"

Jeremy nods toward the paper in my hand. "Something well earned."

The entire room is watching me. A nervous energy runs through me, and I unfold it.

Dear Emma Kingsley,
On behalf of Creative Dynamic Worldwide, thank you for your hard work and dedication. You are the first recipient of a new benefit for selected Creative Dynamic employees: tuition reimbursement.
Thank you,
Jeremy Rossdale

"Oh my God." I look up, but tears cloud my vision, then they spill. Rapidly blinking, I try to match Jeremy's face to what I think this means. "Is the company picking up my tuition this semester?"

He nods. "Funny how the corporate headquarters won't cut one of our best interns a check, but they're open to paying some of your bills."

"It's a tax write-off," one of the accountants volunteers.

"It was Jeremy's idea." Eileen nods toward her boss.

My throat's in a knot. "I—don't. Oh, wow. Just thank you." Not eloquent but exactly how I feel. All choked up and scattered beyond words. "Thank you."

"Enough with the tears. Back to cake." But Jeremy comes over and gives me a boss-appropriate side hug. "Sometimes good things happen out of the blue."

My mind jumps back to Grayson. "Sometimes they do."

Cake in her hand, Sarah steps toward me as Jeremy steps away. "One more surprise."

"Yeah, I don't know if I can handle another surprise."

"You're not going to like it anyway. At first. But Cherry and I are pretty sure it's for your sanity, and she doesn't even know about the Grayson phone call earlier."

"Okay, first off, I need to tell Cherry, not you. She's all nice about him since she thought he was dead, but she's like Ryan. She basically wants Gray dead anyway. And second, my sanity is fine."

"You have three jobs, plus school, plus a kiddo. Let's not bullshit by saying you have a good grip on sanity."

"What are you two up to?"

Sarah beams. "You're going to say no, but don't."

"Sarah…"

"Cherry's going to pick Cally up from day care. She was already going to spend the night at Cherry's, so you *don't* pick her up, and we *do* go to happy hour!"

I snort-laugh. "Yeah, no."

"Seriously, we'll go to Vevy's and have a couple drinks, ring in the big two-one."

"I need to see Cally."

"All you were going to do is pick her up and drop her off."

My bottom lip sticks out. "I'm not sure I'm ready to not see her off to Cherry's."

"A couple hours of very tame fun. I think you deserve it."

Really, I don't feel as though I deserve much. Every single minute of my life is directed toward getting to a better place.

"Just take a break. Take a chance." Sarah sidesteps us into the corner. "Look, I know you grew up with the perfect family, perfect life, all that stuff. But if you don't give yourself a breather, you're… I don't know. Going to explode."

My brow furrows. "I'm not going to explode."

"But you're punishing yourself. It's just a few hours out to celebrate you before you start unpacking."

"I don't know."

"Cally's cool with it, your mom swears. It was her idea actually, even though I'm going to take credit for it."

Gnawing on my bottom lip, I think maybe I do need a breather. Just to laugh. "I'll call Cally. If she sounds like she doesn't need to see me before Cherry's then... okay."

"Yeah?" Sarah goes up on her toes. "Sweet."

CHAPTER 19

Emma

Vevy's is rocking. It's a fancy steakhouse with a bar that makes colorful drinks in snazzy glasses. Creative Direct has a corporate account here to entertain clients, and they spend a serious amount of dough, which is why the bartender has turned a blind eye to my birthday not actually arriving for two more days.

My co-workers mill around, wishing me a happy birthday. Even Jeremy dropped in for two point five seconds and another boss-appropriate side hug. I'm playing the part of the birthday girl, but I can't stop staring at my phone.

At first I was convinced Cherry would call with a crying Cally. So I called Cherry. Twice. Both times, Cally was absolutely fine with not having seen me since this morning. She even told *me* I would be okay. Maybe my snugglebug is growing up faster than I'm ready for.

But that's not the only reason I keep looking at

my phone. For every sip I take, I stare at my cell and slowly drain its battery.

"Thinking about Grayson or Cally?" Sarah asks.

"Oh... um, both."

She nods. "So if you're not going to tell Cherry right away, I assume Ryan will be told... never?"

God, Sarah's right. If my brother finds out Grayson's alive and back in the States, Summerland's favorite rookie cop might just kill the guy.

The shoulder-to-shoulder crowd shifts behind me.

"Happy birthday!"

I turn around and see some of the girls from Emerald's. New faces, but really, there are always new faces. The turnover there is ridiculous. Sarah knows I'm friendly with them, and most of them wouldn't turn down a party, much less the only time I'll probably ever go out for drinks.

"Hey, girls!"

My fake excitement rings true to them, and we do the necessary small talk. This isn't exactly what they'd picture for a twenty-first birthday party, but they're sweet to show up at Sarah's last-minute invitation.

"Bruno sends his love." Dominique, who has been there the longest out of the girls here, holds a card.

My cocktail buzz has me more giggly than I'm used to. Bruno sending a birthday card is like Sarah jumping on the bar to strip—it won't happen unless there's a catch. I'm unsure about opening the card in public, but Bruno has some tact. I think. "What is it?"

"No idea," she says, handing it over. "But we're all dying to know."

I set my drink down and rip open the card. It's on thick card stock with *Emerald's* embossed along the top.

Happy birthday, Ginger. I have a business proposition for you now that you're an old lady. Forget the past, grab the future, and go get laid.
x, Bruno

His scrawl is in thick, dark ink, and I pull the card to my chest as if everyone can see it. My cheeks go hot, and the girls' eyebrows go up. A dozen questioning eyes are on me.

"What'd it say?" Sarah asks.

The Emerald's girls would never ask anything that'd invade Bruno's privacy, but they're dying to know too. It's written all over their pretty, made-up faces.

"Happy birthday and to go have fun."

"I bet." Dominique's smiling. She's the only one senior enough to risk nosing into Bruno's business, even if he's not around.

"Hey." The bartender nods for my attention. "Birthday girl."

"That's me." I tuck the card deep into my purse, and our little stripper circle breaks up as the girls mingle, leaving me to fidget on the bar stool.

"Guy over there sent you this." He slides a shot of something dark with whipped cream on top to the edge of the bar.

I catch the guy's eye and wave. Cute but not my type. No one is ever my type, even on my birthday with a direct order from one boss to get laid and with another boss trying to ease all the responsibility in my life. "Thank you."

He smiles because he knows, with one look, I'm not interested. My mind drifts back to Grayson. Sipping drinks all night has made my cheeks tingly and my heart crave his call.

"Emma," Sarah snaps at me. "Forget Grayson. At least for tonight."

"Right. And what should I focus on instead?"

"Hmm." She scans the room.

Between listening to Grayson growl into my ear earlier and having a few fruity-tooty drinks in my system, I'm slow to control my emotions. I check my phone again. It's seven. Grayson said he'd call back. Will he? I mean, come on, why, after all this time, should I trust him to do anything he says? Then again, he called today.

"Ugh." Groaning and leaning against Sarah's shoulder, I chew on my lip. "Why isn't he calling me back? And why do I want him to?"

She pats my head. "I'd be shocked if you didn't want him to. Be mad and all, but you're messed up over him."

"Messed up? That's one way to put it."

"Well… Grayson's alive. Around, maybe… have you thought about how you're going to mention Cally?"

"Shhh," I hiss, as if maybe saying Cally and Grayson in the same sentence will cosmically notify him of his unknown offspring. "No, I haven't. It's only been a couple hours."

She takes a pull off her drink. "Talk about a game changer."

"No kidding." I keep checking my phone. The closer I get to the bottom of another empty glass, the more my attention focuses on Grayson's lack of a return call.

"You could always call him, ya know." Sarah bobs an eyebrow then stares at my phone that I'm unsuccessfully trying to covertly check. "Yeah, you're totally busted."

Hmm, I should have better phone-checking skills.

I'm pretty sure my happy-birthday happy hour is messing with my stealth moves. Can't help it though; his number is waiting for me. "It's all I can think about."

Sarah finishes the last of her drink. "All you have to do is hit send."

I nod. We shouldn't be strategizing while drinking. "I could call him."

"You could," her voice trills.

"But I won't. Right?"

I've had one too many pink-purple-and-green things bought for me by birthday wishers. Sarah too, just because she's cute. If I drink one more, then I totally will call him. I look at Sarah, my voice of reason, and see she's a notch past tipsy. I gotta get out of here.

"I think I'm done."

She frowns. "But it's your birthday!"

"It's happy hour. And that's probably over by now."

"Party pooper."

Story of my life. But there are cabs outside, and my house needs to be unpacked. I can't afford a hangover or a drunk dial to Gray. Or could I?

I lean into Sarah, squeezing my eyes shut. "I'm going to call him."

"I know, sweetheart." She kisses my head. "I can't believe you lasted this long."

CHAPTER 20

GRAYSON

Highway lights dully glow in summer's twilight sky as I drive down Interstate 95, heading from Maryland to Virginia. Sometimes the military network pays off. After just one phone call from my hospital room to my buddy Parker, I'm pushing down the highway in a two-ton dually pickup truck that growls when I floor it. It's blacked out, decked out, and almost tactical in the way it's been outfitted.

Nothing identifies the truck other than an emblem pressed into the center of the leather steering wheel, the same emblem on the title and registration in the glove box. One word is on all three: Titan.

Uncertainty grows in my chest. I don't know who Parker works for, but I do know Titan Group. *Everybody* knows Titan exists, but that's about it. They're a special ops, post-military outfit. I asked Parker for Emma's phone number and access to a set of wheels. When I'd walked out of Walter Reed, after shooing Mazie away, there sat this truck with keys in the ignition, a wad of cash in the glove box, and cell phone programmed with one number.

It took me less than a minute to call her. That conversation, even with her hesitations, did more for me than the weeks of PTSD therapy bullshit I had to sit through to get released even after the docs gave a green light to my healing ribs and wound.

Her voice. Damn... I still can't shake it, replaying her words in my mind as I fly down the interstate with no idea where I'll end up. A radio station is on, and rock pours through the speakers. My thumbs drum, my heart pounds. Cold sweat spikes on my neck and shoulders. The closer I come to passing Summerland County, the more anxiety kills me.

I'll call her back. But not now. Not when I'm pulled toward Summerland as if the county's got my ass on a leash.

My head pounds, and I rub my temples. Before anything, I need to get a hotel room and get my head on straight. I've got nothing. No home. No Army contract. No team to shoot the shit with. Nothing.

The only shit I'm holding on to right now is survivor's guilt. That's what the nurses at Walter Reed called it. A social worker stopped by with pamphlets and a stern warning that no one could help me if I didn't admit that I needed help. Even Mazie, queen of mental what-the-fucks, nodded.

They warned me about triggers. They said I wouldn't be able to handle letting people down, disappointing others. That it would freak me the fuck out, sending me into some kind of PTSD tailspin if I thought I'd left someone hanging again. Well, newsflash, fuckers—there isn't anyone else to disappoint. I've hurt and abandoned, loved and left everyone there is to leave.

What I need is Emma, which means I need a plan.

I might be uncertain about where I'll work, where I'm going to live, how I'm going to eat after I spend the money in my wallet, but I am suddenly and unquestionably confident about her and me. We just need face time.

Step one's complete, thanks to Parker and Titan hooking me up with a phone number.

Step two: find out personal details and adapt. She's got a boyfriend? Fixable. A husband? Harder to fix, but still it can be done.

My determination surges. It all starts with a call back that I can't make while driving, heading past my hell. A sign ahead reads Summerland County line in five miles.

Damn, that fuckin' place. Nothing there for me, but it's as if I can't stay away. Unwilling to go another mile, I jerk the wheel, hitting the shoulder. Gravel spins in the wheel wells. The smell of burnt brakes filters into the truck. My hands strangle the steering wheel, and I press my forehead onto the Titan emblem.

Can't get the future if I avoid the past. I grab my cell and hit redial. Forty-five seconds later, no answer. Shit. Okay. New plan. Grab a burger and a bed somewhere, wait until first light, try again. And again. And again. Until I get what I need. Her.

Emma

After a quick cab ride to my new home, I'm alone and harboring a serious cocktail buzz. I bypass the kitchen and living room, heading straight for my room. After checking for accidental missed calls a thousand times, my phone died sometime during the drive home. I'm going to flip out if it doesn't charge ASAP.

I plug the phone into the charger and watch it for a few seconds to see if it will turn back on. Nope. Shit, shoot, shit. What if he's calling right this second?

Ugh. I'm going nuts and need to get out of these clothes. One last look at the phone, and I head into my bedroom. It's lonely now that I'm home with no Cally to make dinner for, no two-year-old's stories to keep me entertained.

I chuck my purse across the bedroom and flop onto my bed. But the combination of throwing and flopping while buzzed doesn't sit well, and I need to change anyway. What's a girl to wear when tipsy and home alone the night of her birthday celebration? Definitely something comfy. I change into my jammies and pace.

I unpack a box then check my phone. Still dead. I head to Cally's room, certain the box of her toys is in there and needs to be unpacked first. After ripping it open, I line up all her stuffed animals and dolls against the wall, making her favorite one the center. Packing that well-loved one was a mistake—grinning, I totally blame Uncle Ry-Ry—and I'm not sure how we've made it all week without that doll.

Okay, that's done. Now what? Back in my room, I take off my makeup then check my cell again. Five percent. I shrug, biting my lip. That's gotta be enough to at least turn it back on.

I press the button, and it lights up. I could unpack another box or just stare at my phone, willing it to ring. Damn Grayson. I can't stay away, can't stop thinking about if he called. Maybe it will... now.

Nope. Not a peep.

What if he called, and I missed it? No voicemails... but he wouldn't leave one, would he? I unplug it and move to another outlet before it dies again. Now I can sit on my bed and stare, wishing for it to ring.

Still doesn't. Seriously, he could've called when it was dead.

I scroll to my earlier incoming calls. His number is just sitting there, begging me to hit him back. My thumb hovers. Oh, this is such a bad idea. Nervous excitement rushes through me, and I hit SEND.

It's ringing!

My stomach's in my throat. I'm blushing, I know that, and I'm trying not to grin like a crazy woman. What the fuckballs am I doing? This is so bad. Bad. BAD in a major way. But I can't hang up.

"Hello?" His voice is gruff with sleep.

Hell. It's Friday. He went out and had a couple too. Maybe he passed out. Maybe I shouldn't have called him. He said *he'd* call, but he didn't. So *that* is something. This is a mistake.

Holy shit, I'm losing my mind. "Hey, Grayson."

Silence. Oh. Awkward. I didn't sign up for this. What am I doing?

"Hey."

I hear rustling noises. Grayson's in bed? What if he's not alone? What if he is? Do I want to know this much about him this very second? God. My mind is spiraling.

"Hey. Buzzed you earlier, went straight to voicemail." He clears his throat. It's sleep-soaked and rough. "What are you up to?"

"I've been drinking." Because that honest revelation is what's needed. Ugh. *Head. Slamming. Against. Wall.* I groan. "I mean. It was a happy hour. For me. I guess—"

"Happy early birthday."

God… Just, God. I curl into myself and hide under the covers, letting the deep rumble of his voice echo in my head. "Thanks."

"So… what are you doing for the real deal?"

Nothing I'll tell him about. Cherry's helping Cally decorate cookies and "make" me dinner on Sunday. "Small family thing."

"Your family, everyone's good?"

I close my eyes. It's like we're just catching up, not like our conversation earlier at work. I always thought he'd check in after we found out he went to basic training. Maybe he'd check in with Ryan. I thought he'd talk to *anybody*. But Grayson fell off the planet.

Yet somehow the memories of middle-of-the-night chats stir me. "What did you mean earlier, you're not the guy I knew?"

"I can't explain it. Dead man walking."

My sweet golden boy? Sure, he had his dark moments, his hidden pieces. "What does that mean, Gray? Why?"

"I've changed. Army changed me. War changed me. Walking away from you… ruined me."

My stomach swan dives. "Grayson… you can't say things like that."

"Shit, don't see why not." He groans. "You woke me up, thinking about you in my dream. Or nightmare. Not sure which anymore."

"You really can't say that!"

He laughs quietly. "Baby, I've come to learn it's best to say whatever comes to mind."

"I'm not sure that's true." I stare at the ceiling, wondering what would fall from my lips if I said whatever came to mind. *I still love you. I miss you. I have someone I'd like you to meet…*

"It is." He breathes into my ear. "I've learned the hard way. Lay it on the line, make up for lost time. Fix mistakes."

"Shut up," I whisper, pleading as my heart pounds.

"I was a kid. We were kids, and I was in deep. With you, Ems. And shit was going down at home. I got in my head, ended up enlisted."

"People don't end up enlisted."

"I did."

"How?"

He clears his throat. "That night at Pops's trailer... couldn't breathe, couldn't see. I thought my head was gonna explode. Someone offered me a way out, I took it. That second, it seemed right."

"It wasn't."

"I was stuck... and us, that night on the beach? I thought life couldn't get any better that night. I took that memory and ran. Didn't mean I was any less screwed."

I'm two days shy of twenty-one, and I've never been with another man. It's pathetic, but it's because of him. Hearing his voice, I'm at a loss for the longing I feel. The deep need to be held, loved... "People said you died."

He sucks a breath. "No. I'm the only one who made it out alive. Look, I'm sorry. But, Emma, I'm here now."

My tummy flips, but I don't know how to take *here now*. I need to redirect. "So... how did you get my number?" Does he know about Cally? Surely if someone gave him my cell number, they mentioned his daughter. I want to be the one who shares that. When the time is right. Which is *not* now.

"I called a guy."

"You called a guy?"

"Yeah."

"Who?" What, are we in a CIA movie? *Called a guy.* I rub my forehead. "What kind of guy?"

"Someone who... finds people."

"You found me? I wasn't lost."

"From me you were."

My insides clench. "Gray..."

"I couldn't go home and ask folks I used to know for your info. Hell, I don't want to step foot in that county ever again. So I called my guy. He gave me your number. I didn't pry. I don't know what dorm you're in or if you're off campus. Or... whatever."

Oh. My. God. He doesn't know. He's not calling about Cally. So why now? "What do you want from me?"

Silence.

"Gray!"

"What?"

"Tell me." I know I'm pleading, that I sound as crazy as I feel. "Please."

He takes a long breath. "I should be dead. Every guy in my unit—" Silence. "They died. In front of me. I was shot. Rescued. Transported to the States. Weeks in rehab at Walter Reed. My time's up and—" He clears his throat. "I can't go back. They're gone. And I'm done. Discharged. I'm... just... needing to make things right with you."

I've got nothing to offer. What do I say to that? Tears stream onto my pillow, and I'm not sure why. The explosion of emotion is too intense, and I can't single out one feeling.

"Ems, look, when we were kids, you saved me from home."

"Saved you?"

"Yeah. I'd think about you, and I was golden, no matter what was happening to me. But now it's gone. I can't close my eyes and see your face, can't remember your taste. You're the only thing that saved me, until I was dying and couldn't—couldn't find you. In me."

My lungs ache. I can't speak. My body is dying for him to hold me. I want my tears wiped. I want his mouth on mine. I've never stopped loving him.

"I've hardened. I'm… broken. Haunted. But I never stopped needing you."

Shivers roll through me. "Oh."

"And I'm back with one mission. You."

CHAPTER 21

Emma

Hardened and haunted? Even with that admission, I'm melting for Grayson.

"Emma, are you there?"

I nod, still burrowed in my covers. "Yeah. I'm here."

"Nothing to say to that?"

"Too much to say." I don't know where to start. "I'm not in the dorms."

The tension on the phone crackles between us. I laugh quietly as if I'm nervous, not as if I'm about to lay something heavy on him.

"Okay. No dorms. So how's Trydan?" He clears his throat. "Are you dating anyone?"

"Ha." I'm going to blame the vodka for not keeping that scoff silent.

"No dorms and no boyfriend." Even through the richness in his voice, I hear the curl of a smile. "Not going to complain."

"I didn't go to Trydan." My stomach twists into a

pretzel, and the birthday cocktails may come back up.

"Wait, what?" he growls. "Why?"

This isn't a phone kind of conversation. Why did I bring it up? "Just couldn't."

"You didn't go to college because of *me*?"

I strangle my pillow and press my eyes closed. "No. I mean, yes. Kinda. No. Not really."

"Ems... I..."

"It's not what you think."

"Then what is it?"

He'd make a good daddy. Goose bumps roll through me. I've thought that a thousand times. Cally's my world, the epicenter of my existence. I want to shout that I didn't go to Trydan and I don't care. I push through life, making choices I'd never have made without her, doing things most people wouldn't approve of because I'm going to survive and be better off in the end. My daughter—our daughter—is the best thing that's ever happened to me. But I bite my lip and simplify those thoughts. "It was just... life."

"Fuck me, Emma, you're *here*?"

My stomach drops, and I freeze under the safety of my comforter. "*Here*? Where are you?"

"You're in Summerland?" he asks, deeper, darker, more demanding than I've ever heard come from a man.

Panic pulses in my veins. "Grayson, where are *you*?"

"Five minutes from the Summerland County line."

"No, you're not!" I can't breathe. He's close. Too close. I'm dying to see him, scared to death at the same time. I don't know how to handle this. Shit, shoot, shit. "Ah—um, I'm around."

"Hang on. Give me a minute, okay? Do not hang up."

"Okay." I grab my knees and hide farther under the covers.

My proximity to him is a problem. If I had a hard time not calling him, I'm going to have a sudden urge to find him. When I'm ready. Which I'm not. My head is seriously going to explode. I need to calm down. While I'm waiting for him to come back on the line, I drop Cherry a text.

Emma: MISS YOU GUYS. TAKE CARE OF MY GIRL.

I stare at the screen, but she doesn't message me back.

"Emma, you there?"

"Hey."

"Listen to me, Ems. You never left my mind. Not the day I left or the day I came back. I've thought of you a million times in a million ways."

"Same," I admit. He overwhelms my thoughts when I dance. I move for him, sway for him. Every Wednesday, when there might be hundreds of eyes on me, I'm alone with Grayson. "But I'm already vulnerable enough to you. I'm not sure admitting anything puts me in the advantage."

"No games, baby. I'm past that. We're talking. Just you and me. You want vulnerable? I've killed. Maimed. Mauled. I've destroyed and been ruined. I'm lifeless unless it's about you. Now who the fuck is vulnerable?"

My chest feels tight. The silence around me is overwhelming. I have no creature comforts to rely on. No TV or music for background noise. Nothing. All I have is Grayson's deep voice in my ear, talking as if it hasn't been years, and I like it. A lot.

"I don't know," I whisper.

"This is what I know: your sweet face, your sweet

laugh, God, that smile. The way you used to stare at me like I'm the reason you were put on earth. You're the only thing that can bring me to life." Noise filters through the phone, sounds like he's shaking his head. "Nothing held back anymore. You want the truth, and that's all I have to offer."

My stomach somersaults. He's direct and confident.

"I've survived off your memory, Ems."

Swirling in memories, I swallow away my hesitations. "Same. But probably not in the way you think."

"The night before I was set to go... I meant to explain I'd enlisted. But when we got on the beach... "

I said I loved him. "Yeah."

"Best night of my fuckin' life."

Tears leak into my pillow. "Mine too."

We sit in silence. Well, I'm silent. He's moving around or something. But it's not awkward. I think about that night together and its implications. Who knows where his head is; I can't even figure out my own thoughts.

"Best night ever," he mumbles again, sounding reminiscent. "I'm sure you've changed as much as I have. But I lean on that night when nothing else works."

My heart flutters. I need to get off the phone. I'm falling for this sexy-voiced man and romanticizing him, reliving old memories. It makes my anger hard to hang on to. "Maybe we could talk later, Gray. I'm"—*in love*—"exhausted."

"Don't hang up, Emma. Please. Stay on the line with me."

I don't want to as much as I do want to. My chest squeezes, and I hug myself tighter in my covers cocoon. "Why?"

"Said I was fixing us." His breathy growl makes me dizzy. "It's always been you."

I swoon. A shiver runs through me. It's always been him too. Maybe one day I'll understand why. I probably need intense therapy. I can't admit out loud what it means to hear him say that, but I can't sit around and torture myself. "Good night, Grayson."

"Don't hang up on me, Ems."

Knock, knock, knock. It echoes through the phone *and* my house. I jump, my eyes going wide as I stare toward the wall as though I have x-ray vision. There's no way...

"Not"—one more knock hits. It's as hard and strong as the man on the phone—"unless you plan on opening your front door."

CHAPTER 22

GRAYSON

My muscles bunch and flex, and I have enough energy running through me to deadlift a car or tear the front door off her house. I rock to the balls of my feet on Emma's porch. The small Craftsman house is worn but safe. She's in a semi-decent part of town, and her place has a tiny lawn and windows that could use a security latch.

All I can focus on is the two inches of wood separating Emma and me. I've never been more certain in my whole life that I'm somewhere I'm unwanted. "Open up, Ems."

Thump. I laugh, pretty sure she just bumped her head against the door.

"Tell me this is a joke," she moans.

"No joke, baby. I want see you."

"Wait!" Another thump on the door, and I'm almost certain she's replaced her forehead with her fist. "How do you even know where I live! I *just* moved. Like, days ago. You said you thought I was at college!"

ONLY FOR LOVE | 145

I like that she's smart, that she's thinking and questioning, because I don't want a single doubt after tonight's over. "Pays to know someone. You said you were close, so I pulled in a favor."

"What? Do you have PIs on speed dial?"

Chuckling, I nod at the closed door. "Something like that."

"Spies R Us?"

Now I'm definitely smiling. The girl's still cute. "Titan Group."

"Sounds like they shouldn't know where I live."

"But they do, so let me in."

She sighs. It's more relenting than frustrated, and I know I've won. I just need to drive a last point home.

My hand squeezes the phone. I'll hang up soon as she opens. "Emma, you said you were miles away, not hours. I couldn't stay away. I asked for help, and my buddy Parker pulled a solid."

"Ha. Thank Parker for me."

Cute plus a little bite. Emma's coming back to me. I've got her voice, and I can picture her smile. This is ten times better than any medicine or therapy they gave me for being shot during war.

"I can't believe you're outside."

"Good intel is good intel. Now open the door." Nothing about this moment is planned. My heart's in my throat. Little on earth scares me, but not knowing how she'll react to this offensive maneuver makes me anxious. "I'm not standing out here all night."

"Of course you aren't. My neighbors will call the cops if you stand out there."

I laugh, and my side hurts. But it's a good kind of hurt. The wound is healing; I'm nowhere near one hundred percent, but I can feel my blood rushing, my body anticipating. It's the best I've felt in years. "Come on, baby."

There's a shuffling noise on the other end of the phone. "I hate that you're forcing my hand."

But the door opens.

Emma Kingsley.

More beautiful than when I last saw her. My throat squeezes, and my pulse pounds in my neck, my temple. Fuck me... just... fuck me. Gorgeous. "Ems."

Her eyelashes flutter, and color rises to her cheeks. Her blond hair is wild. It's longer and fuller than I remember, and my palms itch to run over it. I step closer. She doesn't move, doesn't invite me in. Just stares like a wide-eyed beauty.

Here we are. Neither moving. I'm not breathing, and she might not be either. It's intense. Thick tension pushes us together, but as the seconds tick by, we don't move.

"Are you going to let me in?"

"I'm not sure." She blinks slowly but then rushes forward, falling into my arms. She wraps around me, a sob escaping her lips, which are pressed against my neck. "Oh my God. I missed you."

We're locked together. My skin tingles where her mouth brushed it. Her shampoo and faint perfume tease my nose. Her back, her hips, the way she hugs, it feels familiarly perfect. I breathe as I haven't before. As if I haven't been capable of taking in a deep enough or strong enough breath. Nothing's felt right since the moment I left her. Three years of unsettledness gone in a hug. "I'm home."

"Home." She nods against me, sweetly, innocently rubbing her body against mine.

Sweet mother of friction, her moves do good things to me. "Yeah."

Home in her arms has nothing to do with where we stand. This is where I'm meant to be, holding the girl I should never have left. She sobs, and I hold her tighter. My side wound aches, and I couldn't care less. Nothing would stop me from holding her. There was never a second that I didn't love her. She's my everything.

I drop my chin. My lips touch the top of her head and press. It's not a kiss. More of a claim. This woman is mine. I'll beg and plead, do whatever it takes. I've been a dead man walking for years, hurting and hardened, looking for an outlet and suffocating on my mistakes. I've been wrong. Been scared. Been a motherfuckin' fool. The answer to my problems has always been right here, with her.

"Baby." I stroke her hair.

She holds me tighter. "You feel… different."

I've packed on weight, filled out. I'm definitely bigger and stronger than when she saw me last. I let go and step past her. Her eyes watch me take in the barren room. Time has passed, but there's heat coming from her. Need. Want. Arousal. Whatever it is, it's thick between us.

"Wow. So. You're—" Her gaze lingers on my shoulders then my chest. "Like G.I. Joe or something."

A grin tugs on my cheeks. Shit knows I haven't smiled for a long time. "Or something."

Because what am I anymore? I'm not Army. My time was up after I was released from Walter Reed, and I didn't want to go back. Maybe I can do something different. Maybe I can figure it out as I go.

I focus on what's in front of me. The girl I'm never leaving again, her sparse furniture, and cardboard boxes. She's all alone, and I can't stay away. The need to take her mouth and have her body kills me. But more than that, I'd die to know what she thinks.

"What are you thinking?" she asks, her voice hesitant.

"Just wondering the same about you." I leave out the part about her rockin' body making me think dirty things. That's nothing that I'm going to let her in on yet. "You did just move in."

She fidgets. Her eyes catch mine and jump away. "Yeah, not all our, my stuff is here. It's just boxes."

"You look uncertain."

She bites her lip. "I'm a million things. Maybe nervous."

"Don't be." I catch her hand and study her. Her obvious unease fades. "Missed you, Ems." My heart beats faster. This feels right.

She stares up through her eyelashes. "Maybe there's more." Tension envelops us, and I drag my thumb over her knuckles. "I'm just caught off guard."

"More?" I step closer. My boots sound heavy on her barren wood floors as I erase the inches between us. There's a tightness in my chest and a need in my blood. I'm starved for Emma, so hungry that it makes me lose my mind. I came here to win her heart, not jump in her pants, but my mouth's watering like a starved addict's. Everything I'd remember is back, but a thousand times stronger than I imagine. One thing is clear: we've never been over.

"I can't explain it." Her lips part as she retreats, backing into the wall. The quiet thud echoes around us. "It's just you."

Her breasts rise and fall behind a shirt that molds to her curves. She's sexy, sultry, and sweet. I swear to Christ she does it without even trying. My cock's throbbing. The only girl I've ever wanted is this one.

"Can't believe you're here, Gray." Arousal coats her voice, urging me on.

"Feels like I never left."

"I know." She's breathy and quiet, but an intense fever lights her perfect brown eyes.

A scrap of space remain between us, and she presses her palms flat against my stomach. It's soft, not to stop me but to feel me. My head falls back. I take that second to own her touch, memorize the heavy power she holds over me, and I pray that I have whatever it takes to win her back. I need more than the carnal, primitive, possessive explosion that's happening this second. I need Emma in order to survive. I need Emma as mine.

"Baby, say back away if you've got some reason to stop. I have to hear the words because what your face says…"

Her cheeks flush pinker. With parted lips and wild eyes, her head tilts back. "Please," she whispers.

The slope of her neck screams for my lips. "You can say no, Ems, if you don't want me with you tonight. But I'm giving you everything I have inside me, making up for every second apart."

An audible breath heaves from her lips. I cage her with myself, against the wall, and give her a slip of space. She has two choices: duck and run or hang on tight. It's all her call. Until I start. Then I'm never stopping.

"Grayson." Tiny gasps mix with my name. Her fingertips flex, her fingernails digging into my abdomen, then her hands roughly crawl up my torso and clasp around my neck. "Don't you dare leave me like that again." Her face is harsh, then she softens.

"Baby." My hands meet her waist, grasp her sides. I feel her breathing like me. Uneven in cadence and choking on our tension. I touch my lips to her temple, and she quietly gasps, writhing against me. I trail to her ear. "I'm not going anywhere."

Our foreheads touch. It's partly sweet but mixed with a needy hunger.

"But…" she whispers.

"Don't forgive me now." I drag my lips down her neck. "Later, yeah. Now, no. Just let us happen."

She nods against my face. I hug her tight then lift her up, heading for the lone couch.

Her eyes close. "There's so much to... catch up on."

There's fear in her voice. All I know to do is hang on. I swallow her up, and when I drop to the couch, she fits in my lap as though she's supposed to be there. My nose is in her hair, my arms wrapped around her.

"Look at me."

"No. I don't trust myself to." She shakes her head. Silk strands of her hair tease my cheek, but her gaze isn't on me. "You show up, and we end up in bed. What kind of girl does that make me?"

Easiest answer I've had to give all night. "It makes you mine."

Her eyes flit to mine.

"Not a day went by I didn't hate myself for what I did. Not a day I didn't think you weren't better off without me. I watched every man I served with bleed out. My unit was decimated. I was shot, bleeding out. Dying. And I begged God—*begged*—to get this moment with you."

Tears brim in her eyes. "I want to hate you—"

"I'll get us through that."

"I want to hate you..." The tears fall, slipping down her cheeks. "Because I still love you."

Fuck me, my heart squeezes. Everything in my soul hurts. "Emma."

I'm going to die if I can't get closer. Her lashes are tear-dampened, her gaze unsure.

My thumbs move over her cheeks. "I've always loved you, and that's why this will work."

Chapter 23

GRAYSON

Emma's tongue runs along her pink, full lips. I remember them all over me. We had years of friendship but not nearly enough time after things heated up. We're older. Wiser. With experience on our side. I need her and whatever she'll give me because, eventually, it will be all of her again.

"Before, I should have taken better care of you. I promise I will now." I guide her mouth to mine. Our lips touch. Good God, she's so sweet. My tongue slides to her, making me groan when she opens for me.

Her hands wrap around my shoulders, and she repositions to straddle me on the couch. Our breaths are choppy. Her legs press against my sides, and the wound hurts where her knee digs in. I don't care. The pain, the certainty of her riding my cock, makes my body hum.

"Missed you." She's kissing and biting.

Those damn teeth come out when I'm not expecting it. Her hips flex, rubbing the V of her legs against my erection. There's something more sensual about how she moves now, something practiced. I'm intoxicated with her sway, her confidence, and I'm drunk on her kiss.

Emma pulls at my T-shirt. I break us apart and tear it over my head. Anything to give her free rein, to feel her—

"Oh my God, Grayson."

My bandage. Reality check. Not sexy, not even in the least. Eight-by-eight inches of gauze and tape. It's not even needed at this point, but it keeps my shirt from rubbing the fresh scar.

"Was I hurting you?"

"Didn't notice."

"Liar," she whispers.

Her face has always been her tell. She's changing, reacting. Memories bubble inside me, and I'm reminded of the night Pops walked in. Her face had changed then too. But then, it was... fear, disgust, humiliation? Now it's... hell, I don't know what it is. "Emma?"

She looks at my side then trails her eyes over my stomach, up my chest and arms, over the tattoos that weren't there before, the bulk and definition I've put on over the years, and lands on my face. "Tell me the truth, you're okay?"

"Baby," I growl, "I can't think of a single thing that'd keep me from sliding into you."

Her mouth pops open. Three years have passed, and I guess no one's said a dirty word to her. I'll ease her into it, make her wet for it. Her high school crush is gone. I've been replaced by a broken soldier.

Emma's mouth closes into a slight smile, and I know she likes it. Her gaze drops again and retraces the same path—bandage, abs, chest, and tattoos—finally landing on my lips. Carefully, she leans forward, as if she's scared to hurt me, and brushes her lips against mine. Shivers roll down my back. Her kiss is light at first. Delicate. Caring. Then it's stronger, trailing down my chin, down my neck. I groan and roll my hips.

Her tongue glides down to my collarbone, her teeth scratching.

"Christ, Emma."

She slides off my lap, pushing between my knees. I can guess a million ways this could go, but there's not a chance in hell that during our first time back together, she'll end up with me in her mouth. This has to be unquestionably, unconditionally about her.

I expect her hands to land on my belt, but they don't. She moves toward the bandage, kissing my skin, smoothing her fingers over the ripples in my abs.

Chastely, she places kisses on the edges of the bandage then looks up. "I mourned your death."

My eyes sink shut. I hurt that she hurt. "Emma..."

"I never wanted you in pain."

No. Not this conversation again. "Off your knees and in my lap. Come here."

Half a second passes before I take her hand and tug her up. She settles against my hard-on and her arms rise above her head, locking me in a permissive gaze.

I slip her shirt over her head. Full breasts, creamy skin. "My beautiful girl."

A blush hits her cheeks again. "I've always been yours."

Shit. I'm done for, and I drop us to lie on the couch. Her hair spreads on the cushions, a blond halo for my angel, my savior. How did I let this go? I hold myself against her, stomach to stomach, chest to chest. I'm falling for her all over again.

Our tongues lash together, and I kiss her deep. Emma claws my back. My fingers trace up her side to massage her breasts, rubbing her nipples through the lace. With a slide of my hand, I remove her bra and dip my mouth. The harder I suck, the louder she gets and the more she thrashes.

"God, Gray." There's a desperate need in her voice that I feel too.

Enough permission granted to push forward, I tug down her pants. "How are you even prettier than before?"

"That's a good line."

"No, baby." My hands tease over her hips to skim the silk of her panties. "Do you think after everything I've said, I'd drop some line that wasn't true?"

"I… don't know."

My hand cups between her legs, and she groans.

"God, I can't think." She's breathy and drags out her words.

I slip my fingers alongside the fabric. She's wet, and I'm deliriously hard. I swear I'm going to rip the silk off and sink into her. She's ready enough I could. My finger slides against her, and she meets my touch, rolling her hips and rubbing hard as she watches me.

We're side by side on her couch without much room for our tangled bodies. "Good?"

"Like that." Her gasps stutter as I slide a finger into her slick tightness. "Oh. More."

"Yes, ma'am," I growl and give her what she wants.

Time apart has given her confidence, hunger, knowledge of what she wants and how she's going to get it, knocking her sexiness level to stratospheric.

Her mouth is open, eyes closed. I give her two fingers. Her muscles clench on me. She's moaning, building, and crying for more. "Grayson."

"Come, Ems. Come for me so I can fuck you, love you."

She nods nonstop, hair wild. Emma moans, arching her back and grinding her clit against my palm. I work her, do her, let her ride to what she needs.

"God, Gray. God!"

Detonation. With eyes squeezed shut, she comes hard, as if she's needed me to really let go.

Still spasming, her face goes lax as her orgasm lulls. My body hums while she slows.

Beautiful brown eyes blink open. "Every inch of me belongs to you. Always has."

Slowly, I take my hand from between her legs. She's perfect. Naked breasts and amazing body. I kiss her shoulder, her neck. She smells like... mine. To taste and touch and fuck and love. Emma Kingsley is all mine.

"Grayson... there's..." She looks at the wall. "There's been no one... but you."

I freeze. "*No one?*" She cringes. What I said, how I said it, it came out wrong. But three years... my forehead pinches. "Emma."

I've got nothing else to say, but masculine pride fills me in a way I can't express. I owned her virginity, but still it's just me.

She stares over my shoulder. "You think I'm pathetic, but... it's not like that."

I cup her chin, bring her focus back to me, and shake my head. "I don't. I've never been more—" I don't have words. Territorial testosterone is about to make me punch-drunk. "It's not a bad thing. It's fuckin' amazing."

"Promise?"

A dark possessiveness flashes through me. I can't stay off her. My hands cover her stomach, her breasts, her sides... I reach for her legs to spread her thighs. I want to taste her, feel her. I want my dick inside this woman who's only ever had me. I can't breathe for how greedy for her I am right now.

"Grayson, wait."

Whatever she has to explain can be left for later. I need to feel her come on my cock, harder and stronger than she did on my hand. "You need me like I need you?"

She pants and nods. "More than that."

"Bullshit."

I take her mouth hard. This is happening. We're past reconnecting, past talking out forgiveness. Her hands are on my belt. She slides it loose and attacks the button and zipper. Seconds later, I'm hard in her hands. She's pumping me, one fist on top of the other, thumb teasing my crown.

"Fuck me." The couch is too small for us. Restraint. I need it. Someway, somehow. Until I find a mattress. "Bedroom, Ems?"

"Yes. Wait. Don't stop. Please." She's writhing and moaning. "Please."

"Just a little more, baby. Then a bed." Her panties are working their way down, and I'm dying. Our tongues tangle, but I pull back. "Let's go."

"Yeah." She adjusts her panties and sits up with me.

I'm off the couch with my pants hanging loose on my hips. I grab her hand and let her lead me to her bedroom. She's wearing black silk underwear, and that's it. Her ass. What a fuckin' ass.

We're halfway through the kitchen, but I can't resist. I snag her to me. My hands thread through her hair. Her breasts press to my chest. "I can't wait."

"Too close to stop here." She pulls me down a short hall and into a room.

There's a bed on the floor, a dresser, and a few boxes. The lights are dim. We fall to the mattress together, arms and legs tangled. Done wasting time, I snag the sides of her panties, ready to bare her body to me. I've never been more primed.

"I've dreamed of this…" she whispers. "Danced for this…"

My eyes rake over her as I remove the last of her clothes. She's naked and… I tilt my head. What the hell is…

My chest goes tight. Panic curls into my neck, chokes my throat. My mouth goes dry. Emma sits up, heavy lidded. I can't fuckin' breathe, can't believe my eyes. I don't know what to think or do.

"Ems?" I inch closer, praying for a truth that's different than what I think. "What's that?"

Confusion then… fear crosses her face.

"Emma?" My eyes drop, laser-focused, between her hips. She's covering up, moving back. "Tell me what happened there."

"No." Her eyes go wide. Tears fill them. "Shit. Shoot. Just once, I got caught up in the moment."

Oh, fuck no. Please, Christ, don't let it be. Don't let me have abandoned more than just her. "Ems? What is that?"

"A C-section scar."

CHAPTER 24

GRAYSON

For as far back as I can remember, my mom sucked down pills. They made her happy; they made her sad. It was circular, one feeling morphing into the next. A smile. A frown. The whacked-out emotions seesawed back and forth. I didn't know what was wrong with her, but I knew she needed me. Until I killed her.

Right now, kneeling on Emma's bed, hearing the word *C-section*, I know the fucked-up truth. I let people down. It's my lot in life. I don't mean for it to happen, but my decisions are my worst enemy. Pops preached that truth from the day he walked in as I stood over my lifeless mother.

Now tears prick my eyes and raw fear skates down my throat as I stare at Emma. She cowers against the wall, pulling the covers to her chin as though they're a protective barrier. *From me.*

"C-section?" I thought I'd failed her—failed us. Dammit, I was wrong.

She nods. Her tears fall over her cheeks, and she doesn't wipe them. Wet streaks stain her skin pink, reminding me that I do nothing but ruin lives. I have no response. I'm sick. My muscles tense as the urge to run wars with the weight of my abandonment. I don't know which way to go or what to do.

Just another pill, baby. Gray-baby, give Mama her pills. Such a good boy. Precious boy.

A panic attack is coming. I know the signs, the feelings. That moment when I try for a breath and can't take one.

Calm down.

Think.

I concentrate, hoping to focus on Emma... but my vision skews. Black and gray. Hazy and distorted. The walls are caving in, inching closer with every heavy thud of my agitated heart.

"Emma—" My voice shakes.

The room tilts forward. I follow, falling, my head down, my balled fists digging into her mattress. I can't escape the smothering grip around my neck.

"Gray? Are you okay?"

A cold sweat covers my body. I can't swallow, can't function, can't make sense of the room spinning. "Emma. *Ems*, God." I'm not sure I can handle this.

"I'm so sorry," she whispers.

I look up and hold her eyes, seeking the truth that I'm terrified to confirm. "You said you've never been with anybody but me?"

Her head barely nods. Soft blond hair falls over her shoulder, framing her innocent face.

"We." The thick lump in my throat won't budge, and I can't look her in the eye. "Have a baby?"

But I didn't see any toys. A million thoughts crowd my mind. Adoption? Something happened? A protective wave of adrenaline surges through me at the thought of lost years and decisions I know nothing about.

"You weren't supposed to find out this way." Emma wraps her arms around her legs, holding herself. "She's perfect."

My heart explodes, and my eyes burn. "*She?*"

The only girl I've ever loved nods again. "We... have a little girl."

Confirmation.

My fists loosen, and I claw into the blanket, fighting the fall into darkness. My mind screams of everyone I've abandoned. But, God, now there are two girls I love, and I refuse to run from this moment. "A little girl."

"Yeah."

I don't know what to do. I'm aching. Devastated. Curious. Scared. Angry. I'm *everything*, a million times more intense than I've ever experienced. But the guilt. It's going to kill me. Emma and our little girl? Another person I let down, and she's my flesh and blood. I hurt my daughter. Just like my dad. *No.* Just like my mom.

"Gray?" Concern carries in her voice. "Are you okay?"

Shit, no. I'm dying. The only thing I know to do is reach for Emma. She's saved me my whole life, and she might be the only who can save me now. I force myself to look into her eyes, certain of the hatred and desertion I'll see there, but I can't get a read on her.

"Where is she?" My voice breaks. I know it. Can't stop it. Just... "What's her name?"

Emma's face twists; her chin falls, letting her golden hair obscure her gaze.

I don't know what she's going to tell me. *If* she'll share. Not that I deserve anything. But I'll beg. "You have to tell me."

Her chin juts up, and sudden anger radiates from her. "I don't have to tell you anything."

She's right. I left my girl and my child. *My child.* Fuck me, fuck me. I swallow against churning nausea and move forward, crawling toward the epitome of everything I've let down. "I didn't know."

"How would you have?" Emma's ice cold. The emotion is wiped from her face as if she's morphed into a different person. Pulling a blanket around her chest, she scoots out of bed and toward a suitcase on the floor. In a mechanical, efficient way, she pulls on panties and pajamas, semi-shielding herself. Once covered in a baggy T-shirt and flannel pants, she drops the blanket. "What was I supposed to do?"

My mouth opens, but I've got nothing.

"You should go, Grayson." She doesn't look at me and walks out.

I'm left cold, shaking from the news and the aftereffects of PTSD meltdown avoidance. My nerves are shot. My adrenaline's still kicking, changing my begging to anger. "What were you supposed to do? *You find me.* You track me down and say 'game changer.' That it isn't about you and me anymore. It's not about you making me promise on the beach to never say good-bye, or me loving you so damn hard I knew that was the only memory I'd ever need." I follow her into the hall. "Do you hear me, Emma? You. Find. Me."

She spins, arms thrown out. "God, like it's that simple." Her hands tear into her hair, and she growls, deep and devastated. "One day you're here, the next day you're gone. One day you were with me…"

The heavy thud in my heart starts again. My chest aches. "If I had known…"

Her cold eyes hold mine, and she shakes her head. "You don't get to say that."

I heave out a breath, hoping to dissipate the

fight-or-flight reflex that strangles me again. I'm on a roller coaster of crazy that I'm struggling to control. *Thump, thump, thump.* My heartbeat pushes into my throat. A fresh panic attack is inches away. I turn, lean into the wall, and press my forehead to it so hard it hurts. My fists ball. My shoulders tingle. My skin's needled, a terrifying, electrifying sensation ripping me apart. I need to get out of here. Just run. Pound pavement until I can't take another stride.

Help…

I push past Emma, needing the front door and its sweet release.

"She looks just like you, Gray."

God. My heart shreds to a million pieces. Pain I didn't know existed… it's unfathomable. My legs turn liquid. Agony rips through me as I hit my knees. I'm going to implode. I just need to get out the door to fresh air… but I can't.

"Where the hell is she?" Tears stain my words. My throat cracks, and I can't say more.

Emma's steps approach me slowly. Each one takes an eternity. "With Cherry."

"I have to see her." I won't turn around—I can't look at her, not like this—but I have to see my daughter. "Now. *Please.*"

"No."

I'm crushed. My limbs tremble. My heartbeat pounds. Slowly, I pivot, still on the floor, and watch her drop next to me. Resolve paints her face, looking like something I can only describe as a protective mother.

"I don't have to do anything. You're not something I can spring on her. 'Hey, Cally, you have a dad and he wants to say hi.'"

My baby girl's name is Cally.

My mother's name was Calinda.

Emma's mouth pinches closed as the same realization hits us at the same time. This is the biggest, hardest, cruelest what-the-fuck-have-I-done-with-my-life moment, and my heart finally gives out.

CHAPTER 25

Emma

On my knees and in Gray's arms, I'm surrounded by his complete destruction. I don't know what's happening. One second he's angry, the next desperate. I hadn't thought about how to handle our situation, and when he showed up... we spiraled, as evidenced by him still being shirtless. His breaths come too quickly. I don't even think he sees me, even though our faces are inches apart.

"Grayson!"

No response. Like a dead man in a warm body, he's here with me, but something wicked is happening on the inside. I did this to him. The hurt rolling off him is palpable, and this might be shock. I don't know what else to call it.

My hands grip his thick shoulders and shake him. "Gray. Please. You're scaring me." I've never seen anything more vulnerable than him at this moment. "Please."

My cell phone starts ringing somewhere. It's late,

and part of me automatically fears it's Cherry with bad news. But it's probably the diner telling me someone didn't show up. I'm the standard first call to fill any shift. But I let it keep ringing. If it's Cherry, she'll hit redial as soon as the voicemail picks up.

Grayson leans into me. His head fits into the crook of my neck, and he's nearly dead weight. A sob wracks his powerful body, and I wrap my arms around him. I'm not sure that he's in tears, just that he's overwhelmed, and why wouldn't he be? His mother's name did him over. I didn't know much about her, just that Calinda Ford died when we were in kindergarten. I wanted Cally to have a piece of her daddy.

I smooth a hand over the strong muscles of his bare back and up his corded neck. His blond hair is short, though I suspect it's longer than the military would like. I coo in his ear like I do when Cally has nightmares. Hurting him was never the plan. I still love him. I want him. It's this situation—it's hair-trigger tense. We're both set to fly hard in opposite directions, both needing something that can't be had. The past can't be rewritten, but the future... the future is always ours to change.

"I'm sorry," I whisper. "And I love you."

His arms cling to me tighter, like the night at the beach house, before we had sex, before I told him how I felt, what I wanted. If this is shock or trauma or... whatever it is, I don't know, but he can hear me, feel me. Slowly the tension leaves his muscles until we're tangled together on my front floor. His breathing has evened, but his green eyes are sad and downcast, not looking anywhere but at the barren floor.

We stay there for hours maybe before he shifts, letting out a barely ragged sigh. "Bet you're a good mama."

My God, does he always know what makes my heart explode? I nod through the pressure in my chest and the mist in my eyes. "I've killed myself for our girl. Second-guessed everything, pushed myself, lectured myself... ignored the looks, ignored the whispers. But when it comes down to being a good mama? I've given her everything I have."

"Yeah, you're good. I just know it... my mom was, and she wasn't."

I don't remember him speaking of his mom. Whatever I knew had been instilled in my mind long ago, and I never questioned it. As just a fact of life, Grayson's mom had died and his pops is a bastard. I bite my lip, unsure what to say. Gray still won't look at me.

"I was a kid, so I really didn't know better." His eyes well, and since we're splayed on the floor, tears leak sideways into his hair. "She was perfect. Beautiful. Funny. We were happy." He looks at me. "Maybe we weren't. I guess I was too young to know. I was the center of her world, but not really. Her demons were. I just didn't understand it. But... she was the center of mine. Mama's boy."

His honesty shreds me. "You don't have to tell me."

"I eventually learned that she took pills like candy. I even remember bits and pieces. Think I thought they *were* candy. God, she looked the mom part. I remember that. Fuckin' Joan Cleaver lookalike. But something ate her up inside, and she would nap and snack on her candy. I was her little pill boy when she couldn't stand up."

My guts twist as I see where his explanation is going.

"I thought she was asleep. She always went to sleep, and I'd just play until Pops got home. He'd ask me about it, I think. But she always said it was our special secret." His voice cracks. "She must've been dead for hours, and I was sitting at her feet, playing G.I. Joes or some shit."

I squeeze him in our awkward hold on the ground. "It's not your fault, Grayson."

"Of course it is. She couldn't even get up, and I fed her pills. Her heart stopped. Nothing violent, but she could've been saved if I'd picked up the phone and called 911."

"You were a baby."

"I was man enough to hide a secret from my father."

"Gray—"

"I killed Calinda Ford, the woman you named the child I didn't know after. And Pops—damn me, I think he was normal before that. But that night, he spanked the shit out of me for killing my mom. I deserved it, I get that. But for a man who'd never touched me like that before… I didn't go to school for two weeks. Everyone thought I was mourning Mom, but truth was, I couldn't sit down, couldn't move without crying."

Tears pour down my cheeks, into my hair. The burden he's been carrying all these years is that he somehow believes that guilt is deserved. I flash back to the night in his trailer after the Sadie Hawkins dance, when Grayson said he'd first stood up to Pops. We were eighteen, or almost. My heart bleeds for him. More than a decade of that drilled into him…

Grayson pulls a long breath. "I'm not sure Pops had it in him to be a dad. Never seemed into it. Never looked me in the eye. But the day Mom died, I became the enemy. The bastard child he didn't want and couldn't get rid of because I was his last tangible memory of her."

"I didn't know."

He blinks wayward tears away and locks his gaze on me. "And now you do. Won't change anything, but maybe you understand."

"Understand... what?"

"Everything about me."

CHAPTER 26

GRAYSON

I'm spent. Emotionally. Physically. Mentally. I've tapped my reserves, and I'm depleted. But I do have Emma in my arms, lying on her hardwood floor. It's more comfortable than living in a dug-out burrow in the desert. It's more peaceful than my time spent alone in a hospital bed. Emma shifts, and I reposition us so that she's not bearing the burden of lying on the hard floor.

"You okay?" she whispers.

"No."

"You're going to be though."

I nod. "I know."

The night crawls by, and I can't tell if she's asleep. Her breathing pattern never changes, her muscles don't relax. Finally, I shift to see her face. She's out.

"Emma?"

Nothing. The girl doesn't budge. Then I realize she's fallen asleep clinging to me. Her fingers are flexed into my muscles, and her body blankets me in a way that I can't peel away from. Not that I would.

For the first time, everything is laid on the table, and I can breathe.

I stand, and she holds onto me tightly, still sleeping. As carefully as I can, I make my way to her couch, where our night started. I'm not sure why, but I can't head for her bedroom. I don't have permission or some shit. I can't explain it, but it's hers to invite me to. Just like the rest of this house, the rest of her life... I want in, and as evidenced by earlier tonight, I can't ram my way in.

She stirs when I lay us down. Her cheek is glued to my bare chest, her soft hair tickling me.

"You okay?" she asks again, voice sleep-soaked.

"Getting there."

She takes a deep breath as she fully wakes. "I'll tell you a story."

My heart squeezes. "Yeah. Could use one of those."

Silence lingers, and I'm sure it's close to dawn. The night is still dark through the windows, but there's the slight hint of morning.

"Once upon a time, there was a little girl. She has blond hair and green eyes."

God, Emma's stories always take me away, make me feel better. This one feels as if it's going to kill me, but I keep quiet, trying to trust in her to save me from tonight.

"Every day, she wakes with a smile. She puts on her princess hat and lines up her princess dollies, giving them each a good morning hug. With worldly two-year-old advice, she tells each toy to have a great day because the sun is out." Emma sighs. "The sun will always rise, Gray. Even if we have to be saved from ourselves, there's nothing a little princess charm and a hug can't help."

I let her words coat me, sink in. I don't need to be

saved from tonight. I've never needed the here and now more than right this second. "True enough."

Her hand gingerly slides up my stomach, her palm drifting over my light smattering of chest hair. "What I said earlier... I was unhinged. Awful and angry. I'm really sorry."

I kiss the top of her head and inhale the sweet sunshine of her scent. "I deserved it."

"Oh, Gray. I think you think you deserve more than you actually do."

Maybe. "Another conversation for another night."

"I didn't know about your mom. I wanted a piece of you with me every day." She sucks in a heartbroken breath. "You were with me every day. Every night. I couldn't let you go."

"You don't have to."

"Maybe."

"Nothing has to be decided tonight." The darkness in the window is melting to a deep purple. "Go to sleep, baby."

Her arms tighten around me. "Be here when I wake up?"

I hate that she has to ask, but I deserve it. "Promise."

Even as my eyelids hang heavy and I feel Emma relax into a slumber, I can't help but wonder at all the things I never knew I wanted. Holding a baby, naming her. Watching her walk and talk... I hug Emma close, hoping to hell I finally have something to dream about, and I let myself drift to sleep.

Emma

A heavy, warm weight holds me in place, and I inhale a long-ago-familiar soapy scent that makes me melt. Then my eyes shoot open, and I realize I've been sleeping—drooling, oh my freakin' god—on Grayson's bare chest. As smoothly as I can, I fix that problem and try not to panic enough to wake him. Seriously, I'm asleep on my couch with him? The last twenty-four hours have been insane. I wipe the corner of my mouth and hope I didn't snore.

"Morning, baby."

His greeting is grated and gravelly, sexy without trying, and I can feel the deep rumble of his words in his chest since I'm plastered against him. "Morning."

It feels too early to be awake. The sun's up, but it's soft. I'm struck by how odd it feels to wake with a good morning from a half-naked man and not Cally. There's a pang in my heart. I miss her. But this... this is nice. I can't say it's not enjoyable. I love my daughter, but I'm twenty years old, a day short of my birthday, and I've had little time to just be me, not Mommy. Though I really wish Cally was at home too.

"What's that look?" he asks.

Oh, that's a conversation I need a cup of coffee for before we dig in. I sigh and figure vagueness is best for the moment. "I'm off the charts on an emotional roller coaster."

His tongue darts over his bottom lip, and he nods almost imperceptibly. "Know that feeling." But a fire hits his eyes, making them shine like emeralds on fire.

Grayson wraps me in his thick arms, making me sigh against his chest. Our bodies entwine, and it's so familiar. I want to melt and nuzzle.

"We need to talk about the part where you forgive me, Emma."

Because that's the only option. Now that he's back, I'm not letting go even if I'm terrified of him walking away from Cally as he did me. "Working on it."

"Then we move forward one day at a time, and it'll be fine."

I want that. But that's a fairy tale, something I thought we had before. "Before... when we were in high school, my biggest fear was one day you'd find out how I felt and want nothing to do with me."

He nods, making some agreeing-growling sound that set my insides afire.

I swallow the same fear I had when we danced around our feelings in high school. "Time changes people. You don't know me anymore. You might not like this me."

We lie in silence. I'm not sure if he's readying to refute my concern or agreeing as he realizes that for the first time.

"Gray?"

"No, you're right. But some things don't change, baby. You're still you. You've probably got a camera close by, and I bet if we unpacked these boxes, I'd find a hundred pictures of our daughter."

Our daughter. My heartstrings are pulled tight.

His chin touches the top of my head. "You're still the same sweet girl who tries not to trust but can't help it, and you know we have a history that we can rebuild on."

He's right... "Is that enough?"

"Has to be." His confidence is almost enough to

make me believe. "I don't know where you work or who your friends are. I don't know what you watch on television—"

"*Bubble Guppies* and *Mickey Mouse Club*." I look up to appraise his reaction. I'm not the normal twenty-something. Then I remember everything he's said and that I'm probably smashing his gunshot wound and he's too tough to say anything. He's not the normal-average anything. Maybe we're in more the same place than not.

"*Bubble Guppies* and *Mickey Club*." Grayson squeezes me tighter. "I'll have to check them out."

"*Mickey* Mouse *Club*."

A heart-stalling smile breaks across his face. "Right. *Mickey* Mouse *Club*. Ten-four, pretty mama."

In that second, with that nickname, I'm done and in love. That's all it took. "I want this to work."

He lets out a long, harsh sigh. "And thank fuck for that."

"I've never understood how we work like we do."

"But we do..." The rawness in his voice cuts me deep. "Forget the obvious—that you're beautiful and sexier than the dirtiest dream of a destroyed man. Emma, you have a good heart. That's your thing. That's *you*. Some things don't change, baby. You always believed in love. You grew up with the perfect example, the perfect family."

True.

"Our path isn't pretty, and maybe we're still hovering near the starting point, but I'm the man you're supposed to be with."

Butterflies beat in my chest. "But it's not just me, Gray."

His eyes darken. "I have to live with that for the rest of my life, but you better believe I'll spend it making it up to her. To both of you."

I'm in his arms, floating as if this is a dream. "That's a lot to promise."

"Ever heard me say something I don't mean?"

I shake my head.

"I love you, Ems."

He kisses my cheek, his stubble scratching against me in a way so manly, so sexy, I moan. It just slips out. I hadn't even been appreciating the masculine beauty I'm pancaked on top of. I was too busy falling in love over and over again.

"Besides loving you more than you can imagine," he whispers roughly, "I'm laying claim to this dangerous body too, baby."

A heat wave rolls through me. I'm suddenly hyperaware of how his jeans are the last layer before he's naked on my couch. Though my super-sexy flannel pajamas might put a damper on his interest level.

"I look pretty hot in my jammies, huh?"

"Wouldn't be us if one of us weren't downplaying." His mouth runs from my cheek to my ear. "Let me be really clear. I stripped you near-naked in your kitchen. I'd tear this off you this second if I didn't think there was the slightest chance you'd run."

"I'm not going to run."

Shivers run down my arms when his lips dip onto my neck, his tongue dragging down. My body hums as the mood shifts. We've had somber, remorseful, flirty, and now this. Arousal hangs heavy in the crackling air. Tension I can't deny squeezes us together.

His lips tease my neck. "Feels good?"

"Yes." I moan as he shifts to get a better angle.

"Taste good too."

Everything is different from high school. He's

harsher, stronger, more confident. His erection strains in his jeans, and he cups my cheek, his thumb toying with my lip. Each minute passes by slowly. His green eyes darkened, an emerald fire blasting under his blond eyelashes. If I were to picture desire, it would be his face watching me now.

He drops his hand down my chin, around my neck. The rough calluses on his hands grate over my skin, and it's erotic. Grayson studies my reactions, my mews, the way my head tilts and my back arches. His eyes fall to my lips as my breathing stills, and when his hand smooths down my chest, caressing the swell of my breasts, longing ignites deep below my stomach.

"Beautiful, Ems."

In his arms, I believe it. Unlike on the stage where I dance for dollars, this is the truth. I know it in a way that doesn't matter anywhere else on Earth. "I've always been yours. Don't hurt me again."

"Promise."

His hand heads south, and my fingers move to his neck and spear into his thick hair. A groan that I remember from years ago falls from his lips as my fingernails scratch into his scalp.

He closes his eyes, quietly sucking in a breath. "You do good things to me."

His mouth hovers over mine. I feel the softness of his warm breath on my lips. I can almost feel him, almost taste him. I close my eyes. This exact feeling is how I remembered him, so close it would kill me, so close I nearly drove myself insane every Wednesday.

His lips find mine, and he's hungry. One second of softness morphed into a beast. He's over me, his mouth eating at mine, his hands running harshly over me. I love it, need it. I crave him as though he's my drug of choice.

His tongue pushes into my mouth, forcing mine to dance with his, and I gasp into his kiss. He shifts on top of me, and my palms climb up his back. The feel of his flesh under my nails is too much. They dig into him, marking my man as he consumes me.

I'm pinned beneath, scoring his back, groaning as he flexes his iron-hard shaft between my legs. In one quick movement, he has my shirt over my head, and I'm clawing at his jeans, dragging them over his ass.

Grayson dominates me. His hands grab mine, pulling them above my head. I laugh and smile. I try to bite his lips as he spreads my legs wide. My pajama bottoms are still on, but I've dragged his boxers down enough to steal my breath, sear my soul. My heart races because from one quick glimpse and feeling his heavy weight rubbing against me, I know that Grayson Ford is freakin' huge, bigger than I remember, and my nerves explode in my chest.

I need him. The idea of him pushing into me, stretching me makes me shudder, dizzy with want. I'm practically a virgin again for him, and I'm dying. My teeth dig into his shoulder as his hand works under the drawstring of my pants, between my thighs, expertly rubbing my clit.

Shit, shoot, shit. I'm gonna die from orgasm. I can't breathe and bite him harder.

"If you're going to mark me like that, pretty mama, you should know I bite back."

A full-body shiver erupts over me, and I arch for more friction against his hand. "Swear?"

He nods. "To God."

We're pressed together, bare chests and fumbling with our pants. His head drops down, and with a hot, wet kiss, he takes my hard nipple into his mouth, sucking deep enough I wonder if I can come from that.

"God, Gray."

He responds—tongue and teeth—and I'm going to climax from just his hand and tongue. He moves to the opposite breast, repeating his tease and tug, and the time lapse is almost enough to make me cry for him to never stop. But when his mouth takes my nipple, he slips his fingers into me, spearing me deep and hard and letting his thumb rub my nub. I'm seconds away from orgasm. The man's my body's master, and with one strong, circular sweep of his thumb, I explode.

I throw my head back, clenching on him. His mouth leaves my breast and takes my lips and tongue, kissing me hard as his hand still pumps into me. I open my eyes, and his green ones are vibrant again. The fire's still there, but there's a spark and a shine that I know I'm responsible for.

"I'm on the pill. Don't you dare stop."

Everything stills. With one long, hard look at me, he takes my mouth again after mumbling, "Yes, ma'am."

We fight with what's left of our clothes. He's kicking off his jeans, and I'm tangled in my pants, but finally I'm free and wrapping my legs around his waist. He's primed; I'm wet. Our eyes are locked, and he's huge. Nerves hit me again.

"Sure, pretty mama?"

I nod, wriggling myself into position for him to take me. The head of his thick erection is there. I feel it, want it. I'm nodding into his kiss, moaning for more and flexing my hips. My wetness coats the head of him, but not until he moves, just a fraction of an inch, do I feel heaven—and it's going to hurt.

"Just—a little—bit." Tension strains in his jaw.

Sweet Jesus. But he flexes again, pushing deeper into me, stretching me, and my body accommodates him. I'm panting, gasping, breathing through the rush. I've had sex once in my life. With him. Years ago. But my lady parts are in virgin territory again, remembering how insane this feels, how much I love him.

He inches in, and I'm begging for more. My teeth have his lips. My legs are wrapped around him tightly, and oh my god, he's in me all the way and holding still.

"You good?"

"God, I love you." It's all I can say, all I can think.

He takes that properly as permission to go, and he does. Withdrawing slowly, then pumping me full again. One more time, and I'm ready to beg.

"Please," I moan.

He thrusts faster and harder.

I'm clinging to the massive man holding me down, fucking me as if we're starved for each other. A climax starts deep inside me, reminding me that I'm sensitive from just coming. It hits me hard, and I arch back, pulsing on his cock. "Grayson!"

He pumps faster and harder, pinning me down. My muscles spasm and clench, riding his pace.

"Christ," he growls and strains into me.

I feel him come, hotness filling me as he holds deep. A sheen of sweat covers us, and our breaths are frantic. Spent, he falls onto me, not giving me his whole weight but not holding much back. We're connected in a way I've always dreamed of, but this is better than anything I could imagine.

His mouth lands on mine. Not kissing, just touching. "I love you, Ems."

All is perfect.

Somewhere in the background, a noise pulls me from Eden. Grayson moves as though he's trained to kill the enemy. The back door slams open, hitting the wall on the other side of the house, in the kitchen. I warned everyone we needed a doorstopper.

"Shit!" Grayson and I say at the same time.

Rooms away, the entire house seemed to explode with preschooler-sized noise. "Mommy!"

ONLY FOR US

CHAPTER 27

Emma

"Mommy!" There's a clatter of noise that only a two-year-old can make coming from the back door.

I'm frozen with ice-cold panic as Grayson rips on his pants. Two seconds ago, I was in a euphoric lull.

"Emma," he hisses at me. "Clothes."

Right. Shit. Shoot. Oh my effin' God. Clothes. I grab my oversized T-shirt and pull it on. My heart is in my throat, trying to escape. Every bit of me wants to run out the door and give myself a chance to think. Just as Gray wasn't supposed to find out the way he did, Cally is *not* supposed to learn about her dad this way. I hop into my flannel pajama bottoms, and my hands search for the drawstrings. But they're on backward. *Shit.*

Cherry's voice calls out, "Emma. Hon, you awake? Where you at, babe?"

"Breathe, Ems." Grayson hovers over me. I can almost see his pulse pounding in his neck. There's a nervous tension in the air that neither of us knows how to react to.

Cally's footsteps head in the opposite direction of the living room, away from us. "My bedwroom's back here. I wanna show you, Aunt Chwerry."

"I'm breathing," I say to him breathlessly, confirming that I most certainly am not.

His eyes are on the floor. Where's his shirt? Oh, this is not going well.

"Emma?" Cherry's voice fades as she heads after Cally toward the bedrooms.

"You should leave." I bite my lip. "No, you shouldn't." My eyes sink shut, and I'm lost. I can't kick him out the front door. I *don't want* to kick him out the front door.

"Seriously. Take a breath, Emma. It's not how we planned, but it's going to be okay."

Not how we planned? We haven't come up for air long enough to plan. I need to stall or redirect or—

Cherry and Cally laugh loudly on the other side of the small house. My eyes shoot in their direction then back to Grayson. His face is calm, his eyes bright. A curious, almost excited smile plays on his full lips, and I try to understand the magnitude of what he might be feeling.

Gray takes a step forward and cups my chin, letting his thumb softly stroke my cheek. "It'll be okay."

I nod, listening to an excited Cally drag Cherry down the back hall.

"It'll be okay," I repeat as if it's a calming mantra that might save me.

"You want me to head out?" His throat bobs. "I'm dying here. I need to stay. You get that?" His eyes glance over my shoulder. "You're scared. I'm... freakin' out. But I can't leave." He gulps again.

God love him for giving me the option. How hard does it have to be for him? I shake my head and realize that my hands are trembling. I cross my arms and tuck them in tight. "No."

Cherry and Cally make their way closer. They giggle over a lost doll that has been found—the one I put in the center of all of Cally's toys, lined up on her bed.

I need to focus. Time feels as if it's moving slowly, as though I'm swimming through sludge. I try to think. *Okay. Grayson's staying.* "Hey, Cherry, hang on. Hang tight. Be in the kitchen in a sec—"

"We were just—" Cherry falters at the mouth of the hallway and clings to the wall. Her face pales, and her mouth drops open as if she can't understand what's before her. "Um—whoa."

I cringe. Her eyeballs bulge, bouncing between a no-shirted Grayson and me guiltily smoothing my T-shirt.

What am I supposed to say? *You remember Grayson?* Ahh—what the shiznittle do I say?

"You're... here." Though I can tell she almost said "alive."

He nods. "I am."

"Gray's back, Cherry." Nervously, I twist my fingers in the hem of my ginormous shirt.

"You can*not* be serious." Her hand juts to the wall as if she has to hold herself up.

Not the reaction I would've dreamed up. But it's not unexpected. "Cherry—"

Cally is babbling behind her, my guess talking to her doll about hugs and sunshine. Then she bypasses my sister and runs into the room, a smiling blur of blondeness. "Mommy!"

My heart's in my throat, and I have no idea what to do. "Cally, honey, snugglebug, hi."

I sit down on the couch. So does Gray. Cally grips an overly loved doll tightly in her hand, and her eyes are curiously on Grayson as she slinks onto my lap. "Hi, mama."

"Hi, baby," I nervously repeat.

She shifts her weight, hugging me, then concentrates on her doll, apparently deciding that a shirtless Grayson doesn't deserve more than a second glance. My eyes rocket to his awestruck green ones as I watch him see his daughter for the first time.

A lump slowly works its way down his throat. Emotional restraint is visible in his corded neck, and his hard jaw flexes. He rolls his lips together as though he's stifling his words, and his gaze is dancing, mesmerized by the pint-sized explosion who's hugging me and holding a doll.

His reaction is... beautiful. I didn't know a man that sexy, that hard, maybe even that dark and wounded could personify love. But there it is. And it's amazing.

My heart pitter-patters, and my eyes flood, brimming with a happiness that I will remember always.

His gaze moves from studying her to locking onto me. "Oh... my... God," he whispers.

My chest hitches as my breaths stall. Warmth that I can't explain fills my blood. I nod to Gray as Cally pushes back to interrupt my gaze.

"Aunt Chwerry gave me p'cakes."

Other than her brief look, Cally hasn't acknowledged Grayson. This isn't how I wanted an introduction to go, if there ever even was one, but now that it's happening, I try to breathe evenly and focus on her. "Yum, pancakes. You're having a good time?"

Her face brightens as though she's ready to tell a secret. "We had hot chocwolate."

"We have plans to go to the park," Cherry adds, staring at Grayson with unhidden shock. "But we needed a different doll."

Cally shakes her doll for us all to see then turns around to take in Grayson again. They're nearly identical, with the golden hair and the emerald eyes and even the same perfect, pink smile.

"Hi." She shakes her doll at him.

Grayson shifts on the couch as though he wants to inch forward but is unsure. "Hey, sweetheart."

She tilts her head. "Who's dat?"

I cough. Or choke. "He's my friend, snugglebug."

Grayson's smile falters for a brief second, but he rebounds and nods. Cally nods back, mimicking him with a huge smile.

"My name's Gray."

"My name is Cally Kingsley." Her proud, drawn-out cadence warms my heart, and watching her introduce herself to her daddy is the most monumental moment of my life. I'm ready to bawl, and I'm certain Grayson's choked up. His voice sounds tight, and there's emotion straining in his jaw and neck, even when he smiles.

But Cally hasn't noticed a vibe from any of the adults. "Aunt Chwerry lemme have p'cakes for bekfast. Sooo good."

Gray leans forward and drops more to her height, propping his elbows on his knees. "That good, huh?"

"Sywup, too. Lots of it." Her grin reaches ear to ear.

And, *God,* so does his grin. "Yeah?"

Cherry grumbles playfully, softening for what she surely sees as an important thing playing out before our eyes. "It was a weak moment. She's too cute. Can't say no to her."

Cally jumps off my lap and lands on the couch

between Grayson and me, keeping eyes on him. "Have you been to da pwark?"

He shakes his head. "Not this park."

"Like pwaying outswide?" Her little brow furrows as though she's sizing up his answers.

"I love playing outside." He rolls his bottom lip into his mouth. "Guess you come by it naturally."

She has no idea what that means, but she agrees. "You're weally big." Her little head goes up and down, assessing. "You could do the mun-key bars. But you have to wear a shirt."

Grayson lets out a huge belly laugh. I'm hot from head to toe, absolutely sure I'm going to fall over and die from embarrassment. Cherry presses her fingers over her mouth, trying to hide any reaction that's not part of her confusion and concern.

But Gray doesn't miss a beat. "Bet I could handle the monkey bars, Miss Cally Kingsley."

"Bwing him?" She eyes me, urging me on like a little girl playing matchmaker. "And da swings, too."

"Maybe she'll bring me one day."

"Today? Pwease."

He shakes his head. "Probably not today."

"Okay." Cally jumps up, finished with her investigation and invitation. "Weddy for da pwark, Aunt Chwerry!" A second later, she's off to the kitchen. I've childproofed everything in there except for her special drawer, which is filled with things like juice boxes and coloring books.

Before Cherry can get a word out, I shake my head and cut her off. "Cherry. Chill."

Her long, cold stare ruins the moment. "Ryan know about this?"

I assume that Grayson hasn't informed my brother he is alive and in town. Because if he had, I would have heard about it; there would've been a fistfight in my front yard—the soldier versus the cop.

"Prick." Cherry's eyes narrow at Grayson. "So, you're alive. Got it. That just reminds me you're a son of a bitch."

"Stop." I'm losing all the warm fuzzies from moments before.

"No way." My sister the ice queen cocks her hip and rests her hand on it. "When I thought you died, I felt awful for them. I hurt for my baby sister and her daughter. Maybe even for you since you missed out on this—"

"Maybe"—he pulls closer to me, an unsaid challenge to Cherry to back off—"that's what I'm here to make up for." His voice is deep and authoritative.

The tension compounds. I hate conflict already, and this antagonism is so deep that I don't even know how to describe it. "Please let it be. I need to go talk to Cally."

"She'll be fine. We didn't see anything other than Grayson's not having his damn shirt on."

"I'm her mother. I'll judge how she is." God, I want to strangle Cherry right now. "You know what? You have no right to act like this."

"I have no right? I pull shifts so you can work and go to school. We all do. You sleep—what? Like, three hours a night? You are *killing* yourself, and he just waltzes in, and you spread—"

"Don't finish that." Grayson stands, stepping in front of me, a protective growl coming from him. "You'll regret it. There's enough fucking regret standing in this room. We don't need any more of it."

I stand behind him, my palms flat on his back. "Gray…"

Cherry's eyes drop to the wound at his side then back up again. "You ruined her life."

My frustration multiplies, and I expect better from her than to pull that. "Nothing about my life is ruined. It has its hiccups, it certainly isn't what I planned, but it's mine, and I love it."

Her brow pinches. "Em—"

"I get to say if my life's been ruined," I hiss. Then I look over my shoulder as Cally clangs and bangs a few feet away, singing about her water bottle and a milk box from her Cally-drawer. I don't know how to ensure that permanent damage hasn't been done, but I'm positive that the anger rolling in the room is bad for my girl. "Look—enough. None of this is a conversation for right now. Cally can stay home with me, and Grayson, you can go. You too, Cherry."

The singing comes closer as Cally wanders back into the room, all her attention on her hands as she tries unsuccessfully to tear into her milk box with her doll and a water bottle tucked under her arms. "My milk's not listening."

"Snugglebug, why don't you stay home with me. Cherry and Grayson were just leaving." I take the box and pop the straw into it, handing it back after she has propped her doll on the couch with the water.

Sudden tears spring in her eyes. "I wanna go to the pwark. Aunt Chwerry pwomised."

Shit, shoot, shit. I don't know what to do right now.

"Pwease." Her little bottom lip pops out.

I close my eyes and rub my temples for a minute. I hear Cherry take a step, and I sigh, turning toward her. We lock eyes. She's sorry, I'm sorry—it's just that this moment is unplanned.

Cherry grins though I know it's forced. "If you'd like, Emma, we can stick with the Cally-Cherry day of fun. It's my fault we swung by. I forgot to pack her dolly. Lord knows I wasn't going to survive the day without it."

"Pwease, Mommy."

I want to make sure Cally's okay. We've never had this much time apart, and then she walks into a shirtless Grayson. Is she confused? Clueless? I don't remember this chapter in any of the "how to survive teenage single motherhood" books I devoured. I'm sure scenarios like this were included, though not with all the drama. I just never thought I'd love anyone else—and I was right.

Hesitantly, I eye Cherry and give Cally a hug. "Okay. Have fun, baby."

She squeals out of my arms and runs towards the back door. "C'mon, Aunt Chwerry!"

"Coming, honey." My sister turns but watches me. I've had more time than her to process Grayson. I can tell she's struggling with knowing the right thing to say. "Emma... you okay?"

"Yeah." *Better than okay.* I'm on a high from watching Grayson fall in love with Cally.

"You have to call Ryan. He'll find out. He's about as good with surprises as you are."

I cringe. "I will."

"I will first," Grayson says.

"Right," Cherry shoots back, shaking her head. "Details later, Emma." She casts a protective glance at me, shifting it to a challenging glare as she turns to Grayson. Seconds struggle by, but she relents. "Guess you two have a lot to catch up on."

"Aunt Chwerry!"

"Coming, honey. For real this time." She gives us one last hard look. "Bye."

My sister leaves us standing amid tension, conflict, and her judgement. She and Cally giggle in the kitchen as the back door opens.

"Bye, Mommy," Cally shouts then the door slaps shut.

An overwhelming silence coats the room. So much just happened in the last fifteen minutes—just as so much has happened between Grayson and me over the last twenty-four hours. I take a deep breath and collapse on the couch. Grayson drops down next to me. One heavy arm wraps around me as the other hand takes my hand. There are so many thoughts running in my head that I'm not sure where one starts and another stops. What I do know is... I fell in love today. Twice. With the same man who has always had my heart.

He squeezes my hand tight and clears his throat. "I'm... without words."

Know the feeling. Cherry honks twice as she pulls away. My heart is still in my throat, and I'm drifting down from my adrenaline high. "Cally's amazing, right?"

His perfect face and chiseled jaw tilt toward me, but his fierce green eyes remain on the path our daughter took on her way out. "Ems... she's perfect."

I just witnessed a man meet his greatest weakness—and his truest love—and embrace it without thought of complication or fear. He's always been her father, but now I'm sure she'll have a daddy.

"Sweet little perfection," he mumbles.

I can't take any more, and I bury my head into his neck. "What do we do after something like that happens?"

"I don't know. Sit here and think..."

I nod into his strong hold. His soapy scent and abounding confidence make me calm. "That's not how I thought a daddy-daughter introduction would go."

He leans into me as though I'm holding him up. "You've thought about it?"

"Of course." I've thought about our life as if he never left and was there when I delivered. I imagined that he was deployed and came back to our happy little family—as if he hadn't abandoned us. We'd have little flags to wave and maybe paint a welcome-home poster.

He presses his lips to my hair. "Might not be what either of us had planned, but that was one of the best moments... ever."

True. One for the record books.

His cell phone rings, and I sigh. "You need to get that?"

"Not mine. Oh—shit. Yeah. That's me." He reaches to his back pocket and digs out a phone, swiping the screen to accept the call. "Hello?"

He listens, and I watch, curious about who is calling him on a Saturday morning when I didn't think anyone knew he was back.

Grayson pulls himself off the couch and paces. "When?"

More silence, and his brow furrows. "Can do. Thanks." He ends the calls and pockets the phone then crosses his arms over his chest and stares out the window.

"Who was that?" I ask. There's something on his face that I can't read. An uncertainty. Or maybe apprehension. But there's also a determination. It flexes in his jaw and his neck and burns brightly in his eyes as he casts his gaze out onto my little front yard.

He's standing at an angle that makes me appreciate how *huge* he's become—taller and broader than in high school. Everything about him is masculine and magnetic. It's a curious feeling—not having anyone to love or to stare at and then finding some combination of model and action hero who wants to play house with me. And he wants to do more than just pretend.

When he turns to face me head-on, there's

hesitant vagueness hanging on his sculpted face. "I think... it was a job interview."

"What?" I'm surprised—I don't know why. He said he was staying, so that means work and a home and... I haven't thought about how any of this will pan out. Do we date? Do we... what? And what about the Army? Does he have to go back?

I feel myself growing flustered, thinking about the bevy of unknown factors. The internal questions blur and ring in my ears. The pressure of the future suddenly feels oppressive as though answers and decisions need to be made right now.

"Hey, hey—easy there." Grayson's at my side, swallowing me in his arms and chest.

I'm not sure I've ever noticed my heart as much as since he's been home. Right now, it's beating against my ribs as I'm surrounded by his muscles, hidden from the world.

He strokes the back of my head. "What just happened there? Why're you freaking out?"

"I don't know," I mumble, too afraid to voice hopes and concerns. Our relationship-out-of-nowhere seems steady yet so fragile. I'm worried that if I blink wrong, I'll somehow jinx that magic.

"Don't hide from me, Ems."

"A job and... you said you wouldn't leave, wouldn't hurt me. But you're really staying here?"

He nods against me, and I move with him as his body shifts. "Anywhere you are, I swear I'll be there."

"Really?"

He tears me from his chest and levels me with a stare so solemn I'm dizzy over whatever he's about to promise.

"I said I was laying claim to you, Emma, and I want the same thing for Cally. You're the only family I've ever had, and I want that back."

Cally... family... don't blink. Don't wake up.

"Believe me?" His eyes darken in a way that commands my complete attention. "I've done nothing for you to give me that trust, but I need you to anyway."

I'm not pressed against his chest anymore. The warmth that encapsulated me moments ago is gone, but I feel different. Life's shifted—I've been hanging on this roller coaster for years, and now it's as if we're cautiously slipping toward smooth sailing. The lump in my throat eases, and my eyelids lift, my gaze falling on the most handsome man I've ever seen.

"What do you say?" He inches closer.

"I love you, Grayson." Deep breath. "When it comes to us, I'm all in."

He wraps me tight and kisses my temple. "Love you, too. You're the only one for me."

CHAPTER 28

GRAYSON

As job interviews go, this beats out all others. There's a million dollars' worth of weapons in this war room—I'm sure of it. The table is long and sleek. The room is low lit and ice cold. The two men sitting across from me are Titan, but only one of them gave me a name. Parker Black. He's been my phone contact and was the man behind the truck and cash. The other one... I don't know whether he's sizing me up or waiting to share, but we sit here in an intense standoff.

"You're looking for a job." The unnamed man leans forward, his shirt sleeves loose and rolled, exposing colorful tattoos and a thick tactical watch that nearly matches mine. He personifies Special Forces.

I was a grunt and good at what I did. I have the honors and medal that show I mean something to someone. But I'm a risk—even if I don't know what position they're interviewing for. My medical chart is filled with PTSD. My unit can't vouch for me because they're all dead.

"A job? Maybe."

His eyes cut to Parker's before snapping back to me. "How old are you?"

"Not sure why that matters."

"You're Army."

I shift in the cold chair. "Was. Yeah."

"And now you're not."

My tongue runs over my teeth as I try not to react to what he must already know. "I *was* Army. Now I'm not."

He leans back. There's a thickness hanging in the air. This guy doesn't want me here? Fine. Fuck it. Don't care. I'll work the fry basket for minimum wage and work my way up till I own the goddamn joint. I need income, stability, and whatever else it takes to prove I'm solid ground for Emma. So, all of that means I don't give a shit about unnamed tattoo man's evil eye. "What is this? Job interview, waste of my time, or what?"

Parker's lips pinch, but there's a laugh in his eyes.

I growl. "You want the truck back? Take it. You interviewing for a job? Interview me."

The man pushes forward in his chair. His eyebrows pinch. The guy wasn't relaxed before, but now he's a wall of resolution. "You're a young-buck hard-ass. Not what we need around here."

"You know my name. I know his name." I lift my chin toward Parker. I'm done with this. He either talks to me or doesn't. "But who are you?"

"Brock Gamble."

"And how long have you worked at Titan, Brock Gamble?" This will either make progress or hurry up my exit.

"Since I was your age."

"And what the fuck did someone say to you when you walked in for an interview?"

Brock leans forward, a growl coming from his chest. "Didn't interview."

Thought so. I slap the table. "Seems about right. Like you guys didn't know everything about me before I walked in the door."

A hard smile cracks on Parker's face.

"If you're interested, let me know. Otherwise, I've got a shit list a mile long, and I don't have time for BS." I watch Brock's face then give him a nod. "Peace."

No reaction on either guy's face. I push out of my chair. They're going to want the truck back, and I'm not going to have a set of wheels. That's a predicament when I'm trying to prove to this fucked-up county I'm not a runaway dick, but I can work through it.

"Thanks for your time." I turn for the door.

Brock's chair echoes in the war room as he stands. "There's a job. Local."

Local? Now that's interesting. I wouldn't expect Titan to run an op this close to home. I turn back. "What do you guys have going on around here?"

His jaw works back and forth. "Traffickers working their way up and down the coast."

"What kind of trafficking?"

"The kind that brings in Titan."

Not great news. That kind of crime is nothing I want near my family. *Family...* something I've never really had before and suddenly want with shocking clarity. I grew up under the thumb of an evil man, so the bad in the world is not lost on me—I knew about it even before I went to war. But all I can picture is blond curls of a little girl who will one day, somehow, bear my name. I swallow away the life-changing realization and nod. "What do you want from me?"

"I need a couple guys. Just show up for a bachelor's party."

My brow pinches. "Excuse me?"

"Runners use Interstate 95. They start south and stick near the highway for easy access and quick getaway. Establishments, not truck stops. I want them taken down, but I want their network even more."

"In Summerland?"

"Next county over but might as well be Summerland."

Anger boils in my blood. I thought he meant drug trafficking. But... this is more dangerous. "If I agree, I'd do what?"

"Simple—it's just a bachelor party. Make friends. Keep your eyes open. Blend in, and keep mental notes. You can do that?"

"Yeah, I can do that."

The door slams open. A mean-faced man the size of a tank rolls in and stares only at Brock. "Yes or no."

It doesn't sound like a question, but Brock raises a thumbs-up.

The man nods and stares at Parker, who nods. Then he looks at me. "Welcome to Titan."

"Now, that's done." Brock follows the other man as they blow out of the room.

Parker lingers. "Nicely played."

"Wasn't playing."

"That's why you have the job, kid."

Well... fuck me. Sweet.

CHAPTER 29

GRAYSON

Ground zero. I'm here. At Pops's home—a place I'd like to watch burn down to its weed-infested plot. But I couldn't stay away. It was a rust-bucket shithole when I was last here, but years have weathered it to the point I'm surprised it can still stand.

Even with the summer night's breeze swaying the high grass around me, I can't kick the apprehension that has an ironclad hold on my lungs. This trailer is poison. The man inside is my hell. I'm the one who ruined his life. But I still can't fathom how a man can hate his son.

I blow out a harsh, uneasy breath. Since the second I left Titan Group's headquarters, I'd wanted to call Emma. But I also want all my shit in check before I do that. After I confront my demon and get that in order, I'll head her way and prove that I'm every bit of the future she deserves.

I square my shoulders back and climb the rickety, rotten steps. They sway under my weight, and when

I knock on the door, it swings open. The stench of cheap liquor and stale pot is overwhelming. There's a cigarette smoldering in an overfilled makeshift ashtray, and Pops is passed out on the couch.

Damn. He looks like an old man rotting away from the inside out who just suffered through a barroom brawl. His wrinkled skin is checked with gray stubble. His sunken eyes are black, and scratches color his skin. His split lip is yellow and nicotine stained as is the hand wrapped around a generic-looking beer can.

On the coffee table are several empty and semi-crushed cigarette packs, a can of dip next to an empty soda bottle used for spitting, and an almost empty pack of papers. I shake my head. Pot seeds and stems are in a sandwich bag, and there are enough fast food wrappers on the floor to give *me* cholesterol.

"You're a fuckin' mess," I whisper under my breath.

"And you're not welcome in my home." He coughs, swollen eyes not opening. "Out, 'fer I call the cops."

"Right." I pass him and wander to my bedroom. It's the same as when I left it three years ago. Backpack on the floor, unmade bed. An old wallet is next to my backpack, opened, with its contents strewn about. A couple of drawers in my dresser are pulled out. Guess Pops didn't care that I was gone, but he sure wanted to know if I left any cash behind.

My head hurts from a combination of the stink and the memories, and I swipe my bag off the floor and drop to my bed. The bag is open, but there's nothing in it that Pops could want—nothing but a couple notebooks that are worn. One makes my pulse pound. I grab it and crack it open.

A lump grows in my throat as I page through each

scrawled and stopped note. My heart hurts, and I flip through the sheets of lined paper.

Hey Ems,
We need to talk. Last night went bad, and I need to see you.
X, Gray

Pages later.

Emma,
I'm not sure how many times I can try to say this, so here it is. I enlisted—like in the Army. I'm leaving Summerland in a few weeks, and what happened after Sadie Hawkins, it wasn't supposed to happen like that.

That one note had a giant X through it, and I vividly remember sitting in senior English, contemplating whether she'd think that "wasn't meant to happen" part was about us hooking up or about Pops walking in. I didn't finish that note, and when I walked out of class that day and saw her, I went the opposite direction. I'm a fuckin' moron.

I skip through the pages and can see my eighteen-year-old self trying to describe why I was running and why I couldn't tell her I was leaving.

Finally, I'm on the last written page in the notebook.

Ems, I love you. One day I hope you understand.
Yours forever, Gray

I slap the notebook shut and shove it in the bag.

There's nothing else that I need. My space in this shithouse is a stark contrast to the rest of the trailer. Other than what Pops went through, everything is orderly. There are athletic awards and trophies on the walls and equipment in the corner—football pads, baseball bats, and a collection of balls. Taped to the mirror are two pictures. One is a family portrait of the Kinglseys, except I'm in there, too. We were at a lake picnic, and I remember dreaming that they were my family.

The other is Emma. She's not looking at the camera, and she's wearing a shirt I'm positive she made herself. A camera is slung over her shoulder, and she's midturn to me. I snapped it with my phone.

"What'd you do that for?"

My arm drops to my side, phone in hand. I'm not sure that I even grabbed a good shot of her. But she's staring at me, and I just want to say, "I love you."

"Gray?"

"Yeah?"

"The picture? Don't do that. I look terrible."

She looks like mine. She looks like the one I want under my arm, her hand in my hand. I want to kiss her, claim her, do so much with her... to her.

"Prettiest girl I know, Ems." I turn around as she laughs, but I can feel her eyes burning into my back. I walk from her, shoving my phone and fists into my pockets because if I don't, I will ruin everything this family, this girl, has given me.

Short, haggard breaths steal my attention from my memories. I take both pictures from the mirror and put them in my bag before I turn to face off with a heavy-breathing, probably dying Pops.

Standing up, he looks even worse. His skin is

jaundiced. His greasy hair sticks up from his time on the couch. The beater he's wearing is stained, and his jeans look foul.

He sneers. "That's my shit. Don't touch."

"Right." *Such an asshole.* I move to the closet to check for any clothes that might be worth taking.

"Said don't touch, boy."

Screw it. I turn to him. "You knew Emma had my baby."

He laughs. "She tracked you down, too. Little tart showing up here, asking about you—"

Rage fills me. "She what?" I'm blinded by hatred and heartache.

Pops shrugs. "If you were interested in her, 'sume you would've told 'er where you were."

Guilt floods every muscle as my body tenses. I step forward, wanting to take it out on him. "You knew?"

Shrugs again. "Nothing either of us have that'd be good for a Kinglsey baby."

"*I* am good for that baby."

He laughs, and his lungs crackle, full of crap. "Boy, yer not good for shit."

My hands ball into fists. I'm seconds away from obliterating him. I take another step closer, and a fight he's wanted his whole life is coming his way.

No. I shudder. *Not* his whole life. Only after losing my mother.

My head tilts, and I study his drunk, drugged, sad existence. The truth hits me hard. I've always been his burden, but... I'm not his kid.

Randall Ford isn't my father? The idea rockets in my thoughts, clanging and bouncing over every missed father-son moment, every hatred-filled snipe. Pops doesn't understand my intense feelings about the time I've lost with Cally. He never cared about me… for me. There's no biological connection like I have with my daughter.

My boiling hatred slows to a simmer as I process our missing genetic connection. "All this time, you never said a word."

Confusion makes his black eyes cloud. "What da fuck's yer problem now?"

"But I was the only thing you had left of her." The realization is mind-blowing. Slowly, I shake my head. Pieces of my life click into place. *I'm… not… Randall Ford's son.* "You couldn't let me go, and you hated that—" And just as clearly, I understand that I didn't kill my mother. I'd known she overdosed, but I always placed the blame on myself. "She killed *herself.*"

"Shut up!"

"Fuck me," I whisper, trying to handle my thoughts. Whatever pills my mom took, however she got her hands on them, it was *her* fault. In kindergarten, I couldn't understand her addictions, her problems. I was taught sure as the Earth was round that I caused my mom to die. But almost twenty years later… I've had her problems in my head for so long, and now the truth seems so simple. But I couldn't comprehend until I walked away and came back. Guilt thaws off my shoulders. "I'm done with the shames and sins you've put on me."

The same as I'm done with my plan to ruin him, leaving him dead to rot in these shambles.

"You ruined my life, you mother-killing, stupid-ass—"

"No," I growl into his face. "All these years I thought I deserved it." My anger returns, and I could crush his skull. The pounding in my chest pushes me. I want to end him. Adrenaline's choking me. But Emma and Cally's faces pop into my mind. *They* save me, and I rasp out a deep breath, trying to calm my itch to fight. "You're not worth it."

Pops sways. "Son of a bitch, you—"

"I'm done." I pull back, and with my bag in hand, I stride past him, knowing I'll never be back again. I'm not going to touch him, not going to hurt him. I want nothing to do with Pops—no, *Randall*—ever again.

CHAPTER 30

Emma

A million boxes surround me, and I want them magically unpacked. I pivot and stare at each label, trying to decide if any one of them calls for my attention. Nope—not really. My Prince Charming had to run out for the kind of job interview that didn't require more than a quick shower and re-dressing in the same jeans and shirt. We haven't had time to specifically talk about the future, but it feels as if the future is here, and Grayson will be by my side. So... does he move in? And how do I explain him to Cally? Slowly. Carefully.

One call, one night can change everything. I bite my lip, nodding to myself. Whatever plan I make, it's with Cally in mind. I want Grayson to work, but it has to be a relationship—nothing forced out of guilt and regret.

The closest box catches my attention, and I grab it, ripping the cardboard flaps open. "So, we love each other. But are we still in love?"

The box doesn't talk back. Great news: my exhaustion hasn't caused hallucinations.

After last night and this morning, I'd say yes—I'm still crazy in love with the hot guy who rolled through my door and surprised me. I tear through the box, pulling out framed pictures that need to be hung. I lay them in the corner after removing their bubble wrap then sit beside them, popping bubble after plastic bubble. What happens if the feelings go away when the surprise factor fades? Does eighteen years of friendship make up for the three years I spent hurt and alone?

Knock, knock, knock.

My heart jumps, and my eyes shoot to the front door. Surprises have been my friends lately, even if I hate them, so I don't feel the usual annoyance at having an unexpected visitor. I put down the bubble wrap and push off the floor as the knob turns, and Ryan and Cherry burst in.

"Cherry!"

Her lack of eye contact and her walk filled with too much bravado screams busybody. Couple that with my brother scowling as he's pulled in tow, and I'm pissed.

"What?" Her guilty smile falters as she twists to acknowledge our brother. "I had to say something."

"No. You didn't. You're overstepping." I knot my fingers together. "Where's Cally?" Cherry knows I hate changes in my plans, but she still pulls this stunt, using her status as my older sister as if she's somehow wiser and knows better than I do. It drives me batty.

Cherry shrugs. "With Mom, picking out your birthday present."

"Mom knows?" My eyes bulge. "You roped in Ryan and Mom. Nice, Cherry. Think you're overstepping the line?"

"Not really. I didn't even know he was in town."

"I didn't have a chance to tell you! It's not like Grayson's a secret."

"So, he shows up, and *bam*."

"Don't be a bitch," I hiss, trying to remember that I love her, appreciate her. But... *God.* "You have no idea. Don't judge."

Ryan's out of uniform and brushes by me as though he's going to do some cop search. As much as I long for independence, I have to rely on my family. It gives them an all-access pass to my life, though— one of the many reasons they come through the door whenever the urge hits.

Cherry and I both watch Ryan head toward the back of the house as if I'm hiding Grayson in a hall closet. "I had to tell Mom because this is some kind of family-related emergency intervention."

"You're creating drama where there is none."

She opens a box marked LIVING RM but doesn't unpack any of the contents. "This is a big deal."

A big deal? Yeah. But not because of how they're acting. Grayson is home. He's back again like a prodigal son or something. I want to scream. My pulse thumps in my neck. "Unpack a box, or go."

Still, she doesn't unpack but just waits for Ryan. I'm ninety-nine percent sure I remember an episode of *Sesame Street* telling me to expel frustration with tummy breathing. There was even a song. I can't remember it, but I do know I should do something before I have an aneurysm.

I take a deep breath in and blow it out.

Hm. Kind of works. Until my brother comes back into the living room, obviously not fruitful in his boyfriend-back-from-the-dead   search.   The patronizing, overly protective stares of my siblings lock onto me, and no amount of tummy breathing is going to help this moment. "You two are being ridiculous."

Cherry shakes her head. "He destroyed you, Emma. You think we don't want to protect you guys?"

"You haven't given him a chance."

"I don't want to."

"Cally is *his daughter*!"

"I don't care." She throws her arms out. "You are so close to doing everything on your own. Look at you. You don't need him!"

"My God, Cherry, give the feminist theatrics a rest." *Tummy breath.* "I don't need *anyone*. I could do this without you and Mom, but I don't *want* to." *Tummy breath.* "I *want* him here. Just like I want, appreciate, and need you all."

Ryan still hasn't said anything, and that says a lot. Adequately done snooping, he sits on the couch and pats the cushion. "Sit down with me."

I'm at a loss. I'd rather unpack every box in this place, get a million cardboard cuts, and tear up my hands than get a big-brother lecture from him. Seriously, he's acting as if he's a wise old man, when I know that the entire time he was in the police academy he partied like a frat boy. His job is responsible, but he's no old man. "Cut it out, Ry."

"Come on. Sit." He nudges his head. "Cherry, go get a water or something."

She scowls but slowly wanders from the living room toward the kitchen. Very slowly.

Grayson and Ryan were close. When Grayson left me, he left Ryan, too. When Ryan found out I was pregnant, and no one could find Grayson, my brother was homicidal. I can't remember how long that took to pass. Maybe it didn't. Right now, he's silent, his face unreadable—not ready for premeditated homicide but potentially still as deadly. That's not good, considering a rookie cop can't make a mistake like murdering an old buddy. The county police frown upon that, and I need Ryan to remember there's no need to defend his baby sister's honor.

"Can't believe she has you caught up in this," I murmur, settling on the couch next to him.

Ryan's jaw is set. His eyes are hard. A vibrating animosity that could rival an arctic freeze emanates from him. Shit, shoot, shit. Not the greatest vibe to deal with when trying to talk sense to him.

"Where is he?" Ryan finally asks, not looking at me. He leans forward, his elbows on his knees, fingers locked. One by one, he cracks his knuckles. "Or did he get what he wanted?"

Jesus Jones on a cracker—my family is all about the dramatics today. "Don't be an ass. He's out."

"And he's coming back this time?"

"Seriously, stop the jerk routine." So, Cherry told Ryan about Gray showing up on the couch—and that she saw him without a shirt. Now she and I are really going to have it out. What happened to my wild, carefree older sister who actually suggested I become a stripper—at the place where she used to strip? *God!* Where's the girl who knows I'm not a moron and who cried alongside me when we thought Grayson had died? When all this calms down, I'm going to have words with her about sisterly loyalty. "If you two are going to interrogate me, Cherry can stop hovering in the corner. She's going to break her neck trying to listen."

A heartbeat later, she's back in the room, playing like she wasn't climbing the wall to listen. "Hey."

"I'm not a crying teenager knocked up and left alone."

Ryan growls. "Not anymore."

"Cut the attitude, Ry."

His gaze slices through me. It's frigid and meant to change my mind about... who knows what, exactly? The entire idea of a relationship? Giving Grayson a chance and having too much fun with him once I finally have alone time? It doesn't matter. None of this is their business.

Ryan cracks another knuckle. "He shows up, and you erase the past."

"Maybe."

"Shit." Disappointment rolls off of him. "And where the fuck is he anyway?"

She nods as if Grayson not being here is breaking some rule. *Once back, he can never leave?* I consciously do *not* tummy breathe—I hold on to my aggravation. "Like you're the shining symbol of modesty and appropriate behavior."

"I'm not the—"

I shake my head. "Don't say whatever you're about to. Really. I'm done with this, and that goes for both of you. I might be the youngest, but I've got years on you both."

Silence.

"You know it, too. Slumber parties with pancakes and a shiny rookie badge have nothing on being a single mom. *Nothing.*"

Ryan's jaw works back and forth. The tendons in his neck pop as though he's physically restraining himself. Cherry jumps up and paces, wearing a hole in my hardwood floor. We're all silent, and the energy in the room is toxic.

"Now that we've crossed that awkward moment, what else you guys got?" I'm done with their judgment. "Anything? No? Then let's start over."

"No one wants to see you get hurt," Ryan says. "He shows up after leaving for no good—"

"God!" I push off the couch. "You don't know that."

"He skipped town after he—"

"Ryan Kingsley, don't you dare finish that sentence."

"Emma." Patronizing me, he follows me and rubs my shoulder. "When a guy walks away after—"

"You have no idea what you're talking about. He was your best friend, Ry. Do you *really* think that Grayson screwed me, got his jollies off, and walked out like I was some high school checklist? You don't think that *anything* else could've been at play?" I snap at him. "We've avoided this conversation for years now. So, here it is. Let's have it out."

"He left. That's all that matters." Ryan goes back to the couch. "Poof! And the asshole was gone. You were alone at the beach. I'll never forget. Fuckin' never forgive myself."

"Enough with that. I'm so sick of you acting like you have something hanging over your shoulders. Like you—"

"I wasn't sick." His head drops. Hell, his whole body slumps.

I don't understand. "What?"

Ryan rubs his temples, and even Cherry steps forward, curious. A ragged growl pushes from his lips. "I wasn't sick the day you and Gray went to the beach. I wanted you two to work your shit out. So, I bagged on the ride to the shore. You two made up or whatever, job well done on my part. So I thought."

Holy. Effin'. Shit. "Oh…"

"Holy crap, Ryan." Cherry drops to the other side of him on the couch.

Still rubbing his temples, he barely lifts his head. "See? I played a part in this mess."

Now I understand the years of anger and his

constant sense of guilt. I sit down and lean my weight against him and then hug him. "Gray and I.... we would've ended up at the same spot. The same... situation."

He shakes his head. "I pushed it."

"No," I whisper. "We had to work through something that happened before."

Cherry hugs Ryan from the other side. "They did have... a before."

I know she remembers the details from after the Sadie Hawkins dance, from when I came *this* close to losing my virginity.

"Grayson and I were still crazy about each other." I tuck my chin on the edge of his shoulder, appraising the barren room and boxes and briefly wondering how life would be if I traipsed off to college. "I loved him way before I was pregnant. He loved me, too."

Ryan pushes away from Cherry and me. "Guys will say anything to get what they want. You *do* know that. You're not stupid."

A calm lands over me. "I have no doubt that Grayson Ford still loves me as much as he did the day I first kissed him. None."

Ryan's jaw drops.

Cherry tucks her legs under her as she repositions on the couch. "But he still left."

I nod. "But this is the thing: he was gone way before the beach. I just didn't know it, and he couldn't figure out how to share it."

Her head tilts. "Meaning?"

I'm just repeating myself at this point, and I don't know what I expect from them. "This isn't going anywhere. If you can let me be, I have things I want to do." Like find Grayson because I need a hug.

Ryan crosses his arms and leans against the window. He makes an imposing impression, and I'm half-sure he's doing it to warn my new neighbors that I have an enormous older brother standing watch. "Emma—"

"I need to call Mom and have a potentially awkward conversation with Dad. If you want to unpack boxes, have at it. Otherwise, I love you, but go."

"Okay. Fine." Cherry's eyes flash to Ryan, and she fidgets. It's a telltale sign that she's up to something. Besides, that was way too easy. Something's off.

"What?" I ask. Ryan's expression betrays nothing, but Cherry's plans are always on her face. Warning bells are ringing. She's up to no good. "What now, guys?"

"Hm? Nothing." She smoothes her pants while gracefully heading for the front door.

Crap.

Ryan clears his throat. "We were going to go see him, too. But maybe we won't."

"What!"

He shrugs.

Cherry stops tugging at her clothes. "Pays to have a cop brother."

"I don't even know where he's staying."

"Grand Hotel on Main." Ryan's jaw ticks, as if he's holding back an explosion of alpha-male big-brother impulses. "But maybe we'll hold tight for now."

"Yeah, maybe you should," I grumble. "At least you came here first."

Cherry rolls her eyes. "It was a toss-up for who was first: you or him. You won. You always win. Because we love you."

I drop my head back on the couch. "I want this to work, and for that to happen, you two have to back off."

Ryan does his best cop walk, each footstep

sounding heavy. After a few paces, he gives me a tight nod of agreement. "You do what you feel is best, Emma. He fucks up though? No amount of your pleas will hold me back."

"Ryan…"

He shakes his head. His eyes are harsh, and his normal smile is a thin line that speaks volumes to the fight brewing inside him. "Baby sister, it's like you forgot what he did to you."

I swallow past the lump in my throat. "He gave me the best thing I have in the entire world."

A long moment of silence hangs heavy.

"Cally's the best." Ryan rubs his hand in his hair. "But sometimes, you need a second opinion. And don't just rely on Cherry. I *do not* like her crazy thoughts and rationales, about which we are going to talk later."

My eyes shoot to my sister. For one terrifying second, I think she's completely lost her mind and told Ryan that she introduced me to Bruno. That Ryan knows I'm stripping. But she shakes her head almost imperceptibly.

His phone rings, and he turns to answer it, giving Cherry and me a moment to glare at each other over whatever Ryan was talking about.

He struts back around, nodding, phone still to his ear. "Got it." A moment later, he hangs up. His forehead furrows, and the corners of his eyes show the start of stress lines. "Cherry, let's go."

I watch their interactions. "What, are you guys partners now? Jeesh. Stay and unpack a box."

Cherry uses her hands to make fake guns and shoots them in the air as if she's Wile E. Coyote. After her Lone-Ranger moves, she blows the imaginary smoke from each and slips them into imaginary holsters.

Ryan harshly chuckles. "Just remember, mine are real, Emma. As is the badge. Anything hurts you, I hurt back."

I smile as they leave then lock the door behind them, sliding down to the floor. Could have gone worse. I hit my head on my knees. But it could've gone a lot better.

CHAPTER 31

Emma

I'm really proud of all I've accomplished. My cuticles are messed to hell, my fingers scratched and dry. I've unpacked our clothes and Cally's toys, decorated as much as I can without using a hammer to hang up pictures, and I am freakin' exhausted. But... I look around. This house looks like a home. A real home, all mine.

Cally is asleep in her bed with every single stuffed animal that I unpacked. It's almost impossible to find the kid buried in all the plush, but she's there, softly breathing, with a smile on her face.

My phone rings, pulling me out of space. Grayson's number lights the screen, and the first thing I'm going to do after we end this call is program his name. "Hey."

"Hey, pretty mama."

God, I love that. "How'd today go?"

He groans.

"That good, huh?"

"The job interview, that was fine."

"That's good." A job. Stability. I can't help but be nervous that it all might flit away.

"Some other stuff I had to deal with. Basically—" He blows out into the phone. "Ya know, Pops is a piece of shit."

A lump surfaces in my throat. "Yeah. You talk to him?"

"Something like that—so *you've* talked to him."

I bite my bottom lip. Every interaction I had with his father was rough. "He wasn't super conversational."

"I bet. God, I hate that fucker."

"So, why'd you go see him?"

"I don't know." His voice is strained.

"I'm sorry..." I want him to come over. I need him to. But I have work, and I don't know the ground rules for what's too much, what's too needy. He could take a look at all the responsibility my life's laden with and run his hot butt away. With the tightness in his words, I'm not sure what to say. "So..."

"You care if I call you later? I've got a shit ton on my mind."

"Yeah, no. Of course."

"Alright, Ems. Thanks for letting me figure this out."

Whatever "this" is. "Sure."

A quick goodbye, he's gone, and I'm even lonelier. Doesn't matter. My mom should be here in an hour, so I can head to the diner. I toss my phone onto the couch then go into the kitchen for a granola bar.

Working the night shift sucks, but for the first time, I'm struck by three thoughts. The first is about how Grayson—after he and Cally are more than adequately comfortable together—could be here when I have to head to work, so my family isn't constantly helping me. Second—my cheeks heat, and my stomach somersaults—what if Cally and I were more like Cally, *Grayson*, and I? Like, a mommy and a daddy with their baby?

But my third thought quickly cools the others because Gray has no idea that I've been working like this. He's going to feel awful, and I may never tell him about Emerald's. Stripping allowed me to move out from my parents' house, go to school, and save. I would work more nights there, but Bruno has a theory: I'll make more money as a once-a-week special than an everyday treat. Compared to the other girls' take, he's right, and I refuse to regret the decision to dance, even if I don't enjoy it.

There's a quick knock and slide of a key, then the front door knob twists, and Mom walks in.

"Hey, Mom."

"Hi, sweetie."

We share a long moment, but there's little time for a major mother-daughter powwow. Instead, I offer what's in my hand. "Want a granola bar?"

"No." She shakes her head. "I'm exhausted. No idea how you do this."

She's wearing the yoga pants and a baggy T-shirt that she'll sleep in. Everyone helping out is a huge burden. I grew up with a picture-perfect family, and she and Dad don't have a ton of money they can throw my way. We came to an understanding when Cally was born. I work my booty off, sometimes literally—though Mom's not privy to the details—I'll also get my degree, and they will help. If I want to raise Cally in any way comparable to how I grew up, having their assistance is the only option.

"I love you, Mom."

She wraps me in a hug. "I know, honey."

There's a lump in my throat because I'm hopeful

everything will change and terrified at the same time. "You know he's home."

Her arms squeeze. "Yes."

"I really want it to be okay."

Mom gives a deep sigh and a harder squeeze. "And I want you and Cally to be happy and loved." She lets me go and holds me out in front of her. I hope she's assessing and not judging.

I bite my lip. "Are you mad at me?"

"Mad?" Her eyebrows bite together. "No. Nervous? Yes."

"Me too."

We share a quiet look. "Alright, get to work."

"You're early." I toss the remains of the granola bar and smooth my uniform shirt.

"So, take your time. Hit Mickey D's for an ice cream. Read a book. You *can* have a life on your own. You know that, right?"

I shrug.

"This is life, Emma. Enjoy it." Her face is soft. Nothing fazes her. If there's one person on earth who would understand love, it's my mom. She loves love.

"Thanks." I peck her cheek and head for my purse.

"Oh, and I told Cherry that she and Ryan were *far* past the line. I expect you'll hear an apology before your birthday party tomorrow." She clears her throat. "Bring anyone you like."

A lump surges in my throat. "Really?"

"Might as well start somewhere. Doesn't hurt that there will be cake and ice cream to help mend fences."

CHAPTER 32

Emma

It's pointless trying to decide which I crave more: a good book or ice cream. Reading always wins, and I can sit at the counter before my shift and chat with Jan. But the conversation with Grayson from earlier preoccupies me. I slow to the longest red light in Summerland and pull my phone out of my purse. I could call him again and check on him. Make sure what's weighing heavy on his mind isn't killing him.

Or... I could surprise him right now. Like, in person. The Grand Hotel on Main Street is quaint, nice, and on the way to the Delightful Diner. It's one of three hotels in Summerland, and out of those, it's the best. Though that isn't saying much since the worst charges by the hour.

If he can surprise me, I can do the same to him and maybe see if he wants to have a midnight dinner while I work. It might ease his mind. Or maybe I can just make him smile.

My stomach twists. Everything in my life is

scripted—one of the reasons I loathe surprises—and that worked well until he showed up. But Grayson has been a game changer.

The light changes, and I drive three blocks up instead of two blocks over. There it is, the hotel Ryan said Grayson was staying at. Nervous excitement makes me jittery, but I'm going to do it. It'll be fun. Or a disaster. What if he's sleeping? What if he thinks I'm high maintenance?

Calm down.

I park my car on the street as adrenaline ticks through my blood. The hairs on my arm stand up, and I stifle an excited squeal. My heart skips, and my perma-smile isn't going away. I was far from miserable before he came home, but now I'm floating on stupid, fluffy love clouds over my... *boyfriend?*

Whatever his title is, I get out of my car and wander down the street. Grand Hotel's doors have oversized handles, and everything on the inside is the same as it has always been—shiny hardwood floors and richly colored cushions on monstrous couches. The walls are polished wood, and there's bold wallpaper. It smells like lemons, but just a hint, a very clean-citrus scent, not heavy, artificially fragrant cleaner.

So... now what?

Heading to the check-in desk, it becomes clear my plan isn't well thought out. The hotel is just going to tell me his room number?

Hi, where's Grayson staying at?

Hi, I'm his... girlfriend. I swear. Room number, please?

The front-desk girl turns around, making me groan. Jessie Spikes—like a blast from the past, it's everyone's favorite cheerleader from high school. I used to hate this girl and, in my head, had all kinds of bad thoughts about her whenever she was under Grayson's attention. Petty high school BS. Karma gave it back to me hard. When I was pregnant and alone, Jessie was a relentless gossip.

"Emma." Jessie draws out my name, convincing me that as soon as I leave the room, she will be on the phone to blather.

"Hi, Jessie. I was, um, hoping that you could point me to—"

"Grayson Ford?" The bubbling exuberance in her voice can't be contained.

My cheeks heat, and my knotting fingers fidget. I rub my sides, suddenly aware of sweaty palms. "Yes, please."

"Room two oh two." She points toward the double spiral staircase that drips in old-timey opulence.

Well... that was easy. I would have expected a blood-sacrifice requirement for that kind of info. "Thanks. Nice to see you."

I head toward the stairs as Jessie waves her hand, wiggling her fingers as if she's doing some kind of peppy cheerleader send-off.

"Good luck," she says.

Good luck? How pathetic. She must think I'm here to try and win him back.

"Right. Thanks." I can't shake off the years of not-so-behind-my-back chatter. Okay. No need to get all in my head. I focus on my newest favorite memory—the look on his face when he met Cally. Screw the haters.

Room two oh two. I have no need to hide how vulnerable I am and my excitement about the future. I draw in a breath then knock.

No answer.

Well... I didn't take into account he wouldn't be here. I drop my head against the door. *So anti-climactic—*

The door cracks open, and I stumble headfirst, flailing and falling like a moron into his room and landing on my hands and knees. Graceful much? Ugh. Good thing the guy already loves me. My gaze shifts from hotel-room carpet to a pair of shoes.

Women's shoes. The nice kind that people don't wear to work at a diner or when they're carting a two-year-old around all day. My heart freezes, but my eyes drift to the long legs they're attached to.

Oh, God.

There's a woman in perfectly hip-hugging pants, insanely impractical heels, and a shirt that is a blessing to her already gorgeous body—and those breasts have *never* had a baby nursing on them. They are *perfect*, and they are in Grayson's hotel room.

I'm going to puke.

"Hey, down there—you okay?" she asks with a phone pressed to her ear. She lifts a finger, wordlessly asking me to give her a minute.

I jump up, fumbling, spin to the door, check that it's the right number—it is—and turn back on shaking legs.

She's pretty. Kind of gorgeous. But she isn't talking to anyone. The one-minute finger points to her cell and she mouths *voicemail*. Then she says, "Hey, I'm here to surprise you! See ya. Love ya. Bye." She expels an exasperated breath, spins around in an outfit I can only describe as date-worthy, and smiles. "Come in, please—"

"I'm sorry, I have the wrong room." I back up until I stumble against the wall then numbly reach for the door as though exiting this nightmare might help.

"Nope, right room. I'm the one that keeps calling housekeeping." Her accent screams Southern belle, and she tosses her hand as if she's throwing out casual information. She smiles perfectly glossy lips. "I called before, but nothing changed, so I had to call again."

"What...?" Me, housekeeping? I have no idea what's going on. But I glance at my waitressing clothes, and they could totally be taken for a housekeeping uniform.

"The air conditioner stinks like sulfur or something, and trust me, that's a smell Grayson can't handle. Plus, I don't think I could sleep with it." She leans forward as if she's telling a secret. "It's a bit overwhelming."

I'm dizzy. My words won't come. She knows things I don't know. She leaves messages I'm too timid to leave. *I love you.*

"Can't you smell it? It might just be near the bed." She walks away from me.

Unsteadily and stupidly, I take a step forward toward a king-sized bed. A military green duffel bag and a small pink suitcase sit by the bathroom door. "You can't..."

"He has a condition. Sulfur really doesn't help. The bed doesn't even look slept in. I don't think he even stayed here last night."

My stomach lurches. "How do you know him?"

"What?" Her eyebrows pinch. "He's my fiancé."

"Oh, God." Why did I assume all this time had passed, and he hadn't been in a relationship? Even if I'd thought of that, it never would have occurred to me he'd *still* be in one.

"I'm sorry." Her face tightens, confused. "Are you okay?"

Behind me there's a *click-click* of the door unlocking. My legs are stuck like columns of cement. I can't bend my knees, can't run away. Somehow I pivot. Grayson's face is dark and brooding, and his eyes aren't on me. They go straight to her. My mouth goes dry, and my hands tremble.

"Gray!" she squeals.

Gray? My dream of the future shatters a million times over.

She throws her arms out. "Surprise!"

"Shit, Mazie," he growls.

Confirmation. He knows her. That's all I need. My legs come back, and even if my mind's reeling, I can run. I push pass Grayson, sprinting down the hall, skipping down the stairs.

"Emma! Wait!"

But I don't. I can hear Grayson continue to call after me.

At the base of the stairs, Jessie giggles, only increasing my shame. "Have a good night, Emma."

Devastated tears streak down my cheeks, and I'm thankful I didn't park at the hotel. I skip behind the building so no one can find me then weave to my car, which is parked on the street.

Finally, I reach the safety of my Jeep and climb into the driver's seat. Tears blur my vision, and I reach to the center console for tissues. Coming up without, I do find a drawing Cally made last week. The scribbles and scrawl are supposed to be our new house with two stick figures that hold hands—a mommy and daughter clinging to each other. I can hardly make it out but know her intent. The mommy's outstretched hand reaches off the page. There's no one else there for them. That's how we'll always be: alone. Even the pictures Cally drew said that was true.

CHAPTER 33

GRAYSON

I'm standing at the corner of Fuck Me and Screwed after running through the hotel's parking lot and then up the damn block. My fingers are locked behind my head as I scan the empty streets and ignore the pain surging in my side. Blood pulses around the edges of the almost-healed gunshot wound. None of this is important, though. It's only a distraction in my hunt for her. But no matter where I go, no Emma.

I shake out my arms and stretch out the pain. Again, I hit her number in my phone. Immediate voicemail.

Fuck me. I took my eyes off her for one second to say "What the hell?" to Mazie. That was all it took for Emma to melt into the night, a ghost of a shadow that I could not track down. She's not answering her phone—*no*, she's *rejecting* my calls—and I don't know my next move. I'm without allies and completely friendless in this battle zone.

"Damn it," I shout on the street corner and pace a tight circle.

I try her cell phone again, and shit—I hate leaving messages. But this time, after the beep, I'm ready to plead. "Please call me back. It's not what you think."

God, am I the king of "it's not what you think"? I shove the phone in my back pocket and storm back to the hotel. When I bust into the lobby, there's fuckin' crazy Mazie having a heartfelt discussion with Jessie the desk girl. *Fuck me.* Summerland County gossip hags are going to love this shit.

"What did you think you were doing?"

Mazie twists her fingers into a knot. "I was trying to get your AC fixed. Stupid, I know. Can't keep my own shit together, so I jump in yours."

"I didn't mention where I was just to have you show up." I feel eyes on me and pivot. Jessie is staring with rapt attention. I growl at her, and she waves at me with googly eyes. I can't handle this place sometimes. "Let's go, Maze." Sure to fire up the grapevine, I hook an arm around Mazie and guide her to the stairs.

"That was her, wasn't it?"

"Yeah, that was her." Quickly, I push open the door and take in the room, trying to see what Emma saw. It's not hard to picture a bad outlook. There's Mazie's suitcase next to one bed. And, God, the horror on Emma's face. "Damn it, Mazie. Couldn't you have mentioned the pullout couch? Or that you weren't staying *with* me?"

She squeezes her eyes shut. "I thought I was helping. I was worried after you blew everyone off at the hospital. Really, I'm sorry."

My head hurts. Why isn't Emma at home with Cally? Is she working? Where? I've come too far, and

I have too much on the line to lose her—lose *them*. I turn to Mazie. "I have a daughter."

Her head jerks back, then her mouth opens once, twice. "Whoa."

"I can't lose them." My turmoil is brutal, as though the devil's making waves with my soul, causing a hurricane with my heart. I want to scream, want to explode. There are so many things that I want to do—like rip the hotel room apart and beg in Emma's voicemail for a chance to explain. But this volcano of emotion is not a PTSD attack. It's something bigger.

"So, go over there." Mazie's gaze is fierce. She has a million flaws, but she's a steadfast friend who I never doubt wants what's best for me. "I mean, that's what you should do, right? Find her and explain."

"Go where? Her home? She wouldn't leave our daughter by herself. Obviously somebody's with Cally—"

"Cally? That's beautiful."

A lump surfaces in my throat. "I know." I swallow it away. "So, Emma's... out. Work?"

"It's super late."

If she's only now heading to work... I have to wonder again how hard she's had it while I've been gone.

"You have a daughter." Numbly, Mazie trudges toward the couch and collapses. "That's amazing."

My phone rings. Caller ID: Emma Kinglsey. I don't even give her a chance to say hello. "Let me explain."

Mazie pops up and points toward the door before showing herself out.

"Explain." Em's voice is sad and quiet and mistrusting.

"Where are you, Emma?"

"At work."

Damn it. I knew it. "Where's that?"

She hesitates. "Why?"

"Because I am coming for you, baby."

"Grayson, this… you and me. I had some time to think, and I believe in us. I want us. And I have to trust you to get that. Your voicemail said you'd explain, and I'm scared whatever you have to say isn't enough."

"It is." I need to say something that proves she can trust me. That she can give herself to me. Again. Forever. In the middle of my hotel room, I fall to my knees, terrified that what I need to say won't come to me. I close my eyes and—thank fuck—I can see her face.

"She's your fiancé?"

Crazie Mazie and her fuckin' fiancé line. "No. Not at all. It's not like that. I'll put her on the phone—"

"Were you engaged to her?"

"No. She's only a friend. Just like one of the guys. I swear."

"Gray?" Her mistrusting voice sounds broken. "I'm… I—"

My heart's pounding. "I was yours the day we met. Before I knew how deep I loved you, I knew you were my friend. My… *person.* The face I was supposed to see every day. The voice I was supposed to hear every night. If there's one thing that you need to know it's… Ems, I was made for you."

I die waiting as each second passes.

"I'm waitressing at the Delightful Diner. On till four in the morning." She sniffles. "This is hard, figuring us out."

On until four in the morning? My insides are strung tight. "I swear I thought you were in college.

I thought it. Believed it." My words break. "That everything was perfect for you without me. College, classes, fun, parties. Far away from the hell that I was living every day." I pinch the bridge of my nose. "I didn't know you were killing yourself with work. I didn't know you're raising our daughter. So help me God, had I known, there is no military force on earth that would've kept me from you."

She sniffles, and I would absorb her pain if I could. I'd do anything to make this right for her.

"Grayson," she whispers. "I still want the fairytale."

"Good. Because it's coming for you."

Emma

Delightful Diner's door chimes, and I turn around, knowing it's Grayson. There's something about his presence that, even before I see him, makes me react to him. It's as if the air shimmers, and the pressure increases. My skin tingles, and my nerves fire.

Our eyes lock as the diner lulls. Every eye is on him. Everyone in this stinking county thinks they know our story. He ignores them, and his fiery emerald eyes focus on me like lasers, pinning me with a fierce hunger and desire, with alpha possession and domination. It's so real and so palpable I'm not sure how I'm still standing.

"Hi," I whisper though there are twenty feet between us, and bacon and eggs are sizzling in the background.

Grayson's boots echo on the floor. The confidence in his stride makes my mouth drop. With each step forward, I think he'll slow down, that he'll stop this... *charge*. But no.

His arm wraps around me. Hard. The other hand tangles in my hair, threading fingers into the tight bun. He pulls me to his mouth, holding me to his chest. His full lips take mine as though he's underwater, and I'm his oxygen.

Instantly, I'm drowning in need for him, moaning into his mouth. His fingers tighten against my scalp, and the arm supporting my weight has me off my feet and onto a counter barstool.

He tears back, his breathing harsh as mine. His lips hover close to mine, his green eyes brighter than I can remember ever seeing, and he growls, "I love you."

My breaths stutter past my lips, which tickle against his, and I nod because there aren't words to express how much I love him.

His possessive hold doesn't care that eyes are on us. "And I'm sorry for this, what I've put you through. Middle of the night waitressing and raising our baby alone."

Our baby. I want to die hearing that, but I only melt closer to him. "Gray..."

"Ask me anything."

"Are you sleeping with her?"

He shakes his head. "Mazie's a friend. A close friend who's crazy, and it's her thing. She says she's my fiancé. It gets her in places. She knows about you. That's just her. Crazy fuckin' Mazie. I've got no secrets from you."

Oh, boy. I have a doozy for him that involves a stage name and six-inch heels. "I—uh—"

"Forget about her," he says.

"Okay. Trying to forget."

"You can quit this job right now if you want. I'm

going to make this right by you. Starting with you not working nights."

I'm exhausted. I want to go home, crawl into bed, maybe even with him. But that would leave Jan in a lurch. "I can't walk out on a shift."

"Fine. But you don't have to come in like this again." His face is so serious, so solemn that I almost believe that our fairytale might one day come true.

"I have to work, Gray. Bills pile up fast. Faster than I can keep up with them, even with help."

"Not like this you don't."

"If you really want us, you have to know my reality. Forget our chemistry and the... the..." I don't know how to describe what I feel between us.

He tucks close to my ear. "The need to take you to bed? To have you right this goddamn second?"

If I was hot and bothered before, call me primed and ready. Heat crawls up my neck, and I nod. "If you want more than that, I'll break it down for you, explain what responsibility means and then—"

"Fuck that. I accept. Sign me up. All of it. I want you. *Both.*"

I can't breathe. "You're so certain?"

"No doubt." The conviction pouring off him is intense. His eyes are deep, his voice low.

I swallow against the emotion tightening my throat. "Is this really happening?"

"Not sure why you have to ask after last night. But yeah, baby. We're a go. Put a ring on it. Count me as yours. Tell me that we're together. No worries over outsiders, no questions from family. It's you and me and Cally."

My heart seizes. Every bit of me hurts for wanting this so badly. "How do you know this will work?"

He smiles. "You're not saying no. So, how do *you* know?"

Easy answer. "Because I had you with me every day you were gone. I lived for you. I danced for you. I breathed and dreamed so that one day when you came back, it'd be like you never left."

His mouth skirts up to my ear. "You danced for me?"

Shit. Shoot. Shit. I've said too much. But the truth just pours out. "I have something to tell you—"

"Emma, honey." Jan snaps from behind the counter. "Reunions are great, but the tables are stacking up."

I take a deep breath and look around. No way are tables stacking up. No one's taken a bite—they're all watching the Emma-Grayson show. But tips will suffer if tables don't order and turn over, so Jan's point isn't lost on me. "Right. Okay." I inch back. "Want some pancakes or something?"

He tilts his head. "I'll take off. But I can pick you up after your shift?"

"No. Don't do that. But..." I bite my lip and remember the promise not to care about my questioning, doubting family. "My birthday's tomorrow."

He smiles. "Well aware."

"Would you come over with me? Mom and Dad are having a little get-together."

His eyes bounce, hesitant for a second. "Absolutely."

"Cool. Alright. Okay."

Grayson kisses my cheek. "Better get back to work. And don't think I'll forget that you're going to dance for me."

Oh, baby. Don't think I will forget that, either.

CHAPTER 34

GRAYSON

Armed with a birthday-paper-wrapped notebook and a stuffed animal with a big bow, I shake my nerves and park my truck on the street in front of Emma's house. My fingers drum on the steering wheel, and I take another huge swig of Mountain Dew, trying to alleviate my tension. Mega caffeine probably won't help, but it can't hurt. Nothing I've done—walked away from my home, walked into war—has prepared me to hang out with my daughter.

I Googled two-year-olds all night long and found out several things. Kids aren't the easy fun they look like on TV commercials. There are message boards and websites dedicated to kids who won't eat, who won't talk, who have two parents, one parent, same-sex parents, who were conceived accidentally or brought into this world with the help of implantation—a word that didn't mean what I thought it meant. There are mommy "wars," a term that bugs the shit out of me, and parenting styles: attachment, helicopter, free range, tiger...

So basically, I'm terrified of a two-foot-tall dream come true. *Hell*—I'm more worried about what she thinks about me than I've been concerned over anything else in my entire life.

Crap. I take another gulp of soda and fail to ignore my clammy palms.

I pick up the purple stuffed dog and glare at it. "I can do this."

Go time. I breathe out and try to hide my giddy smile. Grabbing the wrapped notebook, I jump out of the truck and head for the door, my pulse jumping faster with each step.

The door flies open as I raise my hand to knock. Emma has Cally perched on her hip. God, they are beautiful. Both girls have sweet grins that make me feel like more of a man than I've ever been. Then Cally quickly loses interest and mumbles something about TV. A nibbling self-doubt surfaces. I need to be what they need, but I'm not sure how to do it. Hence, the Googling.

Emma redirects the squirming girl. "Cally, honey. No more right now."

"Hey." I don't know how to greet them. If it were just Emma, it'd be a hug and a kiss. But I'm sure there's a line that I'm nowhere near when it comes to hugging Cally. My heart squeezes as disappointment settles in. I want to hug her. I want that connection so much it hurts.

Emma sidles up to me and throws her arm around my neck, pecking my cheek. "Hey, you."

"I brought presents." As Emma steps back, I hold up the stuffed animal and the wrapped notebook.

Cally's eyes light. "I 'member you."

"I remember you, too." At her innocent reaction, an easy calm runs through me. "I brought this for you."

Her little head turns to Emma, asking permission without saying a word. After she receives a nod, I hold the purple dog closer. Cally tentatively reaches for it, and when her fingers grasp it, she snakes it to her cheek, curls it into her neck, and cuddles the ever-lovin' stuffing out of it.

"Guess she likes it." And *that* feels pretty damn good.

Emma tilts her head to watch. "It's perfect."

"You ready?" Because I'm not. I'm not hiding, but I'm sure not gung-ho to head into the Kingsley-family hate-Grayson zone. When I called Ryan the other day, there was no answer. I didn't know what to say, so my voicemail message consisted of "I'm in town, bro. Call me." No return call. As expected.

"Let's go." She sets Cally down, and we both watch her run to Emma's Jeep. "Mine has a car seat." She places her keys into my palm but doesn't take her hand away. "Maybe we ditch and go out to eat."

Hooah, I'd love that. But I shake my head. "Nope. Not ditching your birthday party, pretty mama. Move boots."

With her hand in mine, I lead the way then watch Emma as she straps Cally into the car seat. It basically looks like a standard five-point harness. Not that dissimilar to a jumpsuit and pack. I could totally figure that out.

"Easy peasy," she says to me.

"Right." I hold the passenger door open and let Emma slip in then angle to her side as she buckles. I push back the hair that covers her cheek. All my anxiety slips away when I touch her. "Happy birthday, baby. I'll make up for all the ones I missed."

She leans over and kisses me, making Cally giggle and sing words that don't make sense.

"Now, are we ready?" She bites her lip, looking as if she's nowhere near ready to end that kiss.

Neither am I. I glance into the back seat and watch Cally snuggle against the purple dog. "Absolutely." But I can't stop myself, and I lean over to kiss her lips.

When I pull back, her cheeks are pink and her eyes dreamy. Her hand catches my shirt. "We should totally find five minutes alone."

The words go straight south, turning me on more than the two not-so-chaste kisses. "Five minutes?"

She giggles. "Five minutes all alone…"

I brush her ear with my lips. "The things I could do to you in five minutes."

Her breath sucks in quietly, and as I stand up and head for my seat, it's not lost on me that her pink cheeks and dreamy, soft brown eyes are now rabidly hungry.

Her blue Jeep is a boxy older model but impeccably well cared for. There's a dream catcher hanging from the mirror and a photo of her and Cally on the center console. I slide into my seat, push my chair back, and reposition the mirrors. A sense of making myself comfortable in her life settles over me.

Emma's fiddling with the radio, and I back out the driveway and head for her parents' house. The wrapped notebook is stashed between the center console and me, and I catch her glancing at it.

"You didn't have to get me anything."

I take her hand and wish I could fulfill every hope she's ever dared dream. "It's really not much." *But it's everything to me.* "Something I should have given you long ago."

"Oh." She raises an eyebrow. "Any hints?"

How to explain what's in that notebook? "No words to describe what's in there."

Emma

The drive's a short one. Grayson pulls into my folks' driveway as if he does it every day, and then *he* jumps out to unbuckle Cally. It's enough to make my ovaries scream "Oh my God." Seriously. He's this gorgeous, massive beauty of a man, and now he's talking gibberish with my—*our*—daughter.

"There you go." He pats her on the back, and I can tell he took that moment to give her a hug. The loopy look on his face makes my insides go mushy.

She makes her stuffed puppy say "thank you" and runs off up to my parents' front door. He turns to watch, his green eyes glowing with unsaid emotion, and I'm melting all over the place. There's nothing sexier than a hot guy and a cute kid. *Nothing.* So, to watch the man that I adore hug our daughter for the first time... it transcends all other sentiments I've felt for him. It's epic.

Grayson beams and throws his arm around my shoulder. "Gave my girl a hug. Nothing else matters today."

"She hugged you back." My throat catches, and I lean into him. Cally has never known a father, but there is a connection between the two of them already.

"Ready?"

My gaze falls on the house, a place I think of as Cally's fun house. There's a room dedicated to her with a rocking horse and cowgirl hat, a mini-slide, dolls, and games. It pretty much looks like a toy store threw up in there. But this is where I grew up, where

Grayson was by my side almost every day. I fell in love with him in that house; we shared our first kiss in my room.

"Gamma!" Cally slaps the door. "Gamma. Hwello."

We follow behind, slowly walking up the sidewalk. Gray's hand takes mine as I think about how I like him in my driver's seat, how I like him unbuckling Cally, how I like him being part of everyday life. Knowing where we're probably going, together in a forever kind of relationship, gives me the tingles. Even though I've only had days to take in this new reality, I know it's the future.

But despite all that, nervous butterflies tornado in my belly. I have no idea what will happen between Ryan, my dad, and Grayson. *Oh, God...* "I'm gonna puke."

He chuckles low and squeezes my hand. A rush of goose bumps erupts over my shoulders, shooting down my spine.

"Don't do that." His voice is so calm, so steadfast that I actually take a semi-normal breath.

His thumb slides over my knuckles as I hang on to him with everything I've got. "Grayson, wait."

We stop midway up the sidewalk. "I have so much to tell you before we walk in there."

A playful half grin curls on his face. "Right now?"

I nod, adamant that he has to hear how I feel. I have to arm him with the knowledge of how deeply I care before we go in there.

"Okay. Shoot, baby."

"You're not just my best friend, not just the father of my daughter. You're the love of my life." My thoughts are rushed, and I want them to sound perfect. "I haven't explained that to you since you came home." The pulse in my neck rushes. "I can't seem to get the words to come out right. What's in my head isn't what I've said." I take a deep breath and plunge forward. "I need to say I love you. But what I mean is *I love you*—in a way that defies definition and exists only in a world that you and I are in. I'm in deep for you, and I just need you to know that before we go in there."

His eyes fire, and their intensity makes me feel as if I have angel wings, as if I can do no wrong though I'm not sure I've ever been able to pull off even semi-okay.

Thick arms wrap me into a muscled hug so consuming tears spring into my eyes. His lips press against the top of my head, and he breathes in deep. "You smell like sunshine."

"Please don't let me go." I squeeze him tighter, positive that if I'm hurting his side he will never tell me. "I love us."

"Ems, baby." He loosens his hold and lets one hand cup my cheek, tracing my jawbone. "We're okay. No matter what."

I nod.

His laughter surprises me. "You're expecting awfulness in there. A war zone?"

I bite my lip. "Maybe."

"Good thing I've been through that particular kind of hell once before. Nothing thrown my way will change a thing about us."

"Promise?"

He shrugs a shoulder, and his confidence is almost contagious. "Don't need to promise."

"Why?"

"Don't worry about it." He winks. "I've got your back. Into battle we go."

CHAPTER 35

GRAYSON

Talk of battles and war zones before walking in wasn't the best move. It forces me to remember my team that I lost, and then I look around at my two girls I abandoned. The stress that accompanies both lines of thought itches for attention, but I ignore it. I told Emma I had her back, and I'll cover her always. Still, I have no idea what to expect behind that door and am prepared for the worst from Ryan and her dad.

Mrs. Kingsley opens the front door as Cally squeals and jumps into her arms. The tension in my chest expands, my nerves quickening the beat of my pulse.

"Gamma!"

"Hi, buttercup."

"Wook!" She shoves the stuffed animal in the older but familiar face of Emma's mom. Somehow, I always thought the two women were similar, even though her mom looks as if she walked out of a clothing catalog, and Emma is wearing a shirt she probably designed herself.

"That's very nice." Cally wiggles out of Mrs. Kingsley's hold and runs inside, leaving her mom to turn toward us. "Happy birthday, Emma. Nice to see you, Grayson."

I'm strong for Emma and controlling my apprehension, but my knees try to lock up, and my breath staggers. I know this house better than the one I grew up in. Each step farther inside is like pushing through desert sand with a seventy-five-pound rucksack and no sleep for days. My throat tightens as the heaviness of her disapproval hangs over me even though she's done nothing but smile.

Emma's hand slips free from mine, and I'm suddenly on my own. Fuck me. She thought I was supporting her? No way—she was holding me together.

"Hey, Mom. Thanks for doing this."

"Of course." Her eyes move to me. "Welcome home, Grayson."

I can't swallow, can't take a breath. I nod. "Thanks." Disappointment will be my death, abandonment my curse. Once upon a time, I wanted this woman to be my mother as much as I wanted to live in this family rather than my own. Being twenty-one doesn't take away childhood memories. "I'm sorry."

She moves from Emma and wraps me into a maternal hug. Tears I won't let show sting my eyes and throat.

Her hand pats my pack. "I mean it, Grayson. I'm thrilled you're back."

I pull away and need her to understand. "I didn't know. I thought I left her in a better place without me."

She hugs me again and then again pats my back as

if I'm still part of her Kingsley clan. "Alright, you two. Cally's probably already in the cake, which I haven't finished yet, so let's go."

Emma takes my hand again, and we follow her mom. My heart rate is sporadic, and my feelings are scattered. Coming home from war alone was hard. Injury made it worse. Walking into their familiar home, with all its same smells and sounds, is heartbreaking.

Cally and Cherry are screaming and laughing in a back room. Mr. Kingsley stops on his way from the kitchen with platter full of hot dogs and hamburgers. There's a hardness in his posture that's impossible to miss. It's a mistrust that he doesn't need to explain. We stare, locked for a long second, until Emma breaks free to hug him.

"Hi, Dad."

"Happy birthday, Emma."

After they hug, he goes back to his assessment of me. It's awkward, the way we all are. Ems doesn't seem to know what to say. Her mom is behind me, hovering. Finally, Mr. Kingsley nods and extends his hand. "Welcome home."

"Thank you, sir."

"A lot has changed."

I gulp. "Yes, sir. It has."

His eyes narrow a fraction, studying me. I'm not sure whether he's going to throw me out of his house or try to kick my ass. "You plan on sticking around?"

"I'm not going anywhere."

Mrs. Kingsley passes by and tucks herself against his arm. "I think we're past all the Mr. and Mrs. stuff. Certainly no need for *sir*. George and Laura, okay, Grayson?"

I nod. "Yes, ma'am."

She smiles. "Alright then. Like I said, I have a cake to finish. My helper bee yesterday wasn't too keen on putting the icing *on* the cake."

"Where's Ryan?" asks Emma.

Laura tilts her head toward the stairs. "He was in his old room. Some work call he had to take."

Cally hollers for her grandparents, and George nods. "That's us."

"I'll catch you in a minute." I kiss Emma's cheek. "Something I have to do."

She grabs onto me. "No, you don't. Ryan's being an ass."

"Gotta do it, baby."

"I guess." She rolls her eyes but heads toward the sound of Cherry and Cally. I turn for the stairs, taking two at a time, and it's not lost on me how comfortable I am here yet how much tension I'm carrying in my shoulders. The first room is Emma's old bedroom—a place that taunted me all through high school—and then Ryan's. The door's cracked, the light is on, and I'm ready to talk this shit out.

I knock once and nudge it open with my boot. He's sitting on his bed, phone in hand. When his face turns, I'm caught off guard by how different he looks since the last time we hung out. His face says the same thing about me.

"Hey." I walk in.

Ryan stands, pocketing his phone in his jeans. "Heard you were back."

"Back. For good."

"Right." He scoffs. "When you hurt her again, I'm going to fuck your world up, Ford."

Ford. "We were tight like brothers, and that's how it's going to be? I didn't know that, *Kingsley.*"

"You just peaced out. And no one heard from you again? Shady."

I shake my head. "If I couldn't talk to her, no one else in Summerland mattered."

"She's my baby sister." His brows pinch tight. The harsh lines around his eyes are stressed.

"She's my *world.*"

Ryan's mouth opens, but he shakes his head.

I take a step forward. "Not that it's your damn business, but I thought I was doing what was best for her. She didn't need to be tied down to some stupid piece of trailer trash like me that wasn't getting out of this county unless Uncle Sam paid for it. I *thought* she was partying it up, doing college shit, taking pictures, and doing normal-life stuff. I didn't know."

"You never called her. Never came back. Surely your sorry ass got leave, got—"

"Shut up, Ryan." Emma's firm voice surprises me as it bleeds through the room. He and I both missed her hovering at the door. "I made Grayson promise he'd never tell me goodbye. And again, Ry, this isn't your business to butt into."

Ryan starts, "It's—"

"But since you need to hear it again, I *told* Grayson never to tell me goodbye. Right after I told him *exactly* what I wanted from him. You get no further explanation from me or him, Ryan. Okay? Make up, and get over it. It's my birthday, and I swear I'm not going to deal with this from you."

"Emma—" Ryan and I both say.

She snuggles under my arm, and I latch on to her, lines clearly drawn.

"I don't need you fighting my battles." She leans into me. "Certainly not with my brother."

I could say the same thing about Ryan. "This isn't just about you, Ems. It's about us. I'm *done* with anyone thinking it was a one-sided situation."

Ryan focuses on her. "I want what's best for you."

Cally flies into the room. "Unc Ry-ry!"

Emma snakes her arm around Cally in one deft move, lifting her on to her hip. "How do you not see that this is what's best for me?"

Ryan's gaze moves from Emma to Cally and lands on me. "Hurt her again and—" His phone buzzes, and he quickly flips it open, reads the screen, and replaces it. "Hurt anyone again, and we're going to have problems."

CHAPTER 36

Emma

"Well. Now that that's settled..." I shut Ryan's door behind us, but my frustration level is sky-high, choking all my rationality. I should go back and shake my brother. At least that would help me get out all my pent-up aggravation. "God. He's being a jerk."

Grayson's arms wraps around me as we head down the hall. "Let it go."

Cally tugs at the hem of my shorts. "Yur mad at Unc Ry-ry?"

I take another not-very-helpful calming breath. "No, honey."

"Cally-bug bear! Where are you?" Cherry calls from downstairs.

Cally scoots from my arms and hovers at the top of the stairs then turns with her cute face begging for permission.

I nod. "Careful."

She drops to her bottom and half scoots, half

clings to the railing as she takes the stairs slowly. We stand, watching her, and when she gets to the last step, Cherry whooshes in, scooping Cally in a fit of giggles, and runs off. If there's one thing that my sister does well, it's acting like a fun aunt.

Grayson's arm grabs me tighter, and I'm suddenly aware that we're in a full house but very alone at the moment. My senses tingle. He leans over and pushes me against the wall. "Don't say a word."

My mouth hinges open, but I obey. His body shifts as he reaches for my old room's door handle. His hot breath burns against my neck, and the knob twists open. Its click echoes in my ears.

"Stay quiet, pretty mama."

Holy tummy flips. I mouth "trying" while he drags his teeth down my neck. Other than the sound of my needy gasps, we silently slip into the dark room. The lights are off, but the blinds aren't completely shut. Shadows and traces of light are cast across the room, and it feels like a secret enclave.

My eyes shut as his mouth finds mine, his tongue lashing sweet velvet perfection, and all I can do is moan.

He breaks harshly. "Promised you five minutes."

My aggravation melts away, my body hums for his touch, and in between my legs, I'm aching. There's no time for "Should we? Shouldn't we?" Cally's gone with my sister. My mom's finishing the cake, and Dad is manning the grill. I don't give a hoot about Ryan at this point. Thank God I'm on the pill because I would die to get Grayson's hands under my clothes.

Judging by the rough way he's pulling at my shirt and the button on my shorts, we're on the same page. His mouth attacks my neck, and his hands slide down the back of my shorts, slipping under my panties, and he grabs my cheeks in a way that almost hurts and almost makes me orgasm on the spot. I fumble for his belt, purposefully leaning against the erection bulging in his pants. This is totally forbidden. Crazy hot. I'm craving him in me more than I want to breathe.

I shimmy down my loosened shorts, tangling in my underwear as I pull loose his belt and pants. His hands abandon me long enough that he frees himself. My mind stills for that split-second as I take him in. Grayson Ford is masculine perfection. His body, his mouth, the size and girth of him, and that focus on his face when he's hungry for me—it's absolutely impossible to avoid falling in love with him all over again.

He walks backward toward my bed and sits, pulling me on top of him as though I weigh nothing. Our eyes lock, and this is different. This is him taking something fast and hormone-driven and making it beautiful, making it all about me.

"You're in charge, baby."

The control over what I want and what I can give is an aphrodisiac. I move my sex over him, teasing myself. God. My pulse jumps, and my heart clamors. This is power, and he's giving it to me. Crazy, how incapable I've felt, as if I were drowning. But now, a thousand realizations click into place, the most important one being that I can do anything I want—with or without permission.

"You've always been wild," he breathes.

"Only for you." On stage, everything's an act. It looks out of control, but it's scripted and choreographed. Taking him like this, that's wild.

My breath catches as I settle against the crown of his blunt head. I'm aroused, and my body's ready. I press against him, and my mind stills. His shaft is thick, and Grayson groans as my jaw drops. I'm consumed from the inside out. The fullness is overwhelming, and our passion chokes me. God. This was supposed to be a fast fuck, but it's always more with us.

"Christ." He gives a low growl through gritted teeth. My arms latch around his strong neck, and his grip digs into my hips. He shifts, holding me down as he surges up. "Baby…"

"I…" I'm panting, gasping. "I love this."

"Your turn." His voice is soft, but it's firm. "Ride me."

Heat hits my cheeks. I want to be embarrassed. It's vulgar and direct. I'm embarrassingly inexperienced, but I don't care. I love how he makes me feel, how he empowers what I want. This is about me, and even if I fumble my way, I don't think he'll care.

Grayson's teeth nip at my earlobe. "Take what you need, pretty mama."

Driven by the danger of getting caught and the starving need that I can't rid myself of in any other way, I try to embrace what comes naturally, what's instinctual. Because apart from strutting my stuff on stage, I have no freakin' clue what to do.

"What do you want?" He encourages as his hips flex, a subtle and spectacular reminder that pulls me from a cloud of self-doubt.

"You." I lift up from him. Hot streaks of amazing sensation cascade through me. "Shit…" I gasp. "Shoot…"

"Damn, look at you."

I ease down and feel the fullness and stretching all over again. I take a breath and lift myself, using my knees to push up, my forearms glued to his shoulder for balance. He curses under his breath, and I open my eyes to see his squeezed shut.

It's addictive, and I need more. With a ragged, needy gasp, I repeat the motions. Faster, stronger, surer, I ride him as he asked me to. It's heaven, and the more control I have, the more confident I am. It's like breathing fire into my senses.

Grayson flexes around me. His fingers bite into my skin. This is harder and hotter than I thought possible—more than I imagined my body could take and his could give.

I kiss his mouth, bite his lip, and embrace the cataclysmic slide as my climax builds. He smells like soap and tastes sweet. I bury every moan and gasp in a kiss until I can't breathe. My muscles clench, my body rocks. Fireworks sizzle behind my closed eyelids as I come for him, as he pumps and groans just as hard into the kiss.

He flips us over. My back hits the bed, and he pumps into me as he comes. His climax is guttural and delicious. It reignites mine, and in a fury of passion, we're clinging together with our clothes half on, gasping into each other's mouths and riding the wave of insane pleasure.

"I love you." My chest heaves, and I scrape my teeth against his bottom lip.

"Emma." He returns the bite then kisses me just as hard. "Yours forever."

I nod against his neck. "Quickies are nice."

"Quickies are just a promise of what will come," he rasps as we untangle ourselves.

I look around for anything that might help clean up, but this room isn't lived in. There are no real-life creature comforts. "I need to run to the bathroom—" His grin is wicked, and it makes me hot all over again. "What?"

"That was pretty much high school fantasy *numero uno*."

I blush, absolutely sure that my face is several shades past scarlet. "Same."

He laughs and kisses my neck until I'm giggling and shooing him away. For a split second, all of this feels too good to be true. We quickly dress, and he takes my hand and pulls me out of my room. Playfully, Gray swats my butt as I duck into the hall bathroom.

"See you in a minute." I close the door, leaning against it, hugging myself, with an ear-to-ear smile in place. But as soon as the post-orgasm brain fog begins to fade, I realize I sent him to fend for himself amongst the Kingsley pack of wolves—even though most are behaving—and he went without complaint. After what just happened and the conversation with Ryan, I think Grayson's still a true believer that no one can bring us down. All I want to shout is "Hell yeah, amen."

CHAPTER 37

GRAYSON

Night has fallen, bringing with it serenity. Emma's house makes me calm, and after a day with her family—with everyone justifiably looking for a reason to throw their jabs—I need this quiet. She put Cally to bed, and I've continued unpacking boxes, sorting through her things, which look so very Emma. The decorations are often handmade and a little funky. They're reminders of the artsy girl I grew up with. So much is personalized, and her house looks the way I would have pictured it. I work my jaw back and forth, thinking that it also looks as if it could work for *us*.

Cally seems to be taking me in stride, too. We have a connection that makes me believe I'll be a million times the dad Pops was to me. As each hour ticked by today, the kid grew more comfortable hanging on me, which made me fall that much more in love with her.

And her mama. Emma flat-out kills at this mom thing. She really does an amazing job—wiping

Cally's face, wiping her tears, laughing at a joke that no one else seems to understand, and communicating fluently in two-year-old speak. She rolls on the ground with Cally and lets her ride her like a horse. The entire time, Emma smiles, as though she hasn't been struggling to make Cally's life perfect while giving up her own.

"Hey, you." Emma pads in wearing a loose T-shirt and pajama pants that swallow her up. Her face is scrubbed shiny clean, and that wild blond hair of hers is tied into a messy knot on the top of her head. Nothing is trying too hard, and everything about her is gorgeous. She steals my breath when she's not even trying.

"Cally asleep?"

She nods. Then her gaze lands on the notebook I decided against giving her today. It's still wrapped, though the paper is starting to show wear on the edges. "I get to open it yet?"

My gut jumps. I don't know why. It's nothing she doesn't already know. But still, I'm anxious. "If you want. Not a big deal either way."

She giggles and grabs it then jumps on the couch, snuggling into me before I can convince her it's just a silly gift. But it's not, so even as Emma rips the paper to shreds, I bite my lip and wait for her reaction.

Her eyebrows pull up. "You got me a used notebook?"

I chuckle. "Something like that."

"Should I open it?" Her fingers trail over the metal spiral binding.

A long sigh slips through my lips. "No idea."

After holding my gaze, she stares at the notebook then carefully pulls back the cover and leafs through the pages. Not every page is dedicated to an explanation of enlisting. There are rambling notes from Trig and World History, plus some random notes that have nothing to do with right now. I thought about tearing those pages out but decided it would ruin the authenticity of the whole thing. I want her to experience remembering just as I did.

And it's working. Her face softens, and her eyes are laser focused. Her head tilts as she slips back to high school—where we danced around what we felt and where I paid attention to every girl but the one I wanted while she thought the crackling air around us was one-sided. I can almost taste the nervousness of crossing the line, of telling her I was done ignoring us.

Nostalgia hangs over us both as she pages through the notebook.

"I hated Mrs. Rough's World History," she mumbles.

I nod. Emma senses something, probably reacting to my anticipation, and her fingers fidget.

"She wanted me to sit still in class and take notes like this." Her fingers tap on the page. "But I had too much energy to be contained like that. Unlike you, Mr. Perfect Notes Guy."

"Ha. I think I was trying to cover up for something worse at home."

Her face falls. "Wish I'd known more than I did. Or earlier."

"Not a big deal."

She shrugs, blowing off my downplaying of Pops's tendency to beat the crap out of me. I don't want her guilt right now. "Can't corral the creative type with lessons about random medieval battles. Right? You needed to... be dancing or something."

A brief panic crosses her face.

"What?" I'm failing to get her to focus on the notebook.

"Nothing." She shifts before whispering, "What if you came back and hated me?"

"Not possible."

"What if you came back, and I disappointed you?"

"You couldn't."

"But *what if* I did?"

The earnest pleading in her eyes levels me. "Then I'd hate *myself* for being that way, and I'd deal with it." I scoot closer to her and nod toward the notebook. "Keep going."

Her wary eyes relax, and after a long glance, she continues flipping the pages.

There. Her eyebrows furrow as she realizes the notes are to her and what they're about. Then her eyes go wet and shiny. I can almost recite verbatim my many attempts to explain that I'd enlisted, that I didn't want to go, that I'd signed a contract with zero loopholes. Her heavy tear drips onto a page, and her finger traces the side of the loose-leaf notebook.

"Grayson..." She turns page after page, reading my attempt after miserable attempt, giving me nothing now except for an occasional sniffle. But other than that, she's completely silent and lost in her thoughts.

There's a knot in my throat that won't go away. Maybe this wasn't the right birthday present. Maybe—

"You tried to tell me. That night. And this..."

"I wasn't..." Crushing pain in my chest chokes me. "Strong enough to risk losing you."

She closes the notebook and holds it to her chest. Her eyes are bloodshot, her nose red at the tip.

"Maybe this wasn't a great idea for a present."

Another tear slips down her cheek. "It's perfect."

"It's making you cry. Damn sure there's a rule about making your girl tear up on her birthday."

"It's helping me understand. And I'm pretty sure the no-cry rule has exceptions."

"Not likely."

"This"—she hugs the notebook—"makes me feel love down to the very threads of my existence." She burrows closer to me on the couch. "I choose you, Gray, like you've come home to me. Like I chose you then and want us now. What tore us apart had to have happened for whatever reason, and now I'm in your arms forever."

Hugging her to me, I'm not sure we can ever get close enough. "I feel like I have it all."

"Me too."

"What do you think life will hand us next?"

"You should move in here." There's a casual certainty in her voice.

An unnerving calmness runs deep. "Move in here?"

"Fast... but maybe..." She smiles. "You're good with that?"

"Hell yeah, I'm good with that." We're hopping over major relationship steps, but it feels right, almost easy. "First, I told you about that job interview?"

"Yeah."

"I want to be up-front with you. The interview was good, but it gave way to a job... *test*, for lack of a better word. The folks I'd work with, it's not a desk job, and I can't talk about much."

She rests her chin on my chest. "A job you can't talk about?"

"Yeah."

"Like you need a clearance?"

"It's more hands-on than that."

Concern scrunches her forehead. "Is it dangerous?"

I press my lips together, my eyes narrowing, as I try to word what I think might be a truthful answer in my head. "They haven't exactly told me what the job entails. But, who they are—"

"What is it? Like, a security firm?"

"Yeah. They've helped me out since I was discharged from Walter Reed."

"Is that where your truck came from? It doesn't look like you drove it off a showroom lot."

I have to laugh at that. The big, blacked-out, chromed-out fuel guzzler doesn't look very standard. "Yes. It belongs to Titan."

She gnaws on her lip. "So, you'd be in danger?"

"Maybe."

"Like, risk your life every day type danger or... I don't know, something less scary-sounding?"

"If it's what I think it is, there'd be risks."

"You're going to come home from war and just to jump into a job like that?"

"Not if you don't want me to."

She turns her face away and burrows into my arm. "Is it what you want to do, Gray?"

I hold onto her, praying this isn't a deal breaker. I want to provide for her, and working for Titan would do that—very, very well. I miss the camaraderie of a military team, the brotherhood I can't explain and yet still crave. "This is the only thing I know how to do well."

She lies against me quietly as time drifts by. "Anything else you can tell me?"

"There's probably travel."

"How much?" she asks.

"Honestly, I have no idea. And most likely, you wouldn't know where I was going."

Humming against my chest, she sounds as if she's considering the idea. "But you want this?"

"Better than bartending at Seven's or—"

"I hate that place." She studies my face. "But seriously, after everything that you dealt with... *over there*, you want whatever this job is?"

"Good question." My hands smooth over her back. "I have some baggage to deal with."

"Over your team?"

My *dead* team. "Yeah."

"Think you can manage it?"

All of the therapy, the brochures, the stupid pieces of paper where some therapist asked me to circle my emotions that day... there weren't enough options on the page for me even to begin. But in this little house, with my two girls nearby, I know I can face my demons. "I think I can manage it."

"Then I can, too."

CHAPTER 38

GRAYSON

Boys' night out. Job-interview night. I look as if I totally fit in with this group of guys, but it's all for show, and I couldn't feel more out of place than in this bachelor party group. The guys are fine—they're all part of Titan's Delta team and know each other really well. They seem like the kind of guys I'd chill with, throw back a couple beers, and talk about whatever game is on the tube. But since I've been back, readjusting hasn't been easy, and running with this team makes me miss *my* team.

My chest has been tight all day. I left Emma's this morning after breakfast with her and Cally. But the tingle of anticipation has had me pulling at my collar, taking deeper breaths than are needed. Seriously. This isn't something I need to sweat. We're a bunch of guys going to a titty bar, albeit apparently a high-class one, and I'm just gonna sit back and zone out.

I didn't get into details with Emma. Maybe I should have. Hell, I'm not trying to fuck up already.

But it's a job. I'm not headed here to have some stripper grind on my shit.

I hate strippers. They remind me of Pops. His taste in women after my mom died was skank. Cheap vanilla perfume and clear, plastic-heeled shoes. I *hate* this, and we're not even inside yet. Hell, I'm more likely to have a PTSD meltdown from walking around in Pops's slutty world than hanging with a group of men similar to my dead teammates.

Fuck me. I need to take a breath.

"Doing okay, bro?"

I nod at the guy named Ryder. He's Aussie. Says he's a sniper. Acts like it too—cocky dude. I chuckle good-humoredly. The other guys are a fun time, too. Brock, Titan team leader for Delta, is here. There's a guy named Trace who looks too young to have a gold band wrapped around his left finger. Then again, I'm too young to have a woman and a daughter waiting at home for me.

Home.

God, I haven't had one of those in… ever.

I make conversation with a guy named Colin about whether the other dude Javier is getting any pussy tonight. With his face busted up the way it is and the angry scowl every time he looks toward the front door, my vote is no. But I'm the only one voting that way.

The guy to my right, Luke, laughs, shaking his head. "Between the accent, the tats, and the street fighting, Javier found the winning combination for panty dropping."

Right. We cross the parking lot of Emerald's Gentleman's Club. I doubt too much effort is needed for the panty dropping to start.

I take a breath and focus. This is supposed to be fun and games, but it's also a job interview of some kind. Plus, this place isn't far from where I grew up, and Cally and Emma live too close to *anywhere* suspected of selling women. *Sex-trade fuckers.* I stifle a growl as a hand claps down on my back. It ricochets, and a dull stab of pain hits where my weeks-old wound is still healing.

"Ready?" Brock acts as if we're boys, and I suppose he's reading the vibes rolling off me that *aren't* very bachelor-party friendly.

"I'm good." We bump fists right before the blacked-out door opens, and a heavy bass thunders from inside.

Into the belly of the beast we go. I can almost taste the cheap perfume and the itch of glitter. Our goals are simple: size up the staff. Connect them later to any known traffickers. If there's a lead, follow it for information. If there's a chance to build a relationship, milk it. Easy enough.

En masse, we move through the high-roller crowd. It's not as skanked up as I would've guessed, but I still don't like it. There's a general shift as we make our way through. We're big, muscled up, the kind of group that takes no shit. I can feel the eyes on us: strippers sizing up our wallets and security assessing our risk factor. Everyone else just readies to watch a show.

Colin is the groom-to-be, mostly because there were rumblings Brock wouldn't take off his wedding band, that Ryder and Luke would never be able to act off-the-market, and Javier's a no-go because he wants to be here as much as I do. Process of elimination—Colin's our man. We're quickly ushered into a VIP section where a brunette nearly drools over our team as she takes drink orders.

This is all higher class than Pops, but still, it's an in-my-face reminder of how I grew up. I run my hands over my face and into my hair. I want this job badly, and I'm only at a strip club on a random Wednesday night because it means I could bring in a stable income. That's reason enough that I kissed Emma goodbye this morning and told her I'd be back tomorrow.

All day long, we briefed on who Titan thought the runners were and how they were connected. The intel was good, but it had holes that only real life interactions could fill. Delta team is hungry for action, and I have a sense that this job is personal for one of them, but I can't put my finger on it.

Still, I yank at my collar and say thanks when the waitress arrives with the VIP bottle service, placing top-shelf bourbon and vodka within reach. An announcer's salesman voice bleeds through the music. There's the promise of dream-come-true bullshit, like any of these girls would walk off stage and into a guy's lap. The music shifts, blending with it a drumroll beat. The announcer starts in again. *Blah, blah, blah*. It's the main feature. The busiest night of the week for the best Emerald's has to offer. I take a sip of the bourbon, wondering how slowly this night will pass.

The announcer's baritone echoes as my eyes fall on stage to the prettiest, sweetest girl I've ever known. "Welcome to the stage, Ginger Raine!"

ONLY
FOREVER

CHAPTER 39

One Hour Earlier...

Emma

Wednesday night at Emerald's is always packed. Even as I spin circles in my chair, I know that telling Bruno at the last minute is a bad idea. I could fake sick, and then he would *have* to let one of the other girls take my time on stage. But when have I not been honest with him? Never. I think back to my birthday card, in which he mentioned business opportunities. That could be a great conversation opener. Actually, the more I think about that, the more I hope he'll somehow respect my short-notice request.

I don't want to dance anymore. My man is home. Maybe he'll understand that.

Then again, I don't know. Bottom dollar is what makes Bruno tick, and me announcing that I quit at the last minute won't be pretty. I'll just ask him—*no.* This *is not* a request. I don't have a contract, but a pukey nervousness is churning in my stomach. It's only a job in an industry with very high turnover. That's a fact of life. So, quitting is no big deal.

Right. I'm gonna puke all over my favorite black-velvet robe.

Ugh. No, I'm not. But I could use some antacid because I've talked myself into believing this Bruno convo will be such a big deal that it's almost ridiculous.

I take a deep breath and tighten the silk sash over the velvet. The robe reaches high on my neck and dramatically falls to the floor, trailing behind me when I walk on stage as if I'm a queen. It's dramatic, sultry, and sexy. I'm at my best in this ensemble, enhancing it with long, feathery fake eyelashes, smoky makeup, and hair pinned up high. It's a look that is so *not* me but somehow is more me than any other getup I've worn here. No crazy makeup, no spectacular wig—it's just me tonight.

With my matching black heels that give me another six inches and make my little butt look like a serious booty, I make my way toward Bruno's office. That's not his normal hangout at night, but him being there *is* a sign that I'm supposed to find him to talk business. Rarely does he leave the floor when girls are on stage. When he does go backstage, everyone knows because his Rasta-bodybuilder security team tags along.

"Hey." I stop in front of a big guy whom I secretly call Hercules.

"Hold up, Ginger." His hand comes out to stop me.

"Bruno in his office?"

"He's busy."

My very shakable confidence is fading. *I quit. No dancing tonight. I have a boyfriend out of the blue and won't do this behind his back.* Simple enough, but I have to tell Bruno *now*, or this will become a bigger problem. "Please. I'm short on time, and it's important."

He shakes his head. "Later."

Shoot. I square my shoulders back and lift my chin. My game face is on, and I'm ready to talk shop, even if I'm basically in my underwear and holding my favorite hooker heels. "Come on. I need to talk to him." I give a *blink, blink* of the feathery eyelashes. The man doesn't budge. "Please. It's business." *Business* is Bruno's favorite word. No—*money* is his favorite word. Whatever. It doesn't matter. "And it's time sensitive."

His brows bite together, his eyes wary. "Said he had business to talk with you?"

"Yup. I even got a formal invite for the conversation, so..." I gesture to his hand. "Can I get a pass?"

He turns sideways and speaks into his mic. "Bruno?" He shakes his head to say there's no response—which is already obvious.

"Please," I mouth. "So important."

He studies me then nods. "Reggie, you back with Bruno?"

He waits, listening and nodding.

"Ginger says she has an invite." After a long pause, he nods as if he's agreeing with something. "Says a formal invite. So?" Seconds tick by. "Alright."

He's handsome, big, and looks like all of the rest of Emerald's muscle men. We never shared more than a couple of polite words. I wouldn't call us close friends, but when his eyes land on me, he's... searching. A whole new type of worry mixes with what I've already got going on.

"You're sure about this?" he asks.

I bite my lip. "Yes."

"Alright, Ginger. If you're sure." Slowly, he takes a step back.

Jeez.

"Second door on the left."

My eyes narrow as I recall the last time I was down here. That wasn't where Bruno's office was, but whatever. I pull a reassuring breath. Here I go. "Thanks."

The hall's lit poorly, and the walls are painted the color of red wine. I pass the door I recognize as Bruno's office. It's open and still very much looks like his in-use office. But farther down, voices murmur, and there are two security guards standing at the second door on the left. Both look at me with hard jaws and hesitant eyes. *Shit. What the hell is going on?* My stomach twists.

They silently step aside, and I move through the door. There's a velvet curtain that I pull aside and—

What is all this? A plain stage sits in the middle of an open room. The walls look partitioned, and they are deeply shaded. In the middle of the room, in nothing but a thong and heels, is a girl I've never seen before. She's so young. Like, *so* young. She poses, jutting her hip out as if she's modeling, but there's an uncomfortable vibe in the room.

"Sold!" A low voice I don't recognize scares the shit out of me, and I jump, only to have a hand wrap around my mouth. I'm yanked against a stout body and dragged into a dark alcove. As quickly as we go, my eyes can't adjust. I can't see anything, but I recognize the scent of Bruno's clove cigarettes.

"What are you doing in here?" he hisses at me then drops his hand from my mouth, spins me around, and grips my shoulders. His fingers bite into my skin, and he shakes me hard—way hard—and I can't keep my head from jerking.

"Ow, stop," I plead, but he keeps his hold on me.

"Damn it." His accent is heavy as his grip tightens. "What are you doing?"

"I needed to talk to you."

He growls, and I'm trembling. My throat's constricted. Panic and dread blind me. It looks like Bruno's running prostitution rings, and that's a way bigger deal than selling hand jobs upstairs. But the word *sold* in particular freaks me out. I gasp. "That's an auction?"

"That's business. Everything is business. I own many businesses, and you do *not* have permission to traipse your ass down here."

"I just wanted to let you know—I'm sick. The pukes. I've gotta go. Can't do tonight." No way am I quitting unless it's in a bright room in public, surrounded by people. Not when he's shaking me like a rag doll in the dark. "Please. I need to go home."

His eyes narrow in the dim light, and he releases me. Nerves make my hands sweat and my stomach churn. I don't know what's happening down here, but I know it's not legal. A million really bad thoughts run through my mind, starting with the idea that he's selling people and ending with the fact that there are people I didn't know about in the basement, *buying* girls. "Is this the business proposition you had?"

He laughs, releasing my shoulders. "No."

I want to run, but I can't help but try to look back at the stage. "Is she okay?"

"Of course."

"She didn't look it, Bruno."

His dark eyes narrow. "Watch yourself, Ginger."

My gut drops, and I take a step back. "You always call me Emma."

"You're going to go on stage, and we're going to talk about this afterward."

"My stomach—"

"You. Are. Going to go on stage, and we'll talk about this later."

"Bruno," I whisper, knowing I'm completely blocked in by him. Even if I could get by him, he has several of his security guys posted along my way out, and they'd stop me as soon as word of my escape bled through their earpieces. "You're scaring me."

"I think we've both known from day one that I'm a scary motherfucker."

"Not to me, you're not." My eyes burn with tears. "I'm sorry I interrupted."

He remains silent. My knees are shaking.

"Okay, I'll just head upstairs."

He steps wordlessly to the side, and I scurry by him. None of the three guards I passed on the way in slows me down, and I haul ass. Finally, I reach the top of the hall and turn toward my locker and vanity. I rummage through my purse, choke down a few swigs of water, and then do a super-fast redo of my eyes. The girl facing me in the mirror is terrified. I barely recognize myself. I'm suddenly scared that I have no idea what to do.

"Two minutes, Ginger," comes the familiar call from up the stairs.

My hands shake. I call Grayson, even though he's at work on some super-secret job. It rings... rings. *Shit, shoot, shit!* No answer. I have no idea what to say. His voicemail picks up. "Hey. Hi. Um. If I don't talk to you first, I need you to talk to Cherry." I take a long breath and tears sting my eyes. "I love you."

"Ginger! Come on up, girl." The call echoes down the stairs.

Shit. My God. I find Cherry's name and hit Okay. It's ringing.

"Hey, Emma—"

"Something's wrong." My mind spins. "I don't know what's happening here, but—"

"Ginger, get your ass up here now!"

One of Bruno's security guards comes out from the dark hall. "Everything okay?" But there's nothing nice or concerned with his question. His glare says, *Hang up the damn phone.*

I smile. "Just checking on my kid."

I don't know why I feel the need to throw that out there. It's just a quick reminder to everyone that I have loved ones who would notice if I didn't come home. God. I'm totally overreacting. No one's going to kill me or anything. But *shit*—what did I just see?

"Emma?" Cherry's voice is pinched with concern.

"I have to go. Have Ryan pick me up later. Okay? Call Ryan. He's my ride."

"Emma! What's going on—"

I hang up the phone shakily. I'm overreacting. I'm overreacting.

Another guard steps from the dark behind the one glowering at me. Crap. I'm not overreacting. "Just on my way, guys. Jeesh, everyone needs to calm down."

CHAPTER 40

Emma

"Ginger Raine!" the announcer's voice booms.

That's my cue, and I'm not sure how my legs move forward. But they do, one shaky step at a time. My muscles quiver, my stomach churns, and I'm heading for disaster. I can't dance—not now, and hopefully never again on this stage.

Trussed up like a sexy, vampy princess, I move to center stage, completely cloaked from the neck down. The train on the robe spreads behind me as I sway. The music pounds. The lights dim, and shadows dance. Every night I've performed on this stage, I've been heartbroken and purging myself, torturing myself over the man I couldn't stop loving. But now he's back.

I shouldn't be here. But I'm too lost in fear to walk away. My absurd interaction with Bruno has me in a tailspin, and I can't push away my thoughts. Grayson. Bruno. I'm frozen—I cannot move or see. I can't do this job and can't make my body start to dance.

Murmurs from the crowd burn my ears. Laughter

too. The announcer drops a joke—I can't even understand the words. I'm frozen, and my mind runs faster than my thoughts of escape. Consumed by an overwhelming wave of emotion, my mouth dry, I can do nothing but think that I've got to get out of here. The announcer's laughing too, saying I'm a Ginger Raine impostor and calling for the real one.

I know the music. Only seconds have passed by, but it feels like hours since I walked on stage. I fold my arms and hold my sides, and my gaze falls to the VIP faces looking up from center stage.

Grayson Ford stares back at me.

GRAYSON

One second I'm confused and glaring at the stage in disbelief. The next, I'm growling and gripping the wooden railing as I stand, ready to explode.

"Emma?" The word bellows out from my chest.

Hands grab me. Muffled words fall deaf because there's a rush of blood in my ears. That's my girl! *On stage.* None of this makes sense. Sweet, innocent Emma. In what world is this happening? In what world did I *cause* this to happen? *Fuck me*—I want to tear the walls down and maim any man who has ever seen this before.

I fight against the hands that knock me down, swinging my fists for release. I don't look anywhere but on stage. "Emma?"

A fist connects with my jaw, and my head snaps to the side. I wasn't expecting the blow, and it knocks some sense into me. I'm here with Delta. There's a job to do.

But I don't give a shit. I push out of their hold, ready to storm the stage. Brock and Ryder take me down. *Fuckin' A.* I hit the floor. I'll kill this entire team. "Get off me!"

Fists fly. My body growls as I attack, cursing and pleading. The team hits back, keeping me in place until Brock gets me in a choke hold. He leans close. "Get your shit together, Ford."

Not a chance.

Brock flexes his arm around my neck. *Goddamn it.* My pulse slows, and my head pounds. I fight the choke hold until he pushes away, dropping me back.

I fall to the floor again, and Ryder crouches down. "If that's your girl, you've got to pull your shit together."

My eyes swing back to the stage, but she's gone. Close by, Colin and Javier play down the scuffle to security, telling them they've got it under control, and it's just a bachelor party beat-in, an old joke from college.

I jump to my feet and shake it off. My eyes search for Emma, but security steps into my line of sight.

"You good?" he asks.

Fuck, no. "Yeah, man. Fuckin' fine."

He eyes our group. "No more of that shit." But he takes off, muttering in a Caribbean accent, "Fuckin' VIP fuckers."

Ryder slaps me on the back. "Guess you're the groom now."

I need to find her. "No. Got something to do."

Brock's in my face again. "The best thing you can do is play your part. Don't call attention to her, and don't call attention to us. You got me?"

My eyes search the crowd. Nothing. Nowhere. "Where is she?"

Brock hits me in the sternum. "Hey, asshole. Got me or not?"

I can't find her, and all their eyes are on me. An avalanche of worries hits me. What does she know? How could she hide this from me? "I got you."

"Good, because first, we have an in we didn't know about, and second, what you didn't notice was something was wrong with that girl."

Yeah—she got caught. "God," I roar, angry at her, furious with myself. How did this even happen?

"Pull your shit together," Ryder says. "Shit, get yourself a lap dance. Two birds, one stone."

Brock's eyes bounce from Ryder to me, and I watch him mull the idea over before nodding. "Smart move."

"No." I shake my head.

"If you don't, someone else will." Javier laughs, and I lunge for him. He throws his hands up as Brock and Ryder catch me again. "Kidding. Shit, new guy. Calm yourself. Christ."

I pull back from Brock and Ryder, rolling my shoulders. *A lap dance.* Fuck that. Her ass is mine in a private room. "Got a better idea."

Behind me there are a few *shit*s and an *ah, hell.* But I'm out of VIP and heading to find her when our waitress steps in my way. "Where's the girl?"

"Ginger?"

"Don't care what you call her."

She blinks but doesn't move. "Okay…"

"Find her."

"Sure, handsome. Come with me." Making a stupid move, she puts her hand on my arm, and I snap it back. Surprise and maybe concern colors her face. "Just wait in there."

I follow her gaze, and I seethe. My teeth gnash, and my mind tumbles. Has Emma been in there?

Doing what? God. Fuck me. What the hell do I know about her? I can't handle this, and even though I stomp toward the room, I'm still reeling. The private room is dark and warm. The light is dim, and there's an armless chair, almost like a bench, and blood thumps in my neck as I drive myself insane wondering and questioning who has been in here with her.

The door opens and the love of my life, dressed the same as she was on stage, walks in, face toward the floor. Her shoulders slump, and my heart falls. It's really her.

Anger consumed me until I could reach out and hold her, and now—I'm broken. Devastated to the point I can't breathe.

"I'm sorry." It's a whisper from her sweet voice, and it's my undoing.

I roar deep from the depths of my soul. It's a primal growl that must shake the damn building. I rip my fists into my hair and drop to the seat.

"Emma. What the fuck? What the fuck? Goddamn it…" I turn my head up, and she's watching me, eyes sad and tears sliding down her cheeks. I crash through the lump in my throat, and once more, but this time in a hoarse whisper, say, "What the fuck?"

Her delicate hand wipes away the tears, and she carefully takes a step forward. "I was going to tell you."

"Why?"

She bites her lip. "Please yell at me later. Leave me later—"

"Ems—"

"I'm in trouble."

My skin prickles. "What?"

She looks above my head, around the room. "I tried to leave."

"You're forced here?"

"No."

"No? Christ. Fuck, Emma, why?"

"I saw—" She cuts herself off and steps closer. "Why are you here?"

"Work."

She pinches her eyes closed. "Don't leave me. No matter how mad you are, please, please don't leave me here alone."

"What the fuck is going on?"

Again, her eyes dart above me. She's guarding herself, watching her words.

Knock, knock, knock.

Emma pivots to the door, trembling enough that I can see it despite her clothes. "Shit."

I push through the anger, the guilt, and all of the questions about her past and concentrate on the scared girl in front of me. "What's going on?"

"Just act normal."

CHAPTER 41

Emma

"Act normal?" Grayson's raw voice rakes over me, and I watch him transform into a super-scary alpha dude as the door handle turns.

We have exactly half a second to pull this off. "Normal," I answer.

I run my hands over my cheeks to wipe away rogue tears, and then I thread my fingers into my hair while moving my hips. Whoever comes through that door will see me dancing, not acting terrified of Bruno or emotional over the man in front of me. Truth is, I've never been more vulnerable in lace and heels than at this moment. The walls of the tiny room close in on me, and I'm doubly concerned about the hidden camera. Someone's always watching. My body moves, but my gaze is frozen on Grayson. His twisted expression makes me feel as though he doesn't even know me—because he doesn't. Not anymore.

I want to cry. I want to run past security and forget whatever I saw downstairs. But instead, I hold my head high, faking it to keep myself safe. I can do this—I've danced for Gray every Wednesday for years. I step closer to him as the door opens wide.

One of Bruno's men clears his throat, as though I don't already know he's here. "Everything okay in here, Ginger?"

I take a deep breath and hope for a miracle: that I don't look terrified of the Emerald's thugs or shell-shocked over Grayson. I tilt my head and give my most sultry, sinful smile, dropping my voice playfully low. "Think so. We're just getting acquainted. Aren't we, baby?"

"This can't be happening," he whispers against my ear.

With as much sexiness as I can manage, I place my hand on Gray's chest and turn to look at him, batting my eyes and hoping to God he plays his part. Otherwise, they'll call the session quits and pull me backstage. At least, security will *try* to remove me; I have no idea how Grayson would handle that. The amount of testosterone in this tiny space is overwhelming from these two massive men.

But security backs down. "Flag if you need something, Ginger."

"We're good. Aren't we, honey?" I bat my fake eyelashes and will Grayson to agree. We can make it through this.

Grayson growls some kind of agreement, and Muscle Man nods to me. I smile as if this is just any other Wednesday at work.

"Alright." He closes the door, and Gray and I are alone. Except for that camera.

I know what I should be doing, but the look on his face says not to. "They're watching," I say.

He growls. "What do you mean, you're in trouble?"

"I mean if I don't give the lap dance of the century right now, I'm in big effin' trouble. Gray. Please."

"I hate this."

I lean closer. "You're at work, too. So, we should work."

God—despite everything that is going on, I still notice he smells fresh, like soap, and I roll my lip into my mouth. It'd be completely absurd in this situation to feel *any* arousal. But with Gray protecting me, and all this intensity, I'm not *un*affected. Oh boy... I close my eyes, and the low base of the music that surrounds us rolls over me. "You said you wanted me to dance, and here I am."

"Not like this, and you know it."

I move my hands to his temples, fluttering my fingers to the edge of his blond hair, then slide my palms to his cheeks. The strain in his jaw radiates as I continue touching him, moving down to cup his neck and letting my thumbs smooth over his throat. His pulse pounds under my skin. "Camera, Grayson. Play your part."

He's so tense. "Emma—"

The show must go on, whether he's game or not. Swaying my hips with the slow beat, I take his hands from his lap and drag them to my side then to the sash on the robe. I'm nervous, and this is unexpectedly... arousing. He doesn't want to be here, and neither do I. But there's a rush of emotion screaming for us both to release. I can't explain why, but this is more than a set of practiced moves. This is my dream. This has been me dancing for him forever, and now it's really happening. My mouth waters, and my heart rate increases. "Right now, I'm Ginger." My robe hangs open, and I smooth my fingers over my stomach and up to my breasts. His eyes lock onto me, and I see it—the war within him. Grayson likes this as much as he hates it. I push his knees and move between his thighs then press him back against the chair. "Relax."

"I can't—"

My mouth is next to his ear, my fingers toying with his hair. "Let me dance for you. Not because I'm scared to leave this room." My tongue catches his ear lobe. "Not because your new job means you have to roll with it."

"No."

"This is my fantasy, Gray. How I survived while you were gone."

His body goes rigid under me. "I didn't—"

"You didn't know. I know, baby. Stop saying that." I back away from him and drop my robe. His eyes burn over me, and I know he'll give me the answer I want, because no matter how angry or frustrated he is, this is Gray and I. I refuse to let him continue beating himself up over *our* mistakes. I bear responsibility too, because I could've told him about my life. I could've found him—and done more than hope and dream about him. "Gray, don't you know? No matter where in the world you were, what you did, or how long it's been, I've existed for you to come home to again."

I straddle his lap and kiss him—deep and hard. I refuse to let him tell me different. I won't pull away from this kiss. I'm dying for his tongue, for him to take my mouth with just as much need as I have. Excitement has made me dangerously oblivious to what's happening outside this room. My fingers curl into his shirt, and I roll my hips, begging and daring him to want me right now.

"Fuck me," he says against my kiss. Then he owns my mouth and grips my sides. "Can't stay away from you."

I'm consumed by his kiss, drunk on the powerful, almost painful hold he has on me. Raw hunger unleashes from his body, and if I thought I was in charge—*I was wrong.*

I shiver, excitement rolling across my body from my shoulders down to my ankles. My eyes shut as he bites my lip and flexes his hips, holding me down, making me groan in insane need as I rub against his erection.

"God, Ems…"

His massive chest rises and falls in a way that matches mine. We're a shade away from gasping and panting. "I love you, Gray." Such sweet words in a filthy place. "As much as you love me."

"Hold that thought because you might forget that in a minute."

What?

Grayson's hands lock on my bottom, and he squeezes. Hard. *Oh, God.* My back arches, and the bite of pain from his strong grip makes me fly high. He grinds me against his shaft, and the friction is far more than a tease.

"Because I am furious." He bites against my shoulder, drags his teeth up my neck.

My mind spins. I can't think, so I act only on instinct. "Holy shit."

One of his hands runs up my spine. The other drops lower. I'm writhing in place, dizzy over him. Not once have I ever been turned on at Emerald's. Every move, every tease was mechanical, but this is extraordinary.

"What else don't I know about you?" he growls.

All I can do is moan—and then I remember where we are. I should stop and remind him I need rescuing, but I can only think of the needy ache building in me. "There's a camera in here."

"Behind you or me?" He bites my shoulder.

"You," I gasp as bites harder.

Quickly, he stands up, his head swerves, then he grabs the nearly hidden camera and rips it free. "Done."

Well, *shit, shoot, shit some more.* Bruno won't be happy about a dead camera in a private room, but Grayson unbuckles his jeans, and I don't care about anyone outside this room. I've had too many years of dreaming about Gray in Emerald's.

He falls to the chair, taking me with him. My legs wrap around him, and my arms do too. I'm surrounded by him, burrowed against his chest, and his hands slide over me as though I'm God's gift to him.

"Pretty mama," he whispers against my ear and pulls my thong to the side. "I need in you."

"Yes." The blunt head of his shaft presses against me. I'm already so wanting that I can't wait another minute.

He squeezes me tight then pushes into me, spearing me, stretching me, making me cry out for more. Grayson drives back then thrusts his massive self back in.

"Damn, woman." His growled words don't sound as if they are mine to hear. But I don't just hear them—I feel their vibrations. They make my nipples harder and set my most sensitive muscles on fire. "You're my world. You know that?"

He sinks deep into me again, and I gasp. I hang on and clamp my mouth to his neck. Grayson pounds into me. The fury and heartbreak are there with each slam of his body into mine. The roughness—the greedy, starving need that he takes me with—is addictive. As his harsh breath burns against my skin, I climb faster, past the point where I can handle it. *Ah, oh, God.* "Grayson!"

I moan, come, and cry his name through clenched teeth. His heartbeat explodes against my chest as he comes, too. We're knotted together, breathing as one and surviving a high so dark it's spectacular.

"Love you," I murmur against his skin. "I love you more than I can understand."

He catches my mouth in a kiss that's as harsh as it is sweet. I'm lost in him and completely exhausted.

Knock, knock. "Hands off the girl unless you pony up some cash," Bruno's voice bleeds through the door.

Oh, shit.

CHAPTER 42

Emma

Before I can say no and try to explain to both men that there's nothing to see here, Gray sets me to the side. We quickly right our clothes, and a second later, the door slams open. Bruno stands there, glaring and assessing.

Grayson folds his arms over his chest. "Got a problem?"

"Know anything about my camera?" Bruno's thick accent rolls off his tongue.

Gray's body language shifts, and he acts as though he couldn't care less about doing a stripper. "Not a fan of an audience."

"Not your decision."

I step forward. "Come on, Bruno. You know I *just* dance."

Bruno's eyes narrow, assessing Grayson, then me. "Finish up."

"We're good," Grayson offers. He turns to me, angling away from Bruno, an odd expression playing on his face. I can't figure out what he's thinking. My mind's still climax-clouded, and I'm suddenly shaking, not wanting to be alone with Bruno.

"Thanks for the dance." He doesn't kiss me but does brush the hair away from my ear, lean close, and whisper, "Back to work. I'll get eyes on you—no worries."

Then he walks away without another word, brushing past Bruno and leaving me uncomfortable under my boss's intense study.

Bruno cracks his knuckles, making the process last forever, and then shoves them back into his pockets. "We need to talk about what you saw."

"I didn't really see anything, and I'm still sick. So, I'll just—"

He shakes his head and opens the door to let in one of the security guys I rarely see. It's a very cramped space, and I take a step back, but his hand lands on me. My feet don't move, yet we're all still moving through the door together as they drag me out.

"Hey, guys." I struggle in his hold. "Let me go."

There's no response, but we're moving away from Emerald's open floor and toward a set of back stairs that only Bruno and his muscle use. *Shit. Shoot. Shit.* Bruno is going to... I don't know what, but it's very bad.

"Think the girl said to let go, asshole," Grayson's voice booms from behind me.

Thank you! I turn toward him, elbowing the guy on my arm. He shakes me, and the twist on Grayson's face says he's about to kill everyone here.

"Not your girl to worry over." Security lifts me and turns.

A gut-twisting roar comes from behind me, and I'm flung to the side as Grayson rips between

Muscles and me. I skitter back, then I spin to leave but slam into a solid wall of man. Dread washes over me. When I look up, I see it's not one of Bruno's Rasta security guys. He picks me up *and hands* me to another—equally big—guy.

"Aren't you a pretty thing," he says casually. He sounds so out of place, especially with his Australian accent, that I have no idea what is happening. I'm in his arms after being passed away from Bruno, and I still feel out of control but not about to die.

The Australian guy nods to someone. "Let's go."

I turn for Grayson, but he's squared off with Bruno and security. What other choice do I—?

"Put. Her. Down," a voice bellows from behind me.

Oh, God. That sounds way too much like my brother. My stomach bottoms out. I roll myself into a ball against the unknown Australian guy. None of this makes sense except—*oh shit*—I remember that I pulled the emergency lever and told Cherry to get Ryan to get me out of here. I pop my head up, praying that my ears are tricking me. *Oh. Shit. Shoot. Shit.* Ryan's out of uniform, with his badge clipped to his jeans and two *very* large guns strapped to his side.

"Put her down, so help me—" His hand is on his holstered gun. "Emma, come here!"

The Aussie blond looks down. "You know him?"

"My brother."

The look on his face says *Oh, shit,* but he tells me, "Alright then."

From out of nowhere, security surrounds Ryan from behind. My brother's an intimidating guy, and there's pure, one hundred percent rage on his war-ready face. We're in a small area full of large, violent-looking men who seem ready to fight to the death. The Aussie edges back with me still in his arms.

Grayson and the other man push toward Ryan till the three of them stand shoulder to shoulder. But they're outnumbered two-to-one.

"I have an agreement," Bruno says. "No badges in here."

"You don't have an agreement with me, asshole." Ryan squares his shoulders. "If my sister wants to leave, she gets to leave."

Bruno swerves toward me. "Brother's a cop?"

The Aussie's protective hold on me tightens, reassuring me, and the dark-haired guy next to Grayson steps in front of me. "Girl goes, place closes down early tonight. We sort shit out."

Bruno shakes his head. "Nothing to sort out."

Aussie guy shifts again, and he's slowly extracting us from what seems ready to be a bloodbath. Bruno casually lifts his wrist toward his mouth. I know that move! Communicating with his behind-the-scenes guys. *Shit*—this is so bad.

I don't know Aussie from a hole in the wall, but Grayson said he was interviewing for a security job with good men. He's protected me so far, so I turn to him and whisper, "There was a girl downstairs. I wasn't supposed to see her."

His blue eyes study me for a second then jump to the guy in front of me. "Boss."

The dark-haired guy pivots, keeping his eye on Bruno. "Yeah."

Aussie and dark-haired guy exchange a look, a passing of information with a shift of their hands and eyes.

Bruno watches them then shouts into his mic, "Close it down."

"Shit," the Aussie says casually, even though we're suddenly moving fast. He dives us behind a table.

Noise explodes from where we were seconds

ago—flesh hitting flesh, people the size of mountains wrestling each other to the ground.

A new guy ducks under the table with us. "Talk fast."

It's another accent—South American maybe. His face has fading bruises. Are all these guys ready to throw punches or what? *Okay. Talk fast. Um.* I struggle with my thoughts. "There was a girl in a room downstairs, and I didn't recognize her. But I heard *sold*..." My stomach drops all over again. "Like she was *being* sold."

His swollen eyes narrow. "You saw a prostitute?"

"Bruno lets girls pro here if they want. This was more like an auction."

"Fucking confirmation." He shakes his head. He rambles into his wrist faster than I can speak then turns to me. "Good girl. I'm Javier. That's Ryder. Welcome to our world, gorgeous."

CHAPTER 43

GRAYSON

It started as three of us versus them. We could have handled it. Then the rest of the team showed up and quickly ended the brawl. Ryan's badge was surprisingly helpful, but when all was said and done, he and I weren't on the team that was going to wrap up this job. I was on a trial run for a job I'm now never going to get, and he didn't need to be in the mix.

Delta goes off to do whatever Delta does behind the scenes, and I head toward a table where Javier and Ryder have safely stowed Emma. Emerald's is chaotic. People are evacuating—men running for their cars, strippers running for their clothes. The place is wild, and my girl's upset and being calmed by two guys I don't know. I'm grateful they're here, but enough of that.

I hop over a railing, and when she sees me coming toward her, Emma's face lights up. *Damn.* Man, that reaction does something to me deep inside. Forgetting about the two men standing guard beside her, I scoop her into my arms, pressing her head to my chest. I need to feel her and hear her voice to know she's alright.

"You're good, pretty mama?"

She nods. Then she sniffles.

God—not okay. Of course, she's not okay. I don't know specifics on why she thought she was in trouble earlier, but if it has anything to do with why Delta is here, I'm going to shred whoever scared her.

Stroking her hair, I drop my chin to the top of her head and eye the guys. "We're good. Thanks."

Ryder angles his head toward where the team disappeared. "Brock's gonna want to talk to her."

I nod. "Later."

Emma pulls back and turns to both men, smiling weakly. "Thank you for... that."

Javier nods, gives her a fist bump to the shoulder, and walks away.

Ryder crosses his arms over his chest. "Shitty circumstances, darlin', but we were serious. Nice to meet you."

"Thanks." She relaxes against me again, but her fingers touch the side of my face, where I'm sure a bruise or two is forming. "That fight sounded like it hurt."

My lip pulls into a half grin, and I laugh quietly. "Didn't think about it, I guess."

She shifts, and her fingers tangle with mine. "Your knuckles are bleeding."

"Shit. Sorry." I wipe them on my pants. "Fixed."

"Tough guy." But she genuinely smiles this time.

Across the room, Ryan is talking with a few cops. They look buddy-buddy, but then his gaze lands on me and slides to Emma. He shakes hands with the men and heads our way. "I take it Ryan didn't know, either."

"No," she whispers.

"He's ten feet away and gaining."

Emma groans. "Oh, God. This is going to—"

"Emma." Ryan's voice is low with concern. "Can we talk?"

"—suck." She slumps against me.

I hang onto her, catching his eye. He'd better watch his ass on this conversation. If I can deal with this, so can he.

"Ems?" I squeeze her.

She doesn't turn toward him. "Everyone's going to be so disappointed."

"No one's disappointed." I say it for her benefit, but loudly enough that Ryan could hear. So help me God, if he says anything to make this worse for her, the truce we have will be called off in a heartbeat.

Emma

"I can't look at him." It's not that I'm embarrassed about what I did. I've made hard decisions, and I own the consequences. But that there is something going on that feels so wrong, and I was so close to it... never seeing it. That Ryan and Grayson had to get into a brawl to save me—*that* humiliates me. I've never been helpless.

Ryan puts a hand on my shoulder. "You okay?"

"Fine." But I still won't look at him.

"Ems," Grayson murmurs into my ear. "Talk to him."

I was in tears when I first saw Grayson—when I connected the guy in the crowd to my Grayson and registered the shock and anger and *What the motherfuck?* look on his face. Now, I turn to face my brother, who looks every bit as menacing as Grayson and has the same fight marks swelling on his face. My throat stings from emotion, and I can't swallow because of the guilt about what I failed to notice all the time I was working here.

"Hey." I roll my bottom lip into my mouth.

Gray shifts me to a chair. "Yeah, so I'll let you two talk."

My fingers flex into his shirt. I don't want him to leave me.

"No, it's fine." Ryan pulls up a chair and drops into it. "Gray can stay. I get it."

Gray nods and slides me onto a chair across from Ryan. The tension kills me, and I'm expecting the worst.

You're a slut.

You're stupid.

I'm disappointed.

I'm disgusted.

But Ryan just stares. Finally, he runs a hand over his face. "Talked to Cherry. She gave me some details."

Aw, shoot. I have no idea what Cherry would have said, so I bite my lip and wait, hoping he'll keep going. His gaze flicks to Grayson then back to me. "Obviously, whatever you do to pull in some cash, that's yours to decide. Same with Cherry. Not my business."

My eyes go wide, and I can only imagine what Cherry said—or threatened—to make our brother stick to that kind of non-Ryan response.

"For real, though—you're okay?" he asks.

I shrug. "I don't know. What about you? Are you—" *mad, embarrassed, pissed* "—working?"

"Kind of. There's a bit of a..." He looks away, as

though searching for the right word. "Jurisdiction problem."

"What do you mean?"

Grayson clears his throat. "Folks I came here with have an off-the-books federal contract on a sex trafficker—"

My back jolts straight. My mind reels. "Wait. What?" He stares at me as if I'm insane, and I turn to Ryan. Same look. "What do you mean *trafficker*?"

Ryan's eyebrows raise, and I see he's lofting the question to Grayson.

My stomach churns. "Bruno had some girls turn tricks. Occasionally. Not everyone. *Never me.*" I blink, dumbfounded. I don't condone prostitution—but to each her own. But maybe I was wrong—really, really wrong. "That's it. Right?"

Gray's head shakes slightly. "Don't think so, baby."

Move over, stomachache. A surge of nausea hits me. "But I know the girls here. No one was forced." Or maybe they were? I was always different, and no one ever stuck around long.

Ryan shifts in his chair. "Looks like it's airing out a couple of dirty cops, too. I don't know. No one's telling this rookie cop shit."

"I'm not stupid..." I can't comprehend this. "I *am* so stupid. Oh, God."

"You're not, baby." Grayson's placating voice doesn't make me believe him.

"I *didn't* know. Until today—oh, God. The girl on the stage. Did they—" I'm not sure what to ask. Was she... sold without her consent? I knew it was wrong. Bad. But it didn't occur to me that she was like—I don't know—*stolen* and forced. "I'm going to be sick."

Quickly as I can, I'm out of Grayson's arms and running toward a bathroom. I hover in the stall and wait to throw up. But I can't get sick. It's just an overwhelming, disgusting hold on me that I can shake.

"What the hell!" I hit the divider wall as hard as I can but don't feel better. I kick the door, and it slams shut just to bounce open again. "Ahhh," I scream then collapse on the toilet seat and completely lose it.

I sob into my hands, unable to breathe for how hard I'm choking. For years, I thought I had everything so under control, and now, under my nose, this is happening. It's disgusting, and those women didn't have a choice. I can't imagine how scared or angry or fucked up they have to be. Drugged? Blackmailed? Kidnapped? I cannot wrap my mind around it.

Knock. "Emma?" Ryan asks tentatively from the bathroom door.

"Go away."

Minutes of crying pass, and there's another knock. Footsteps that I know are Grayson's come to the stall. "Ems, baby, you okay?"

"Please just leave me alone." I sniffle. "Please."

He ignores me and knocks on the stall door. "I'm worried about you."

"Don't be. Just go away." I don't think I've cried in years, and this—no, everything—is just too much to keep in. I want to be alone.

He bumps his fist against the door twice. "Alright, but I'm right outside the door if you need me."

"'Kay."

He leaves me, thank God. I hate how naive I've been. Traffickers? I'm so, so stupid.

Finally, I slump. The motion-controlled lights turned off long ago, and the room is eerily quiet—until the damn door opens again, and the lights click back on. "Go," I choke out, "away."

"Can't do it, sweetheart."

Sarah. *Oh, God.* The stall door swings open, and there stands my best friend—in her pajamas and sneakers. Faster than I can thank her for showing up, she pulls me out of the stall.

"Ryan called, and I met Grayson. So, we have *a lot* to talk about. But first, are you okay?"

Tears burst out. "No."

She wraps me into a hug that I feel down to my toes. "Okay, it's okay."

"I'm so stupid."

"No. You didn't know. And you've been running yourself a thousand miles an hour. The only thing you focused on was Cally, not investigating the ills of the world."

"I should've known. I turned a blind eye to a lot of things."

"You can't be the moral compass to everyone you meet."

I bite my lip. "I don't know anything anymore. Grayson was dead, and now he's not. Bruno's a dick, but really, he's a *sex trafficker*? I mean, come on. Who misses stuff like that?"

"Sweetheart. Stop."

"I feel like the stupidest person alive."

Sarah shakes her head. "Cherry danced here. No red flags. Ryan said something about an Internal Affairs investigation. So cops must have been in on it. There are beefy military dudes here who were undercover, so I say lots of people had no idea about what was going on."

I sigh, letting her logic take hold. "Where's Bruno?"

"I don't know."

"I don't know what to do, Sarah. I don't want to talk to Gray, and I don't want to see Ryan."

"I think we start with getting you out of this

striptastic getup and into some jeans or something. Plus, those are two *very* worried guys who have been perched a dozen feet away from this restroom, waiting for you to come out. I would've paid to see you chase off their efforts, by the way."

I drop my head. My eyes are swollen, and my makeup must be smeared to hell. I long ago pulled off my fake eyelashes. "I need to wash my face before I go out there."

Scrubbing in the sink without makeup remover is fruitless. After two minutes of that, I look so much worse. I shake my head and point to my red nose and puffy eyes. "Hot."

"Eh, not as bad as you think." Sarah laughs. "And let's just take a second to say... Grayson is just as hot, maybe hotter, than your brother." She throws her hands in the air. "No. I don't want to hear that I'm not allowed to say that. There's a time and a place for such admissions, and when Ryan's all growly tough guy with big-ass guns strapped to his hip—let's forget he's your brother for a second so I can point out that, oh my effin' shit, he does that look well."

I have to laugh. "Oh, too much."

"Never thought him calling me in the middle of the night would end like this. But I'll take it."

I close my eyes and ignore the dull, throbbing headache that has started. "Alright. Let's go."

She opens the bathroom door, and there's a lineup waiting for me: Ryan—guns and a badge on his waist—standing next to the hot guy with dark hair and tattoos, who is next to an older-but-still-hot man with dark hair, and finally, there's Grayson—chiseled, brooding, and personifying the word alpha. Four men who look ready to kill.

"Holy mother of hotness," Sarah whispers. "I just died and went to bad-boy heaven."

Chapter 44

GRAYSON

My molars might shatter for how hard I'm grinding them. My head hurts from the last few hours, but especially after Emma hid out in the bathroom. Ryan didn't stand a chance, but his call-in-the-best-friend ploy deserves a little credit. Sarah popped into the bathroom and came out with a beautiful, albeit exhausted and distraught-looking, Emma Kingsley.

Damn. In that second, I want my name on hers more than I want to breathe. Emma *Ford.* That is how it should be.

I take a harsh breath and clench my fists, trying to focus on the situation at hand. Ryan and I were joined by Brock. Soon after that, the man who gave me a thumbs-up at Titan arrived. Turned out he—Jared—owns that whole company. Both dudes didn't give a shit what any of the cops said, and with the exception of Ryan, they cleared the badges out of Emerald's when Bruno and his gang of thugs were arrested.

All I know is Delta got to work tearing the place

apart, looking for intel and whatever else without me. Big surprise. Fight in VIP? Check. A fuck-off from the team because I was sticking close to my girl? Check.

I quickly move to Emma and claim her from Sarah's side. Both girls have wide eyes. Maybe they weren't expecting us to be waiting, but that's how it goes. Titan has questions that only Emma can answer, and I'm not leaving her side. Neither is Ryan.

"Come on." With her under my arm, I guide her to the main seating area, where the lights have been turned up.

"Hang on, buddy." Sarah takes her other arm. "We'll be back."

"Em—"

Sarah scowls. "Seriously, Grayson, give her a minute. We've got to get cleaned up."

"I'm fine," Emma offers. "I want to change."

I narrow my eyes. I know that she'll be fine, but I don't want to let go. Still, I do. "Do your thing. We'll be here."

The two women disappear, and Brock and Jared grab a seat and huddle over a discussion they obviously don't want us to be part of. I exhale hard, out of frustration more than exhaustion, then turn toward Ryan. We haven't spoken, other than the necessary conversation points.

I rock back on my heels. "So, a cop, huh?"

He nods. "Always the plan."

I nod too. "Right."

Ryan shifts then runs his hands through his hair. Slowly, he shakes his head. "I didn't know this crap."

Bet not. "Seems like if that girl keeps a secret, she does it well."

Ryan breaks his scowl with a harsh laugh. "Yeah,

maybe." His eyes jump past me, and the girls' voices enter the room before they do.

They walk in, Emma in jeans and a T-shirt. She's wiped the streaks of makeup off her face, but her red eyes are still puffy. Her smile has resurfaced though. It's more confident than I would've expected. I don't know why I expect her to still be shaken. I should have remembered that Emma's a fighter. She's resilient.

"Alright." Jared stands and walks her way. "You met Brock." He gestures with his head toward the Delta team leader. "I'm Jared Westin. I want to know what you know. Let's chat."

The man has an edge that shows the world he'd kill first and ask questions later. But in that grumbling request to talk, there's something about the way he asks that implies that she should trust him.

Emma nods, and Jared looks to me as though seeking my permission. Fuck if I know why. He hasn't said more than five words to me. There's no way I have this job, so why does he care? But I nod.

Sarah wanders over to us as Emma joins them on the other side of the room. I glance around. Not a damn good thing has ever come out of these places. I hate them. Just when my molars are grinding again, Sarah squares up to me.

"Hey, we need to talk." This little girl half my size and weight has her hands on her hips, and she's scowling at me as if I were the one with a secret stripper job.

My eyebrow rises. "About?"

"You. Buddy."

Christ. Over Sarah's shoulder I catch a glimpse of Ryan fighting a laughing smile. *Shit.* I paint on a smile and get ready for whatever comes my way. "Alright, sweetheart. I'm game to talk."

"Oh, no way, Mister Back In the Picture. I'm immune to the looks-and-charms thing you have going on, and I'm crazy happy for Emma and—" She catches herself, momentarily slowing her lecture-slash-ass-chewing.

"Cally," I volunteer.

Her eyes narrow. "I'm crazy happy for them, but if you hurt her, I'll find a way to destroy you."

Part of me would rather defend myself to her, but I get it. Actually, I'm glad Emma has a girl like Sarah at her back. "If I hurt her, you won't have to bother. Those girls are my world."

"I won't let her get burned twice."

Ryan walks over, watching Sarah. "Easy, killer."

That defense is unexpected, but he seems to know how to disarm her. She takes a step back even though the expression on her face says she'd rather take a step toward him. Then her finger bobs from one of us to the other. "If either of you gives her hell for this, I'll put you in the ground."

Ryan rolls his lips together. "Got it, gangsta." Then he adds a sincere smile. "No one plans to jump on her case."

Alright. Okay. Emma's brother will keep his cool, and I'll find a way to handle my own feelings about finding my girl here. I release tension I didn't even realize I was holding. After seeing how Ryan reacted to my homecoming, I had no idea how he would deal with this. My wager would've been on *not well*, so his admission to Sarah is a shocker.

"And the two of you." Her finger bobs back and forth between Ryan and me again. "If you act like assholes to each other, it *will* hurt her. Then I'll have to find a way to take out *both* of you, and really, I'm not cut out for this dropping-bodies stuff."

I have to bite my lip. I have no idea if this girl is

for real or Emma's version of my crazy friend Mazie. But Ryan moves to her side, hooks her under his arm—which makes her blush and smack his chest—and laughs. "It'll be okay, Sarah."

"No cute stuff, Ryan. I'm immune to you." She ducks away, leaving us to watch her, but then she looks over her shoulder. "I need to call Cherry and tell her everything is okay."

Glad I'm not the one calling Cherry, I nod. Ryan waves. She's left us with our hands in our pockets, standing awkwardly.

"Immune, huh?" I joke, trying to alleviate the uncomfortable tension.

Ryan chuckles. "I wouldn't say one hundred percent."

I glance around, not sure what else to say. He shifts in his boots and clears his throat. We could stand on opposite sides of the room and waste time on our phones or something. But we're stuck. *Shit.* Honestly, I miss the guy. If I'd ever had a brother, it would've been him.

There's a tightness in my chest because I'll never say those words, but losing him as my brother has been a heavy burden. There's been too much loss in my life. I lost my team, lost my time with the woman I love, and lost the early years with my baby girl. And all because I couldn't open my damn mouth.

The muscles in the back of my head strain, locking up my neck and shoulders. My palms tingle and sweat. I'm slowly being sucked back into the darkness of all I've abandoned, everyone I've hurt. My throat aches and burns. I want to swallow. I need to take a breath. But I *will not* lose my shit in the middle of a fuckin' strip club.

Mind over matter.

Gray spots blur my peripheral vision, and my chest feels pinched.

Once upon a time, Ryan was my brother. I have fucked up life to the point where I can't fix it. *Shit.* I pull a breath through my teeth. *Fuck me. Fuck me. Goddamn.* This will not happen now.

I pinch my eyes closed as my heartbeat slams in my chest so loudly the whole damn establishment must think there's a mortar attack. I push myself to pivot away from Ryan and squeeze my eyes tighter than before.

Mortar attack... the blasts, the blood—morbid memories floor my senses. It's all I can concentrate on. I picture Maddox's face as he reached for me—as if I could save his life. *Goddamn it.*

My fists ball in my pockets until I think my hands will crush themselves.

A hand claps hard on my back. I'm in a complete spiral, falling apart within eyeshot of those I am desperate to impress. I stagger away in the same direction Sarah went. I can't clear my head enough to look for an exit, but I need to escape. My steps wobble—I know they do. I can't stop that. But I growl forward, focusing on my breaths and footsteps, trying to survive this moment.

That hand claps my back again, even though I'm moving. At least, I think I am. *Shit.* This is so bad. But I have complete tunnel vision and can only follow Sarah's way out.

A weight leans against me—no, I lean against it. Somehow, I move with purpose toward the back hall, away from Emma, away from Titan and Delta. They don't need to see this. My head hangs low. I'm panicked and ashamed, but when I look up—it's Ryan.

I seal my eyes shut. My breaths heave through my clenched teeth.

"Open your eyes, man."

Anguish and anger torment me—I can hear the explosions ripping my team to bloody pieces—and I can't get away from my own mind. I can't stop thinking about everything I've screwed up.

"I've got you, brother." The words are quiet. But *God*, they are strong.

His hands are on my shoulders. My mind desperately wants to stop living in the past. My knuckles ache, and the pain centers me and tears me away from their last breaths... *I've got you, brother.* My heart slowly slides from my throat, and I take what feels like the first breath I've had in days. Then I take another, and I open my eyes.

Ryan drops his hands and backs away a few steps. We're alone. I fill my lungs completely and drop my head back. "Fuck me."

Seconds tick by...

"It was bad over there." He doesn't really ask me but just kind of acknowledges the hell I lived.

I nod. "Yup."

"That happen a lot?"

I don't answer.

He looks toward the lit end of the hall, where it opens to the main floor. "No one noticed."

I drop my gaze to my shoes. "I've fucked my life so many ways, I don't know how to fix it."

"Nah. It's fixable." Ryan shifts, shaking his head, and crosses his arms. "We both care about her."

I nod.

"And we both carry a huge burden for her."

I have to laugh. It comes out sad and angry. "Think I've got you beat on that one."

"Yeah." He tilts his head back. "See, this is where I fucked up: back in high school, I was a cocky ass. You too. Right? And she was—God, Emma's always been so sweet... I didn't get you and her. I liked it and wanted that, 'cause it made her happy, but I didn't see... the whole thing." He sighs and knocks his head against the wall. "When you were gone, I could have killed you. When she cried on my bed—it slaughtered me. And that conversation, that she was knocked up... shit."

A lump forms in my throat.

Ryan clears his voice. "I forgot that you and I were boys. That you grew up as my brother."

"I left. I deserve that. Abandoned every fuckin' person."

"It didn't cross my mind that you loved her—even though we were close friends. A you-and-her long-term thing? I was too young to understand anything of that magnitude. But her pregnant and heartbroken?" He drops his arms then cracks his knuckles. "What I'm trying to say is I pushed for you two to hang out back in the day, and now I've done the opposite. And really, I need to step the hell away."

His words hang in the air as I think back. Since we're airing memories, I speak up. "There was a lot going on back then. Since I was a kid, Pops would beat the crap out of me." I rub my temples. "I ran from that. That's why I left. I might've been the person you knew when I was at school or around your family, but at home, I was worthless. Except when I was with her."

I sigh, letting my eyes close and my mind drift back to the night at the beach house—the night I almost didn't run.

Emma's warm body wraps around me under the blankets, and I watch her sleep. The things you notice when trying to memorize someone... her breaths are sleepy and soft. Her lips curl slightly as she holds onto me. Hours have passed. I meant to leave at midnight, then two in the morning, then four. But now dawn is pushing through the night. The darkness from the window is a purply blue. Moving from this bed is literally the hardest step I've taken in my life.

But we promised: no goodbyes. She wants and needs a good life, free from people like me who come from places like the ones I come from and who have to hide their real lives from their best friends...

In one push, I roll away and turn back. That soft smile on her sleeping face fades. She's still asleep, but it's not just an expressionless dreaming face.

I cannot believe this is how it ends. "I love you, Emma."

But she'll go to college. Get a degree. Maybe stay away from stupid Summerland County and go... I don't know. Become a famous photographer or a Broadway dancer. She can be anything she wants without the likes of me to hold her down.

I let my fingers run over her cheek and—her sleepy smile returns. I capture that image in my mind and turn before letting go, not daring to risk seeing the loss of that smile.

I grab my shirt, find a pair of pants, tuck everything into a backpack, and can't help but turn around. Her smile is gone, as if even in her sleep she knows I'm leaving her.

Screw it. I've kept too much inside, and it hasn't worked out well for me. "You were my family."

Ryan nods.

"Pops was miserable. He taught me nothing and tried to ruin me. But man, your dad's the one that taught me how to live. I might've missed some of it without him. I needed to figure out how to..." I shake my head, trying to find the words. "How to undo the deep scars I got from the bastard who raised me.

Your dad didn't tell me how to live or how to handle my problems, but he did let me watch. And he let me participate in your life." I take a breath. "Anyway, Emma and Cally are my family now."

Silence hangs between us. Ryan works his jaw back and forth. "I had no idea."

"Why would you?"

His forehead furrows. "I just thought Pops was a prick... maybe? Shit."

"Don't try to figure it out. The bastard isn't worth it."

Ryan's voice is low. "God, man. I'm sorry." He concentrates on me, and an earnest confidence crosses his face. "Families make mistakes. They walk away. They come back." His eyes narrow. "And blood doesn't make a family."

CHAPTER 45

GRAYSON

As if those were the words I needed to hear, the weight of guilt recedes. Blood doesn't make a family, and I've known that my whole life but never realized it. "Are we good?"

Ryan throws his hand out. "Yeah."

That's all that needs saying. We shake on it. "Alright then."

He dips his head, nodding toward the open room where Jared and Brock are chatting with Emma. "You good to go back out?"

It's my turn to nod. "Yeah, let's do it."

I take a deep breath and head down the hall. I've said it a dozen times—I hate strip clubs because they remind me of Pops—but right now, I want out of here for different reasons. I'm exhausted and more emotional than I'll ever admit out loud. And I really fucking *need* Emma's body against mine. She makes me sane. The simple fact is that I'm meant to survive with her by my side.

Across the room, Jared and Brock stand up, then

Emma. She's smiling. Both men look pleased, and whatever their questions were, they must've asked them the right way. They're pros. It would've been nice to work with a new team. Throwing punches at potential new team members probably means I have no shot at that job, a fact that was confirmed when Delta went to search Emerald's at Brock's request, and the order pointedly did not include me. It sucks. But like the way it worked out with Ryan, a new team will happen when it's meant to happen. I have to believe that my near-complete mental breakdown in this stupid-ass strip club happened so that Ryan and I could move forward. A new job will come when I hunt it down and find it.

I rub the back of my neck as Sarah comes back from the same hall we just came from. Ryan heads her way, and I miss most of what she says. My focus is intent on Emma.

Yeah, she's sweet and gorgeous, but damn, the woman is strong—a survivor. It makes me love her all the more. As she walks over, her eye catches mine, and I get my arms around her as fast as I can. Sliding to the side of the room, she melts against me. Her soft curves press to me as if we're pieces of a puzzle. "You good, pretty mama?"

"A lot better."

"Good. I want as much distance as possible from here."

She turns in my arms, gazing across the stage. "Don't hate this place or what I did. Emerald's isn't who I am. But I *am* better for it. I'm stronger because I pushed myself."

Holy. Shit. I love this woman. "Way to make my asshole mistakes sound like some shitty stepping stone in life."

"Ha."

Holding her to me, I wave bye to the men standing in the room. "Ready?"

Her smile curves as she leans back into me, but then she pops onto her toes and kisses my cheek. "I'm going to get my purse and keys, okay?"

I squeeze her before letting go. She runs off and grabs her things, saying her goodbyes, and then she's back in my arms, and I'm dragging her out the door. Fresh near-dawn air hits us. I drink in the cool morning and turn to look at Emerald's a last time, briefly thinking back to the moment I saw fear in her eyes. Never again can I let that happen. Once again, I'm consumed by a dizzying need to run my hands over her, to make sure she is fine.

We make it to her Jeep, and I manage to stow her safely in the passenger's seat before my hands clasp her cheeks, and my mouth takes hers. I breathe her in as our lips brush against each other. Her tongue caresses mine, and I push away the sudden spring of fear. Life's too unknown, with hidden enemies and unseen terrors. The idea that I could lose her again... it's unbearable.

"I love you, baby," I murmur against her lips. "I'm not the best guy out there."

"You might be."

"But Jesus fuck, I promise you, Emma. I will be the best one for you. No more working shit jobs, no more paycheck to paycheck. I'll figure it out."

Her eyelashes lower as if she's lost in thought. But then her hands cover mine. I realize I'm clinging to her.

"We'll figure it out. I didn't work this hard here because it was my only option, but because I needed to control what I could of my future." She studies me. "Does that make sense?"

Her words roll through my mind. She doesn't

need me to survive, but she wants me by her side, making it better. There's a big difference between those two things. "Yeah, I think it does."

"Sweet." She settles against me, her legs hanging off the passenger's seat as I block her in. She sighs against my chest and asks, "What's next?"

"Guess we go home."

She leans back. "*We* go home?"

"Yeah, baby. We go home together." My hands run down her shoulders, holding onto her biceps. "Us, under the same roof."

"With our daughter."

Point, Emma. My heart explodes in my chest. "Don't be too perfect, pretty mama. Otherwise, I'm likely to propose in the parking lot of a strip joint. That'd be an awkward story to tell our kids."

Her face lights up, with big eyes and an unhinged mouth. She silently mouths *our kids.*

I kiss her on the forehead, buckle her in, and shut the door. Kids. Plural. She's my family. I want her as my wife. I'm not sure how I'll pull it all off, but it will happen. I toss the Jeep keys in the air as I walk to the driver's seat and climb in.

She leans against her door with sleepy eyes. "What a night. Glad it's over."

I chuckle. "Me too, baby. I can't handle any more right now."

"We'll get a couple hours sleep before Cally wakes."

"Perfect." I pull my wallet and phone from my back pocket, turn the engine over, and notice a light flashing on my screen. No one has this number except the Titan guys and Emma.

And Mazie.

I slide the screen on, and there's her text: THERE'S A GUY LOOKING FOR YOU. POPS IS DEAD.

CHAPTER 46

Emma

My thumb hovers over the button to snap another picture, but really, I'm studying Grayson, wondering what's wrong. Is he angrier about Emerald's than he let on, or is he continuing to rehash all of his regrets?

I kick off my flip-flops. The cool grass scratches the bottom of my feet and tickles my toes. Summer is my favorite season, and I bask in the warmth of the slipping sun. There are a million excuses to go outside, a million things to take pictures of, especially around sunset. *Especially* when Grayson is manning the grill on the back patio.

But as much as I'm enjoying the view and taking pictures of Gray flipping burgers and Cally trying her best to do rolls in the grass, Gray's smile isn't genuine.

I snap another picture and check back in the viewfinder to study him. Sexy man. But that's not a true smile. I haven't seen one on him since we left Emerald's yesterday.

I hold my camera up again. "Smile."

Again, a smile without a spark. I'm unnerved, and despite all of his words, I have to wonder if the guy who was so quick to want to join Titan needs more excitement than Cally and I can offer. Sure, grilling out is fun. Having a beer in the backyard while watching our kid is my dream come true, but now that real life is settling in for Gray and me as a couple, is he having doubts?

"Everything okay?" It's the thousandth time I've asked him that today. Maybe he's not over the Emerald's thing. Maybe he is upset that Mazie took off back south, and I wasn't overly interested in hearing about it. I rolled my eyes when he called her this morning. He said something about her checking out of the hotel room for him, I think. Maybe, maybe, maybe. My mind spirals as I let the camera hang on my neck.

Are you mad at me now? Hurt or bored or antsy?

No matter how I've asked, all of his answers are the same. He isn't mad, angry, or holding a deep grudge because I shook my booty for cash at Emerald's. Honestly, I'm surprised he let me off the hook for that, but then again, he made it perfectly clear we've both made our choices and we should move forward. I like that. Except my sixth sense is going berserk.

He flips a burger. "Yeah, I'm good."

I bite my lip, scared to ask the only question I have left. But it has to happen, especially with him staying here. I walk closer, even though I'm already way out of earshot of our girl. "If you're not ready to do this, we don't need to talk to Cally."

His spatula-holding hand drops, and his eyes go wide. "What? Why?"

"Because something is off, and I don't want to

rush this." I go back to biting my lip. "I don't want to ruin us because we rushed. Everything is really perfect right now, and I know that doesn't last forever, but I don't want it to stop so soon."

"Baby." He drops the lid on the grill, puts down the utensil, and pulls me into his arms. "It's not like that. I promise. This isn't rushed. Hell, it's far past due."

"But there is something."

He doesn't answer, and my gut drops all the way to the floor. "Please, just tell me."

He's holding me, but mentally, he's drifting. "It's really nothing."

"You're killing me."

His chest expands with a giant breath in, making the tight T-shirt stretch over his sculpted body. I watch as he holds it in, dropping his head back to look at the sunset sky, then lets it out. As he does, I feel as if he goes with that lost breath.

"Just tell me," I whisper, hoping my words will somehow bring him back to me.

"Pops died."

"What?" That's not what I expected to hear, and I have no idea what to say. *Good riddance? Are you okay?* I'm not sorry. Really, I don't know what I am, so I stare up at the orange-pink sky and lean onto his chest.

Finally, he pulls back, opens the grill, and pulls the burgers onto a waiting platter. When he's done, he tosses the spatula down with a clatter and lowers the lid. I still don't know what to say, so I walk behind him and wrap my arms around him. My hands clasp against his chest, and my chin rests on his shoulder blade. Under my backward hug, his body relaxes, and he turns, letting my hands drop to his side, though I refuse to let go. I can see a thousand emotions warring for prominence on his face.

"See?" His lips twist into... not really a frown, but definitely a furrow. "Confusing, right?"

"Grayson..." I release my hold on him and run my palms over his stomach, up his chest, and down his shoulders, finally stopping on his biceps. "Your dad died. He was awful, but still, he was... your dad."

His face skews even more. "Yeah, about that. Turns out, he wasn't."

My eyes peel back. "What? What do you mean?"

"That Mazie-diner night? I saw him earlier, and it clicked." He spins me around and nods to Cally. "How could I feel something so deep for her in a matter of seconds, but he... never once did he care." Grayson turns me back to face him then pushes my hair off my face. "Anyway, I called him on it. He didn't disagree. Randall's not my dad."

"Well..." I lean against him as he lays his arm over my shoulder. "God, Gray. I'm not sure what to say."

"Confusing, right?"

I angle into him and study his expression. "Yeah."

"I hate him." His lips press into a flat line, making their color fade. His eyebrows bite together. "The bastard was mean. A nasty, angry drunk. He hated the world and hated me. But, God..."

"What?"

"I think he really loved my mom. She was with him, right? So, he couldn't have been all bad, maybe, a lifetime ago."

"You don't know that," I whisper. "People stay in relationships for a lot of reasons. A weakness, guilt, a soft spot."

"Guess it doesn't matter."

"So, who's your biological dad?"

Grayson shrugs. "No idea. If he knew about me and still left me, fuck him for that. If he didn't know I existed, then that's the way it goes."

"So, is there a funeral? Or what happens?"

"Nothing. I'm not planning it."

I nod. I never thought about what happens when a person no one cares about dies. "How'd you find out?"

"Cops knew what hotel I was staying at, and Mazie was still there. Front-desk girl directed them to my *fiancée*."

"Wow."

"She said sorry again, by the way. The girl feels like shit about how you two met."

I watch Cally play in the grass with her toys. "If she's your friend, I don't hate her. I was just caught off guard."

"She's nuts. That happens a lot."

I laugh. "Okay. But about Pops."

"What about the asshole…"

Gray's right to feel that way. "So, which has been bugging you—Pops dying or knowing he wasn't your dad?"

"Actually, neither." He pulls me under his arm and holds me close.

I love the way he smells and the way I fit in the crook of his arm, and right now, I love how I can feel how calmly his heart beats. "But something's been up."

"I've been thinking about Cally—or really, about me. If we're going to tell her that I'm her dad, then I want to think about what kind of dad I'll be. I'm terrified my past will come back to haunt me. But, you know, mind over matter. I won't be Pops. I just refuse."

My eyes slip closed. Sometimes, I can't believe the amount of love that comes from this guy. It was like he was meant to be a dad, to make up for all the evil inflicted upon him.

Grayson's grip flexes into my shoulder. "Think I can be a good dad, considering my example?"

"Of course you can." I put my hand over his. "Plus, he wasn't the only example you had growing up."

"Ryan and I talked about your folks a bit—"

Ryan? That catches me off guard. "You did?"

He nods, folding me to him and pressing his chin to the top of my head. "Your dad treated me like a son sometimes. Doing guy stuff. Camping, basketball practice, stuff like that."

"I know." Having Gray as a sort-of brother made for some confusion when we were growing up.

"But I've also made some bad choices. Like enlisting when I freaked out and walking away from you instead of telling you the truth."

"That was years ago," I say, hating that he still can't let go of his guilt.

"They were still my decisions." Grayson moves so that we face each other. "I want a good life with the two of you more than I want to regret my past or worry over how Pops will affect my future."

"You can do that."

"I have to believe if you want it badly enough..."

Deep inside, I ache for him. "The only thing you need to do is forgive yourself." I want to beg him, to force him, but I can't. All I can do is make sure he knows that I believe in him. "I need you to do that, Gray. For all of us."

He stares at me in a way I can only describe as adoration. It warms me from the inside out. He needs me as much as I need him. "Grayson, however it happened, this is us. We either make progress toward our future or we drown in our excuses. You're not going to let Pops dictate your life. Right?"

"I won't."

"I'll say this as clearly as I can. The wrong choice,

bad people… I don't know, sometimes we deal with those things because they bring us to the right spot and make us ready for the future."

He blinks. "You believe that?"

"Down to my soul, Grayson." I watch him, willing my belief to sink into him. "And when you do too, I'll know our life can be okay."

CHAPTER 47

GRAYSON

Another new day in my new life, and it's pretty effin' sweet. I'm dribbling a pink bouncy ball in the living room. Cally is hiding behind the couch, completely sure that I cannot see her and giggling up a storm. "Where she'd go? Anyone see Cally Bear?"

"Rwar!" She roars her loudest, and damn cutest, bear growl.

I spin the opposite direction. "She's over here?"

Giggle. Squeak. Giggle.

Jumping to the TV, I look around the cable boxes and pretend she's slipped behind the flat screen, all the time dribbling the ball and bouncing it between my legs as I turn—which always makes her squeal louder. "Where'd she go? Cally Bear?"

Giggle. Squeal! Giggle.

I spin. "Ah, there she is!" And I bound across the living room in two strides, throwing myself onto the couch and tapping her head with the pink ball that I have palmed in one hand. "Gotcha, kid."

"Got me! Got me, got me." She takes off and runs around the room after snagging the ball from me, and then she circles and dives onto the couch.

I grab her up, hold her in the air, and her legs plank and her arms are flying.

"Whee," she screams. "Highwer!"

Tipping her to the side, then bringing her back up, I'm dropping airplane noises like I was meant to do this. Because I was.

She tosses her head back, laughing as I land "the plane" on my chest, and she bounces, begging for more. But Emma's sleeping in, and I'm sure that too much more will wake her.

"How about this? You hungry?"

Her eyes go wide and her head nods wildly.

"You already had breakfast though." I pretend to shake her little shoulders. "Are you sure there's room in that belly?"

"Yeah!"

"Hmm, I don't know. Maybe we make room." I tickle her, and she laughs so hard I'm concerned she might pee. "Alright."

I jump up, tucking her under one arm. Her legs bicycle in the air as if she's taking her trike down a racetrack.

"Let's see what we can do for a mid-morning snack." I put her on the kitchen counter and take a step back, analyzing Cally's perch on the edge. Nope, that has disaster written all over it—broken bones, missing teeth. Emma would kick my ass.

"Jump on." I turn and hook her onto my back. She climbs up me like a tree, locking her arms around my neck, and we head to the cabinet.

Snacks. What to do for a fun snack? Easy—the girl likes pancakes. She flipped her lid for syrup with Cherry, so... here we go. I grab some granola with

M&Ms in it and some vanilla extract, then I hit the fridge for… chocolate syrup.

"What do you think, kiddo?"

"Good!"

On my way to the pantry, I grab the bananas. Surely there's got to be pancake batter in Emma's kitchen, right?

I search cabinet after cabinet. What the double deuce—no pancake batter? Big fail. *Damn.* "No pancakes. Time to regroup."

Cally's hand extends and points to a container. I grab whatever it is, hoping I can do something fun for a snack and—I read the label. "Add water and shake." *Well, alright.* My girl found me pancake batter. "We're a go for pancakes."

"Go!"

I head back to the counter, where my pile of extra ingredients sits, and I search every single cabinet and drawer for a measuring cup, finally finding it in the last one. Doors are open, and things are reshuffled. Cally laughs in my ear, and I act as if we're not going to survive if we don't make pancakes. She pushes me to pull it together, and I can see myself in her as she issues a strategy to get what she wants.

The kitchen resembles a disaster zone. I peel the bananas and pour the granola onto a plate, plucking out the M&Ms, then fill the measuring cup. "Water."

"Water," she repeats and helps me pour it in, singing, "P'cakes, p'cakes, I wuv p'cakes."

I drop some extract and M&Ms in, add a squirt of chocolate syrup, then screw on the cap. "Now, shake." Her arms hook around my neck, and we stomp around the kitchen, shaking the pancake batter until the powder mix has liquefied. We probably go a few minutes more than we need to, but what the hell.

It takes a few minutes for me to get the griddle

going. Cally bores quickly during that part of the pancake-making process and sits under the table in her "fort" with her dolls, talking to them about chocolate syrup. In the last few minutes, while she's worked alongside me and played on her own, I can see Emma's sweetness and my tenacity in her. This is pretty much the most fun I've had in a kitchen. Ever.

I make a few circles of different sizes, just enough for a snack, and flip them through the air and onto plates. *Most* of the pancakes make my target. A couple hit the floor. All of the tosses earn a giggle.

"Ready to decorate?"

"Weady!" Her arms shoot up, and I grab her around the waist, hoisting her high before landing her on the counter.

I'm sure there is a rule about counter sitting, but... I keep a hand on her and decide to check in on that rule possibility later. "This is what we do. Bananas—" I drop the slices onto the plate "Take some of these, and toss 'em on."

Cally grabs and smashes the bananas then tosses them onto the pancakes and eats what's left in her hand.

"Good?"

She nods.

"Sweet. Next, the chocolate."

Her eyes go big, and based on the excitement exploding on her face, I decide that squirting the chocolate onto the plate is really a Cally-Daddy four-handed project. After enough chocolate syrup, I grab two forks and the plate and piggyback her to the big-girl chair.

"You good?"

She scrambles and shuffles, scooting around in the chair as I set the plate down. After a quick arrangement, we get down to serious business. I chop up the pancakes, and we dig in. They are unreal. Seriously, I am a master dessert-pancake snack chef. "These things are genius."

"Yeah." Her head bobs up and down. She's eating with her mouth kind of open and chocolate smeared on her chin and cheeks.

"Someone's going to have to hose you down."

She giggles and stabs more pancakes off our shared pile. "Good." She chomps on her pancake. "Weally good."

"I agree." We clink forks, and after a couple more bites, I let mine drop to the plate. It clatters, and I lean back in my seat. She does the same and leans back, mimicking me.

"We did a good job, Cally Bear."

"Yeah."

"You like me okay?"

"Yeah," she says. Her sugary grin warms me from the inside out.

"Think we should go wake your mom?"

"Nooo," she giggles and shakes her head.

"You sure?"

"We can jwump on her."

I laugh, raising my eyebrows. "We *could* jump on her."

Covered in our snack explosion, she squeals and slides out of her chair. "Mama!"

I bound behind her and scoop her up. We head into Emma's—no, our—bedroom and jump on the bed. Cally lands on my pillow, and I cage myself over Emma as our girl ducks under my arms and snuggles into her mom. "Tickle!"

We tickle Emma, and she squeaks and laughs, sounding exactly like our daughter. It's in that sticky, laughing moment that I have no doubt I'm going to do this parenting thing right.

CHAPTER 48

GRAYSON

Today is the day, and I haven't been able to sit still as I pace from the living room to the kitchen. Hell, not only is today the day, but the hour is upon us. It's time to try to explain to Cally what's happening and where the future goes. I get it. She's two—albeit a very mature two-year-old, in my opinion, but two nonetheless. I have no idea if she'll understand anything I tell her. If she does, maybe she'll like it and maybe she won't.

The sound of a squirming kid plays from the monitor. "She's up."

Emma's smile lights my world. "Yup. I'll go get her."

I nod and take a sip of my Mountain Dew then cap it, deciding that I don't need any more caffeine. I'm wired enough. I'm seriously going to jump out of my skin. I bounce on my toes then pace the kitchen.

"Hey, Snugglebug." The lights on the baby monitor jump as Emma pulls Cally from her toddler bed. "Up, up, up, and at 'em."

"Wuv you, Mama." The sweet, soft sound of her sleep-soaked voice makes me give a stupid grin. I know I have this goofy look on my face right now, but I'm just... pumped. This is really happening, and even though Cally won't *really* get it, I will. Thanks to these girls, I have another day that I'll never forget. It's enough to erase the bad ones that have clouded my mind for years.

Emma rounds the corner into the kitchen with a sleepy-eyed Cally held to her chest. Her blond hair is mussed with bed head, and her just-waking green eyes are identical to mine.

"Do you want some crackers, baby?" Emma asks.

She nods but not before Cally smiles and waves hi to me. There is no doubt: this kid is going to be a daddy's girl.

"Alright." She places Cally in a chair and fastens a buckle on her lap. "Let's get you situated in the big-girl chair with your snack, and then we have a big-girl conversation for you."

I drop to a chair at the table and perch on the edge. My blood thumps, and my knees bounce. Emma calmly lays out a plate of crackers and a milk box.

"So..." Emma sits on the other side of Cally. "We have something fun to tell you. It's big-girl news."

Cally's megawatt smile flashes, and she excitedly nods, using some real words and some fake ones to explain how she can handle whatever we have to share. My hand crosses the table and takes Emma's. Cally's eyes briefly drop to the handhold, but her crackers are also in her line of sight, so she takes one of those.

"Snugglebug, you like Grayson?"

She nods and gnaws on her cracker, letting crumbs fall. "Uh-huh."

"I do too." Emma squeezes my hand. "I love him."

I squeeze her hand back. "And I love your mommy," I tell Cally. "And you, too."

Cally smiles but keeps gnawing on her cracker. Emma flicks the crumbs off the corner of Cally's mouth with her free hand. "He loves both of us very much, and he's going to stay in our house."

"Forever," I add. I'm not sure why, but I just had to get that in there—more for my benefit than for Emma's.

"Forever," Emma agrees, and we both watch Cally. "We'll be a family. So, like a mommy and a daddy, and you're our baby."

"Like *my* baby." Cally takes another mouthful of cracker.

"Right." Emma nods and smiles. "Just like you take care of your baby, Grayson will take care of you. Make sense?"

She nods and goes on to babble unknown words in a singsong tone. I don't know that she understands anything we said, but God, the kid has no idea how tied in knots I've been, and that one simple nod has done a hell of a lot to loosen the pressure.

"Because *I am* your daddy."

Cally watches me, munching on her cracker but now also very inquisitive, as if her growing brain is pulling together all the pieces of this conversation. "Okay."

Her silliness has stilled, and I can feel this conversation inside my chest, so deep it's killing me. Talking about telling Cally was one thing. Hearing it out loud—*fuck me*—that's some kind of miracle that terrifies me. I clear my throat. "Are you okay with that, Cally Bear?"

She toys with her cracker, and it dawns on me that these are just words. She must know a ton of dads, but having her own wasn't a part of her world until now. The complexity of this moment is probably well behind *my* years.

"Daddy," she says, her little mind assigning that to me.

I nod, my throat burning. "Yup."

Her green eyes shine. I know she's too young to get any of this, but it *looks* as if she's assessing me just as she did the first day she met me. I can't take a single breath until she finishes her two-year-old analysis. Blood rushes to my ears, and my collar feels tight. I've been through basic training, been shot hanging off a helicopter, been beaten within an inch of my life, but right now feels as though it could break me if it went wrong.

Finally, she grins again and makes her cracker dance across the table.

"Okay," I say, almost gasping for air.

"Okay," Emma says, too.

Title of Daddy has been officially bestowed. Emma bites her mouth and wipes her eyes. I lean back in the chair, my conscience clear, my heart full… probably for the first time ever.

Cally finishes her crackers and ignores her milk box. Emma unbuckles her, helps her slide down, and then puts the milk in the fridge.

Clapping my hands together, I realize I've got to do something, or I'll lose my mind. "Alright, good talk."

My little girl launches herself onto me, and I drop back to the chair, letting her crawl into my lap. Her little head rests on my chest. *Aw, shit.* This girl makes my eyes burn.

I drape my arms around her. "God, I love you, kid."

"Wuv you too."

Just when I thought I couldn't feel anymore, she said that. My life's complete.

CHAPTER 49

Emma

Weekends take on new meaning when there's Grayson to wake up to. I'm draped across his muscular chest. The scar on his side doesn't hurt him at all—so he says—and his eyes are closed. His hand lazily drifts up and down my spine. It has been years since I just lay in bed. But Grayson's made it something we do. Nothing—we do absolutely nothing, and it's mind-blowing. Just as unbelievable as when we stay in bed and do *everything*.

I've picked up a normal work-and-school schedule. Jeremy at Creative Dynamic and Jan at the Delightful Diner were both far more excited than I expected when I asked for a little down time. We still have bills coming in, but with CDW picking up the cost of tuition, I have breathing room as Grayson hits the job hunt hard.

He hasn't said as much, but I think he's bummed about how everything turned out at Emerald's. But he won't utter a word of complaint, because his "screwing up"—his words, not mine—when he saw me on stage paled in comparison to the danger I'd put myself in. One day, he'll let go of all of the guilt. He's not there yet, no matter what he says, but he'll get there.

"What are you thinking?" His morning voice is gravelly and rough.

It makes me want to curl closer to him and hang on. "Nothing much. Why?"

"You're tense, baby."

"Oh… I don't know. Thinking about how I like lazy mornings in bed with you before Cally wakes, and I'm hoping you've forgiven yourself." I sigh, feeling my breath against his skin. "Not sure if you'd ever tell me."

"Not sure you need that burden. Think I've done enough."

I push up on his chest quickly. "See? *That* is what concerns me—you think I'm not strong enough, or that you haven't hurt enough—"

His mouth takes mine, and the words fall away as his tongue softly sweeps mine. The kiss has a harsh mix of urgency and caring. I melt against him, letting him flip me over and thread his fingers into my hair. His massive body weighs heavily against me but not enough that I'm pinned down. I'm just deliciously immobile—with his hardening erection pressing against me.

Gray breaks his mouth from mine, trailing his lips and tongue down my jaw. The morning scruff on his face scratches me, and instantly, my nipples ache. I part my legs to allow him to settle between them, and I writhe just enough to elicit his growl. It's deep, dark, gritty, and makes my entire body shiver.

His teeth tug my earlobe. "I have something to tell you."

"Hmm." I gasp as he bites again, and his hips flex, slowly thrusting his shaft against me.

"Truth is…"

"Gray," I pant. He's doing insane things to my neck. Between the tongue, the teeth, and the scratchy morning shadow on his cheeks, he's irresistible. I'm drowning in need.

"Our conversation with Cally? I'm good. Scared every day to do the right thing by her, but no more heavy burden."

"No… more…" I moan as his hand slips devastatingly slowly up my side. "Burden?"

"Yeah, baby." Finally, his hand palms my breast, massaging, before he lets his fingers tease me harder. His thumb runs circles over its peaked swell. "You want to talk some more, or you going to let me make love to you, Emma?"

"God, I love you."

"Thank fuck for that." His mouth takes mine again, and I move my hips, flexing and rubbing against him. His shaft teases, and I'm drowning in desire.

"Please," I whisper into a kiss.

"Whatever you want." Slowly, Grayson sinks inside me.

It's heaven—blissful, soul-claiming heaven. His hands find mine, his kisses deepen, and he thrusts, taking his time to draw out each of my kiss-muffled moans. This can go on all day. I'm lost in him.

His arms pull mine overhead, my body stretched beneath him. Grayson rocks into me, I arch back, and the climax I desperately seek builds. My thighs wrap tightly around him as the world spins away. The room goes white, and I fall apart, climaxing and breathing raggedly, locking my legs around his waist. As I tumble through the tidal wave of my orgasm, he thrusts harder and then finds his release as well.

Our hands are still locked, our bodies still connected, and we're gasping and kissing and promising the world. Finally, he collapses against me completely but rolls to hold me close to his side. "You're mine, Emma. But really, pretty mama, I'm all yours."

CHAPTER 50

GRAYSON

I tap the pen on my list, sitting at the coffee shop where I've been making notes about where to look for jobs. I've had a few offers come my way, one of which I will eventually accept. Summerland doesn't have many opportunities for men like me. I let out a deep breath and tap the pen again. I could do security on Emma's campus. Ryan said he could pull some strings and get me a job with the county. I've been asked to teach self-defense at the local gym, though I'm not at all qualified for that. Going to war and being a built guy doesn't mean I know the moves to keep a woman safe from a bad situation—though Emma said the job offer had nothing to do with me knowing anything about teaching self-defense. I roll my eyes and tap on the paper again.

A footstep behind me catches me off guard. I turn and blink, slowly standing from my chair to meet Delta team's Brock Gamble.

My head tilts. "Hey, how goes it?" I don't have time to rehash what went wrong on the Emerald's op a few weeks ago, but I knew it was only a matter of time before they wanted their belongings back. I stopped using their phone when I got my own, but damn, I'm going to miss that truck.

Brock nods. "It goes."

"Good." What does this guy want?

"Was trying to get a hold of you. But the phone's turned off."

I shrug. "It wasn't my phone. I needed to drop it to Parker but didn't have the chance." Or rather, I didn't make time, not wanting an awkward conversation like this.

"That so?" He shifts, his boots scraping across the tile.

"Parker could've pulled my new number."

Brock's narrow gaze is cold. "I have no doubt he could."

This conversation blows. Not only is it awkward, but I also don't want it in a damn coffee shop where the Summerland County rumor mills will churn. Word will get back to Emma, who will stress about money.

I reach into my back pocket to grab the truck's key and loft it to Brock. "Suppose you're here for that."

Brock catches the key but stays quiet.

"I fucked the Emerald's job. Lost the Titan opportunity. I get it." *And seriously, dude, just leave.*

"Not exactly." He tosses the key back.

I catch it but don't drop my hand. Not trusting the situation, not seeing his point of view, I'm wary and tired of wishing the Emerald's job had gone a different way. Working on a black-ops team based near my family? A job like that is impossible not to wish for, but I'm realistic enough to know it's not going to happen.

Hell, the job doesn't matter. I'll flip burgers to make Emma happy… even though I hated putting that on the list of job possibilities.

"Sit down, Ford." Brock drops into the opposite seat. He rolls up his sleeves, showing off his ink. "Sit already. Jesus Christ."

So I sit. Crossing my arms, I'm unsure of what he wants. "What's up?"

Brock leans forward, placing his elbows on the table. "I heard the audio playback of you trying to save your dying team."

A boulder lodges into my throat. "Alright."

"I heard you go try your damnedest out there."

My chest feels tight. "Tried. Did not succeed."

"Son, shit like that happens. Short of hell's angels showing up and letting you off the battlefield, you can't survive. You weren't supposed to make it. No one on that team should be alive. You understand that?"

"Seems like some better men should've had my place."

He tilts his head. "The fact that you think that… confirms this conversation."

"What conversation?"

"Anyone who handled their shit like you did in Kirkuk deserves a place on my team."

"Excuse me?" I'm dumbstruck. He doesn't look as if he's fucking with me, but between the fistfight at Emerald's and my history that screams PTS-motherfuckin'-D, it doesn't add up.

Brock slaps the table and stands. "Keep the truck. Keep the job. Consider the ride a signing bonus."

"Wait." I stand up and meet his eye. "You shouldn't do that."

He laughs, throwing his head back. "Jesus, fuck. You're going to fit in. You wanna tell me why I shouldn't have you on my team?"

"I have a medical chart that's ugly."

He gives me a curt nod. "I've seen it. You'll be okay."

He's *seen it*. So, the whispered rumors about Titan are true. "I screwed up the Emerald's op."

Brock shakes his head. "That night could've gone a hundred different ways. We went in there for information and came out with a whole lot more— arrests, actionable intel, a network. These traffickers... they're like the string in a dirty fuckin' sweater. It keeps unraveling. Join Delta, see it to the end."

This is too good to be true. "What's the catch?"

"No catch. The job's the job. You'd be stupid not to take it. You're not stupid, are you?"

In my mind, Pops's resounding affirmative answer to that question barks, *Yes!* But I pinch that memory away. "Not in the slightest."

He sticks his hand out. "Then welcome to Titan."

CHAPTER 51

GRAYSON

Summer's slipping away, almost gone. Our bags are lined up behind my truck. It's shocking how much is needed for two adults and a kid to travel to the beach. I'm ninety percent sure that Cally has more packed than we do. The sun hangs low in the early-September sky. Emma's in the grass with Cally, and even though they are playing, she's lost in thought.

"Hey, pretty mama."

She snaps out of her fog and smiles. "Hey."

"*That's* a lot of stuff." I gesture with my head toward the luggage.

She laughs. "True."

"Everything okay?"

She scrunches her shoulders. "First family vacation. Kind of awesome."

I stride to her and drop into the grass, pulling her into my lap. She smells like summer, and her back relaxes into me. "I got you a present just in time for the beach."

Emma turns. "What is it?"

"Come on. Let's roll, and you can open it on the way."

Truth is, I'm just as excited for her to open it as I am for everything this weekend. I have two Delta jobs under my belt. Both pay in a way that lets Emma take a deep breath and open a savings account. She still gives a nervous glance at her receipts and our bank balance when she buys anything more than Ramen noodles, but I think she's coming to grips with our new comfort level.

Our little house is definitely our home. Quality time for the Kingsley family no longer revolves around arranging babysitting for her work schedule. Still, Emma refuses to buy anything special for herself. I'm done with that.

There's a brand new, fancy-ass camera waiting for her in the passenger's seat of my truck. I kiss her neck them jump up with her in my arms. "Cally Bear—" I drop my head to Emma. "She gotta pee?"

Emma laughs. "Already did it."

I learned that lesson the hard way once before. And it required me running with her in my arms to the restroom at Home Depot. We made it, but it was *way* too close. "Cally Bear, it's go time, kid."

She squeals and runs toward the truck in our driveway. Patiently, she waits by her door as I carry Emma over and drop her on her feet. I'm convinced that Cally likes riding in my truck more than Emma's Jeep because we're higher up. I've playfully debated it with Emma. She loves her Jeep as much I dig my truck. "Ready for the beach?"

"Yeah!" Cally jumps with her arms in the air.

"Guess we need to buckle you in then." It takes a couple seconds to get that job done, and as I click in the last part of the car seat, I catch Emma's face lighting up.

Holding up the wrapped box, she beams. "Daddy bought me a present."

Cally squeals. "It's yur camera su-prise."

I laugh, shaking my head. "Surprise."

"*Camera?*" she mouths, eyes wide and overacting for Cally's sake.

New lesson learned: don't tell Cally any secrets. Emma tears the paper off and opens the box, which was opened already once before when I put the pieces together and charged the battery. "It's ready to go."

"Cheese!" Cally shouts, and I duck close to her for a picture.

"Perfect." Emma snaps one quickly and then a few more as I kiss my girl and jump in the driver's seat. This weekend is going to rock.

Emma

Our lazy beach vacation has been perfect. The weekend is almost over, and I don't want tonight to end. Tomorrow we go back home, and I can't help but remember the last time we were together at the shore, when everything was so out of control and so perfect simultaneously.

Cally's asleep, and I'm lounging in Grayson's arms outside on the deck overlooking the beach, feeling as though this night is supposed to make up for the one when he left me. There's a glass of wine in my hand, and the baby monitor sits on the nearby table. The stars shine overhead, and a cool breeze rolls over us. I tug up the blanket and let the heavy weight of his arms tuck me in and hold me tight.

My shoulders are a tiny bit sunburned, and we've grilled for almost every meal since we arrived— basically, my beach-time ideal. "This is how you're supposed to do a vacation."

"Hooah to that."

His breath tickles my neck, and I snuggle closer. Grayson has taken up wearing his board-shorts uniform that I love, and I haven't for a single moment taken for granted how ruggedly handsome he is *and* how amazingly sweet he is to Cally. Life is perfect in a way that I never saw coming. "Love you, baby. Thank you for this."

"Pretty mama, it's you that deserves the thanks." His lips press to the back of my head before he takes a pull from his beer.

The ocean crashes around us. "Did you think we'd ever be at the beach again?"

"I don't know," he murmurs. "I thought about what was best for you last time we were at the beach together, and I got it wrong that time. I'm not going to try and predict the future again. Maybe I'll just pray I get it right."

I shift to gaze up at him and touch his cheek, letting the weekend's worth of scruff scratch my fingertips. "Everything was supposed to happen for a reason."

"I'm a lucky bastard you think like that."

My head tilts. "I think like that, and every day I wake up to you, I smile at all I have."

"At every hurdle we've cleared."

"Yup." I sip my wine and burrow against him. "Want to go inside?"

"Not yet."

"What *do* you want to do?" I ask, teasing him because there is something I definitely want to do, and it involves going inside and losing the remainder of our clothes.

"Just sit here for a few more minutes." He sighs, holding me firmly, then breathes in deeply. "So, you like your camera?"

It hasn't been out of reach, and I've been completely addicted to it, starting with the ride out to the beach and through every moment since. "Of course I do. I love it. You're too generous, baby."

He chuckles against me. "Got any good pics?"

"I think so. Maybe I'll wake up early and grab a couple at sunrise before we leave." I cast my gaze into the black, inky ocean. "I got a couple super-cute ones tonight while you guys were grilling." Grayson and Cally made dinner with aprons over their bathing suits. Cally mixed her bowls on the ground, sitting across from him while he manned the meat and veggies.

I reach for my camera, curious about how those turned out. I flick the switch on and turn the setting to show the photos on the small screen. There are a couple of pictures I don't recognize of Cally making faces into the lens very, *very* close up. I laugh. "Snugglebug got the camera when we weren't looking."

He shifts us so we can both see. Slowly, I start clicking through the pictures. More Snugglebug pics, then there are some of Cally *and* Grayson. "Busted. You were there!"

Laughing, he whispers against my neck, "Guess so."

Then one by one, I click through. Cally and Grayson pose in their daddy-daughter selfies. Then they hold a piece of paper between them with

Grayson's outstretched arm holding the camera. Black ink clearly stands out in block letters.

WILL

What the...? I click to the next picture, sure that this is not what I think it is.

YOU

Oh my God...

MARRY ME?

I spin toward him. "Gray!"

His smile shines in the light from the camera's screen. "We had an art project while you went to the store."

"You're asking me to marry you!"

"We are."

We are. *God. Shit, shoot, shit.* My heart can't take too much more of a good thing.

This guy nails us with everything he says every time he tries. I can barely breathe through the rush of happiness. I'm choking on surprise tears and throwing my arms around his neck. "Of course I want to marry you."

His body shifts as his arm reaches down, below our chair, and his hand returns with a small box. He flips the lid open with his thumb, and there shines in the moonlight the most perfect ring. It's not classic—it doesn't have a single diamond—but it's so me.

"For you, baby." He pulls me to his mouth, and I kiss him, packing as much emotion as I can convey. The camera slides to my side, and my hands clutch his face. He drops the ring box between us, and his fingers thread into my hair, tugging just enough to make it hurt, just enough to make me bite his lips.

"I've always wanted to be your wife."

"Good answer," he growls.

"Now, *I promise you*, it's time to take me inside."

CHAPTER 52

One Year Later...

GRAYSON

"You ready, buddy?" Ryder lines up a row of shot glasses on the coffee table. "Move boots, boys. We've got places to go."

Brock walks by and smacks me on the side of my head as I push off my couch. "Easy there, killer." I pretend to smooth down my hair. Then I join the guys standing around my living room.

Javier. Colin. Ryder. Ryan.

Groomsman. Groomsman. Groomsman. Best Man. Plus a couple of others. *Fuck me.* What a solid bunch of men to share this day with.

Ryder pours scotch for each of them and raises his glass. "To those you love, those you've lost, and those you'd die to see again. Cheers to getting the girl you've always wanted."

The room fills with *hooah*s and *hooyah*s, then we throw down the shots. A couple of back slaps later, I nod. "Let's do this."

Emma and I opted to get married at our new home. Cally calls it her castle. Ems calls it our forever home. I don't know if the place needs more of a name besides *mine* to go along with everything inside it. My house. My girls. Shit, *my heart* pounds in my chest, and I'm ready to claim my woman as my wife.

We move from the living room, where the walls have Cally's framed art and Emma's photography hanging proudly. There's artsy, handmade stuff all throughout as we head toward the back and pass a sign that says Ford Family, and then there's another that we pass in the kitchen that says, "Happiness is Homemade." But it's not just her artistic touch that makes this place amazing—it's that Emma struggled over every detail, from the carpet to the paint on the walls, and the result rocks.

Just like this wedding. She wanted it close-knit and homemade, to make memories and to celebrate. I don't need the ceremony any more than I need this house. These walls aren't my home; my home is living and breathing. It's my family, my life— everything I ever wanted and was too scared to go after. Emma and Cally are it for me. Where they are, I will go. They will always know how much they are loved and protected and that each breath I suck down is dedicated to making them the center of my world.

"No, no." Ryder's growling voice pulls me from my thoughts. "Well, shit. Everyone out."

"What?" I'm pulling the tail of our group. They keep going straight to the back deck, but I turn around to see—*Emma.*

Her white-lace dress is fitted down her body, leaving her arms bare, and she carries a bunch of flowers and jewels bundled together in one hand. I'm speechless. The heavy, slow thump of my heart echoes in my ears. There are no words for how I survived life to get to this point.

"Hi," she whispers. "Couldn't stay away."

I snap out of my awe and take two steps to pull her into my arms. "You're gorgeous."

Her eyelashes bat, and her cheeks blush.

"And sexy. Christ. You're all mine."

She nods, her teeth tugging on a glossy pink bottom lip. "You look handsome."

"I look like I'm yours." Her pink smile lights my whole fuckin' world. "You okay, Ems? What's with this?"

"Cally told me a story before she went off with my folks." Her eyes brim with tears. "And she gave this to me, too. She wants you have it before we start."

Emma pulls out a picture from where she's been holding it with the bouquet. As she unfolds it, I see our new house and, in front of it stand Cally, Emma, and me. Cally is in the middle, and we're on either side, holding her hands, but our outside hands rise over the little figures' heads and clasp in the air. All connected.

"Before you first came home"—her voice shakes—"she drew me a picture of our old-new house. And on it, there I was, holding her hand, but my other hand scrawled off the page." She closes her eyes like she's trying to keep it together. "And tonight, she told me a story about a king who was lost until two princesses came to his rescue. Eventually, they lived happily ever after." Tears slip down her cheeks until she laughs quietly. "Oh, and the princesses had a puppy. I think that's her way of asking for a dog."

"Smart kid." I swallow away the lump in my throat. "Our girl wants a puppy. Guess we're getting a puppy."

I take the picture from Emma's hand and fold it neatly, sliding it in my pocket, then pull my bride to my chest and drop a quick word to the guy upstairs, who I had once thought abandoned me. Hell, I thought that more than once. I prayed for a new life, prayed for an easier struggle, but the truth is that over the years, I always focused my thoughts back on Emma.

My whole life, while I thought my pleadings were going unanswered, my saving grace was with me. She was my answer.

I take a deep breath. "I love you with my whole heart, Emma. Hope you always know that."

She nods against my dress shirt. "You're my everything."

I walk us back to the kitchen table and put her in a chair then kneel in front of her. "What I have to say out there is yours to hear first."

"What?" Her eyebrows lift, and she puts her flowers on the table.

She deserves so much more than recited lines. If I can capture a tenth of what I think... "You've always been by my side. From the day we met. And God knows there were years of secrets and storms and pain and tears, until I came out the other side."

"Gray..."

"I'm a better man, and I exist for you, for us." I hold my breath and watch her silence. "You've got to know there's no more important thing I can do than to take you as my wife and Cally as our daughter." My chest hurts; my lungs burn. My throat is tight as I choke on the decades' worth of sentiment. "I love both of you so deeply that my survival, *my sanity*, would be gone if I couldn't be yours."

My voice cracks, and her lips find mine. It's a soft kiss but packs a powerful punch. She whispers, "We're yours forever."

Emma

I never believed that Grayson wanted me when we were in high school until he said almost those exact words and kissed me so sweetly that years later, I still get the shivers thinking about that day in my bedroom. But tonight, I believe every word that pours from his sweet mouth.

"Come on, baby." I stand up and press against his chest. "Let's go get married."

He slides his arm around me as I pick up my bouquet, and we head outside.

My dad is by the back door, and as my eyes settle on him, warmth bleeds through me. He nods to Grayson then shakes his hand. "I'd say she's the best thing I have to give away, but she's always been with you. Guard them with your life, son."

"Yes, sir."

"I have no doubt."

Dad kisses my cheek and leaves us as I see my Mom—who I left when I detoured to see Grayson—send Cally our way.

"Look at my dress," Cally says as she spins. The skirt fluffs out until she slows and grabs my hand. "I look like a princess!"

"Absolutely." Gray crouches down. "You remember what to do?"

She nods enthusiastically, pointing to the side of the wraparound deck that feeds into the backyard where our guests have gathered. "Walk over there and stand near Aunt Cherry."

"Exactly." They exchange fist bumps, then he

kisses her cheek.

This isn't a typical wedding. No one is seated in rows. There's not even an aisle. Instead, a semi-circled group of all kinds of people awaits us—a nod to how we want to live. The guys from the Delta team—the men Gray refers to as his brothers—wear dark suits. Then there are the other Titan families we've grown close to. My family is interspersed with a few close friends. I'm sure Ryan has his arm around Sarah, Cherry has caught the eye of a few of Gray's buddies, and Mazie is drooling over the groomsman lineup.

As Gray and I walk out together, I find that my assumptions were correct. Even my boss, Jeremy, is here—*with* our secretary—and, yeah, this all works for me because it carves into stone what we want: an all-inclusive family.

The ceremony was planned to be casual, and there are kids running around in the grass, most of the girls wearing princess tiaras with ribbons that fly around their heads when they move. Everything about this is perfect for us.

As Gray leads me into the center, our crowd quiets, and my parents' minister says his bit. I don't focus on the words. Instead, I watch Grayson, memorizing how his blond hair is mussed perfectly and his bright-green eyes dance as they watch me. Then he says his vows, a heartfelt summary of what he just professed to me in the kitchen.

Now it's my turn. Every face fades away except for his. My hands are locked in his protective grasp, and he pulls me closer.

Before I open my mouth to pledge my life to him, a memory surfaces and trumps what I'd planned to recite. "I remember the first day I realized you were *my* friend, not just my brother's. We were at recess, and some kid pushed me off the swings."

"Jerk," he whispers, grinning.

I laugh quietly. "You chased him away, picked me up, and set me back on the swing. I think you even gave me a little push. Then you ran off to play. But you looked back... that was the day I fell in love with you." I smile and take a deep breath. "There's this saying: stars can't shine unless they're cloaked in darkness. I'm not sure that's true. They're always there, always shining. It just depends on whether we can see them. And that's us."

He squeezes my hands, his thumbs running across my skin.

"Our love has always been there. You said storms, but I say life, and Grayson, I will walk through a hurricane with you, no matter what challenges come our way, because I love you. I'm yours as much as you're mine, and I want to be the family that holds you, that picks you up and cheers you on. I want to be Mrs. Emma Ford."

"God, Ems." He shakes his head as though he can't believe he's here listening to all that I've said. He pulls me close and kisses me deep. Somewhere along that kiss he dips me back. It's one spectacular kiss.

I'm sure the ceremony carried on, and that his Delta boys gave him hell, but I'm lost to the rest of it, and he never lets go. I love this man. He gave me the fairy tale, but *God*, he's given me so much more. Cheers to our forever love.

The End

Note To Readers

From the very bottom of my heart, I am throwing *huge* tackle hugs of thanks your way. The Only series was a leap for me, and this couple had their claws in my heart. I couldn't stay away. Hopefully I will have news on similar books in the future (sign up for the newsletter to stay in the know!).

If you are new to my books, check out Sweet Girl. It's FREE at all retailers. If you loved Grayson and Emma, you will go crazy for Cash and Nicola.

Or if you're already a Titan/Delta reader, thank you for trying something new.

Titan hugs and happy reading. XO.

BOOKS BY CRISTIN HARBER

The Only Series:
Book 1: Only for Him
Book 2: Only for Her
Book 3: Only for Us
Book 4: Only Forever

The Delta Series:
Book 1: Delta: Retribution
Book 2: Delta: Revenge

The Titan Series:
Book 1: Winters Heat
Book 1.5: Sweet Girl
Book 2: Garrison's Creed
Book 3: Westin's Chase
Book 4: Gambled
Book 5: Chased
Book 6: Savage Secrets
Book 7: Hart Attack
Book 8: Black Dawn

Each Titan and Delta book can be read as a standalone (except for Sweet Girl), but readers will likely best enjoy the series in order.

ABOUT THE AUTHOR

Cristin Harber is a *New York Times* and *USA Today* bestselling romance author. She writes sexy, steamy romantic suspense, military romance, new adult, and contemporary romance. Readers voted her onto Amazon's Top Picks for Debut Romance Authors in 2013, and her debut Titan series was both a #1 romantic suspense and #1 military romance bestseller.

Join the newsletter! Text TITAN to 66866 to sign up for exclusive emails or visit www.CristinHarber.com

www.ingramcontent.com/pod-product-compliance
Lightning Source LLC
Chambersburg PA
CBHW020520260626
47156CB00006B/2071